Mike Grist is the British/American author of the Chris Wren thrillers. Born and brought up in the UK, he has lived and worked in the USA, Japan and Korea as a teacher, photographer, writer and adventurer. He currently lives in London.

HAVE YOU READ EVERY GIRL 0 THRILLER?

<u>Girl Zero</u>

They stole her little sister. Now they'll pay.

<u>Zero Day</u>

The criminal world is out for revenge. So is she.

Learn more at www.shotgunbooks.com

MAKE THEM PAY

A CHRISTOPHER WREN THRILLER

MIKE GRIST

SHOTGUN
BOOKS

SHOTGUN BOOKS

www.shotgunbooks.com

Paperback ISBN - 9781739951139

For Su

1

DEADHORSE

Chris Wren sat in his truck in Deadhorse, Alaska, lit only by the glimmering green tendrils of the Northern Lights above, planning his next kill.

Pythagoras.

On the Blue Fairy's dark Internet of abusers, he was one of the worst. Active since the beginning. His track record was phenomenal, with hundreds of children destroyed in his wake. Maybe he would have some answers.

Wren rubbed his bleary eyes. He was worn out, hadn't been sleeping well recently. His hands shook like an alcoholic's coming down, smeared with blood still.

Whose blood?

He couldn't remember. The last three months were a blur of Blue Fairy interrogations. He'd been in Florida for one, then California, then New Mexico, hunting the 'Pinocchios' who'd targeted his children, who might know something about his father.

Apex of the Pyramid death cult. The man who'd ruined Wren's young life, and even now hung over his children's' lives like some sword of Damocles.

His phone started buzzing in the glove box.

Wren ignored it, looking out at the rippling green aurora as it danced across the deep Arctic sky. It was almost painfully beautiful. So much beauty in such a dark place. 1 a.m., and the sun had only gone down a few hours back, with sunrise coming in four. The company town of Deadhorse on the northwest coast of Alaska in mid-January, a place for oilfield workers, ice road truckers, the occasional coach full of Japanese tourists and now Christopher Wren.

He'd pulled up five hours earlier after a long-haul drive up from the States, shown his fake passport and special permit at the town limits. The guard had been chatty, said he was the only tourist in town this deep into the winter, boasting that the rivers were so frozen even the fish were hibernating. Wren hadn't known if that was a joke or not.

The phone kept on vibrating.

Wren popped the glove box and picked it up, a burner bought a few weeks ago. He thumbed the screen and the vibrations stopped. An alarm, the same time he'd set night after night. He tapped in the phone number on the glass for the hundredth time and stared at it. 4 a.m. here, 7 a.m. back east in the Delaware duplex, where his wife Loralei would just be waking up, laying out her yoga mat for a morning routine. Their kids Jake and Quinn would be asleep still, almost as if nothing had changed.

Except everything had changed. They weren't in their family home in New York anymore. His wife and kids had fled when Loralei found out what Wren did for a living, the CIA's international assassin of cults, gangs and cartels. 'Saint Justice', they called him.

Already Loralei had found a new man. She didn't want Wren's protection, despite or perhaps because of the threat he brought to hang over their heads. She didn't even want to let him see his kids, at least not until the threat had passed. Until Wren found his father and put him down like a rabid dog.

Wren smiled, pulled off his gloves and set them on the counter, then pulled out his wallet. It was fat with bills. He fanned through them. "Pull the record of receipt. You tell me. That's all I want, then I'm gone. No mention of the whisky crates I saw down the side. It's a dry county, last I heard. That's one count in the smuggling column. So get out your books. Slide a finger down. Five hundred says it never happened."

He eased the bills out of his wallet, laid them on the counter. Five hundred. A week's work, maybe. Consider it overtime. He pushed them closer.

"There's blood on your hands," the old guy said. It didn't seem to faze him.

Wren noticed it too. "It's not mine," he answered, like that made it all right.

A long moment passed. Wren's breath steamed the glass. One more corrupt official to bribe, or threaten, or whatever it took, and he was already thinking ahead to his plan for Pythagoras. Active for decades, with dozens of children destroyed in his wake.

The guy would talk, he could feel it. The link back to his father was achingly close. The route back to seeing his kids.

Then he heard a siren.

It was far off, but growing closer. More than one. He refocused.

The smug glint in the old guy's eyes had come to the fore, now. When had that change happened? Wren cursed silently. He'd let himself get distracted by the big picture.

"You hit the panic button," Wren said. "Under the counter."

"Company security," the old guy answered, offering the slightest shrug. Montanan accent, maybe? Wren wondered. Moderated by long years away. It took all sorts to populate a pipeline station. Loners, largely, men drawn to the verges of society, to the allure of the maddening wild.

The sirens drew in.

Wren didn't react. Didn't run. "I can give you the order number," he said, smiling now like it was funny. "I have the signature of the receiving agent, one William Hartright. Would that be you?"

"Man before me."

"Care to show me some ID?"

The guy almost cracked a smile. "Wouldn't care to, friend. But you'll be needing yours. Last fella came in asking about shipments, he left with two rounds in his chest and a bag over his head. Helicopter, FBI lettermen, the full contingent. We shoot first out here. Terrorism demands it, this close to the pipe-head. Tourists come on our good graces, and you just blew right through."

"I made threats?" Wren asked. "You'll testify at my trial?"

"It'll be a write-in." The guy let his smile through now. Feeling his own power reaching out. This was what happened when you asked about laptops in Deadhorse. "And if you're carrying a weapon, like the pistol weighing down your belly pouch, on federal land like this? That's a straight up terror charge, ten to fifteen years in solitary, if they don't shoot you outright."

Wren nodded, thinking through his position. The FBI threat was empty, at least in the short term; there wasn't a field station any closer than Anchorage, which was a. two-hour flight away. Maybe the local cops, enough to secure a remote pipehead and keep three thousand rowdy pipe workers in line, but that'd be a handful only, ten at the most, say three or four on duty at any one time.

It didn't worry Wren overly. On the other side of it, this guy had punched the alarm button to call them out, on the strength of what, a couple of insistent questions and some old blood on his hand?

Something else was going on here, and Wren decided to lay his cards on the table. "The laptop guy, how much is he paying you?"

The old guy smiled. Showing his hand too. "More than you can afford."

That was a tell, and it made things easier. This guy knew about Pythagoras. He was loyal to Pythagoras. The sound of sirens wafted in like a bugle call, growing louder.

"Usually they run now," the clerk observed.

"Nowhere to run," Wren answered. "We both know that. Not for me, not for you."

The guy frowned. Wren almost laughed. Sometimes he felt sorry for the people who crossed his path. "What is he, Pythagoras? A foreman on the pipeline, maybe a director of the company?"

The guy leered at the name. "I wouldn't worry about him. Think about yourself, son. Get your story straight. Explain that blood to the feds."

That was all the confirmation he needed. The guy knew who Pythagoras was, and the meant only one thing: he was in the Blue Fairy too. Wren felt the world flip around him as permission was granted. It always felt like that, when a civilian became a target.

"Explaining the blood's easy. I've been killing my way across America." He said it flat, knew from experience it would come off intimidating. "Pinocchios, like the man you're protecting." A flicker of annoyance. "You saw the Blue Fairy livestream off Pleasure Island, I'm thinking. That means you saw me, Christopher Wren, by the altar, shackling in one of your boys?"

The guy paled noticeably. His eyes widened. "Wait, what?"

Now it was Wren's turn to grin. "I look different in real life, right? Ever since then, I've been cleaning up the mess." He placed both his stained hands palm-up on the counter. "Maybe this was from Des Moines? Or Cincinnati? I thought I washed all the blood off, but it sticks, you know? It gets in the grain. I drove straight north afterward. Slept in the car. Three days driving just to see you. William Hartright. That's you, right? You've got what I want. Give me Pythagoras, maybe you get off easy. A man like me, Hartright, you sure you want to go hard?"

The guy blanched a little but forced a laugh. "Bullshit. You ain't him."

Him. The boogey man who brought the Blue Fairy down.

"Let's find out. Your toy town cops'll be here soon, no way you've got FBI lettermen on standby, and maybe they'll try to bag me." He reached into the belly flap of his jacket and pulled out the SIG .45, laid it on the counter. Hartright's eyes flashed to the door. The sirens were getting real close. Coming around the lake. Not far to go. Maybe on snowmobiles, blue lights flashing? Wren would like to see that.

"The glass is bulletproof," Hartright said.

Wren snorted. "Not against hollow point bullets. Three shots and I'm through, then the fourth finds your heart. Probably you should run." He pointed back into the warehouse. "You've got two exits plus the loading bays back there, but what if they don't open? Those locks are easy to jam with a heating filament. You can do it with an industrial light-bulb in seconds, and who's to say I didn't?" He paused, charting the guy's sharpening breath. A bluff, but the guy wouldn't know that. "Now you're really thinking. What kind of crazy fish you hooked. Hartright, you don't want this. Roll belly up now and I'll let the feds have you. Otherwise you're dealing with me, and I'm not that big on forgiveness."

Hartright gulped, took a step back. Wren could almost see the thoughts flying in his head; too much to take in, narrowing reality down to an immediate calculation. It had been a normal, quiet night in Deadhorse, and now everything had changed. Things were life and death, and who was ready for that kind of decision?

Wren always tried to make the math easy for perps, and tossed his wallet on the counter, like lead on the scale. The sirens sounded to be right outside.

"Take it all. Must be three thousand in there. Give me what I want, I'll give you a day's head start before I call you in."

Hartright wilted like an orchid under studio lights. Events were compounding and jamming him up. Wren fixed him with a steady gaze. It was all in the pitch, all in the delivery.

One of the sirens bleeped and cut out at the door.

"Your call," Wren said. "Either way, I'm getting what I want, but how angry do you think I'll be if I have to kill these guys? Their blood'll be on your hands. Pretty soon after, yours will be on mine. You won't like that."

Footfalls on the steps outside.

"It's on your word now. You pushed the button. Better decide."

Wren slipped the gun back into his belly flap as the door opened.

3

TOYTOWN COPS

A kick; the door swung wide and a gun came in first, left hand clamped underneath, finger already squeezed to the trigger. Two in the doorway, a young white guy in front and a black older guy in back, both wearing navy security outfits with golden badges.

Company cops.

"I need you on your knees right now, sir, with your hands up," said the lead guy. Twenty-five at a push, with rough stubble, swollen shoulders and a rounded back from unbalanced powerlifting. He shuffled in through a meltwater puddle, making room for his colleague; mid-fifties, maybe a family up here.

"This is all an accident," Wren said. "Right, Mr. Hartright?"

The cops looked to Hartright in back.

"It's him," Hartright said, his tone dead cold. Wren glanced over his shoulder and saw Hartright was now holding a gun. "Christopher Wren. The guy who brought down the Fairy."

That was unexpected. Wren turned back. The lead cop's eyes immediately flared wide and now his knuckle bruised white, riding the trigger hard. So they all knew him. In a second the world flipped once more, changing Wren's calculations. These weren't just toy town cops anymore, responding to an alarm. He'd stumbled upon a Pinocchio nest.

"He's what?" the cop in back asked.

"The guy from Pleasure Island," Hartright went on. "I didn't recognize him at first, but he says he's been killing Pinocchios up and down the country. Bastard boasted he's got their blood on his hands."

This revelation stunned the room further. The older cop kicked the door closed behind him, gun beaded now on Wren's face too.

"Fellas," Wren said, with a slight nod. "I didn't recognize you without your masks."

"You're sure?" the older cop asked. The young one's brows beetled hard together and his lips curdled to a sneer. Maybe Wren had killed some of his idols.

"It's me," Wren confirmed, "and you're all screwed."

This made for another odd moment; Wren stood with three guns pointing at his face, making threats.

"It's a bluff," Hartright said in back. Empowered by the layer of glass between them. "He's alone, here under a fake name. He's got a SIG .45 in his belly flap but that's it."

"That's not it," Wren said, keeping it cool and calm. The lead cop made a step forward. His face had turned blotchy red, like a parboiled sausage. "I have got a SIG, but I'm not going for it as long we all go easy."

The guy blurted a laugh and stabbed with the gun. "Easy? Wait until Pythagoras gets here. The things you did! You mother-"

"Be quiet," Wren snapped, and strangely the cop did. They all did. Afraid of his reputation, maybe. He worked the angles swiftly. "If you want to live through this, you need to stay calm and think, before this depot becomes another oil lake crater in the ice. You take me out, and fire rains down from the skies like a Biblical plague. I've got two MQ-1 Predator drones circling at twenty thousand feet, it'll be a minute or so before their missiles hit; you think you can clear the blast radius before that happens?"

He eyed the men. Didn't matter that there were no drones. It was a cozy fall back bluff he'd used many times before; deliver it confidently enough, it gave everyone pause. It helped that plenty of times it hadn't been a bluff. "Maybe not, and we're all pink mist. This block becomes a crater, Deadhorse's latest dark tourist attraction."

Silence. The front guy licked his trembling lips, eyes darting to Hartright.

"Bullshit. He's bluffing."

"We're in a hostage situation now," Wren went on, "whether you like it or not. I want Pythagoras. You want to survive the day. I could be convinced to let you go, if you give him up easy." He paused on that a second. "Well, not go. Like I said to Hartright here, I'll give you a day before I call down the FBI. I think my boy here would like that." He nodded at the lead cop. "Am I right?"

"Like it?" the guy blurted. His eyes burned with rage. Wren figured pushing him to the limit was his next move, get him hot enough to break the logjam, and smiled as patronizingly as he could. "I'm going to tear your damn head off."

"Figures," Wren said dismissively, and looked to the older cop in back. "Get this joker out of here. He's going to get you all killed."

"We need to see the proof you've got the drones," the guy in back replied.

Wren gave a short, sharp laugh. "I'm proof. The fact that I'm here. So get him out, he's a liability. Then we talk."

"Simon," said Hartright, behind the glass to Wren's left. A

Hartright jawed at the air. Looking for an avenue to argue his way out of. Ten minutes ago his life was normal. Good, maybe.

"Where's Pythagoras?" Wren asked.

"He shot you!" Hartright insisted, paling further.

"He missed," Wren answered. "Now decide."

Hartright's eyes flickered, then he ran.

Wren didn't wait to see if the back doors would open. He knew they would; the heating filament story was all part of his bluff. Instead he strode through the main door and looked out over Deadhorse and Colleen Lake. The cold air was bracing on his ungloved hands. The SIG instantly absorbed the cold and bit into his palm. He put it back in the torn belly flap.

The lake stretched on forever. It looked like fresh snow was in the offing. Out here, you wouldn't know. A deep breath brought a sharp pain in his lungs. So cold it hurt. He listened out and heard the slam of the rear door go, then advanced down to the snow-coated road, where one patrol car, a sedan with its blue lights still spinning, and a snowmobile with lights of its own were waiting.

No other blue lights spun up across the little town. Maybe just two guys on duty at a time. Someone might place an emergency call, muster them out, but Wren figured he had time.

He took the snowmobile and caught up to Hartright in thirty seconds. The machine ate up the distance, the snow making every surface navigable; off the road, over the sidewalk, up a low embankment. Around the back of the depot he went, down a fence encircling a heavy vehicles pool, where he ran down the older man beside a heaped pile of glinting gray sand.

He hit Hartright with the snowmobile's nose. Enough to send him reeling. Killed the engine and dismounted. Hartright scrabbled at the snow, crazed now and babbling like them all, desperate to survive.

"Please, listen, I can help you! I'll tell you whatever you want to know."

Wren already knew that. He had just one question, and it didn't take long to get the answer.

eighty. Any time kids were on the line. He looked over the controls, took the cyclic, set his feet on the anti-torque pedals and pushed the engine start. The rotors engaged and spun up fast, straightening out and chopping the falling snow into a downward cyclone that frothed like whipped cream off the pad.

He cycled it up and the machine lifted hard, bucking wildly in the wind. Wren adjusted the cyclic, sweat beading on his forehead, trying to control the machine before it splattered him across the pad. Take-off and landing were always the hardest parts, when dealing with the backwash of your own downdraft.

It was only going to get harder. Finally stable, he turned the machine toward the house. Ramming speed could be fun, but there was little chance he'd be able to jump clear safely. No. Instead he approached slowly, winging the finer controls and working calculations. The rotational diameter of the blades was about forty feet. That was the kind of thing he could judge by eye. Hit solid reinforced cement and the blades would snap. The bird would roll, crash, and if he didn't burn up in the resulting fireball, he'd get chopped to pieces as he tried to flee it.

He'd just have to avoid hitting cement.

He hovered in low over the snow-covered gardens. Here a statue. There the replica of a Japanese pagoda. He brought the helicopter up to the top floor of the three stacked concrete boxes, to the biggest floor-to-ceiling window overlooking the Arctic Ocean. Through the tinted glass he picked out a richly appointed office; a stately desk, shelves stacked with leather-bound books, tall Ficus plants framing the window.

The helicopter roared in a sound chamber of its own making; the echo of its rotors bouncing back off the glass. He pulled in close, the edge of his rotor blades only yards from the window. Snow whipped madly down then up, caught in complex crosswinds dictated by the angular shape of the building. Wren bit his lip and edged closer still. It would be tight; the turning circle of the blades versus the width of the window.

No time to play patty cake. He worked the cyclic and the helicopter jogged left, hovering within inches, leaning in until-

The blades struck the window and screamed, and spun, and glass crashed and sheared and metal whined and the whole machine juddered away, blades rattling madly.

Wren fought for control as the Dhruv reeled, hit autorotation after thirty seconds of heart-stopping battle, then peered through whirling snow at the window. There was an ugly gouge where the tips of his rotors had smashed clear through the glass, but only a gouge. Shatterproof triple-layer glass backed with polycarbonate, he figured, as if he'd raked a serrated knife down a pat of cold butter; all he'd done was leave a scar. He laughed out loud, imagined trying to work the Dhruv on another horizontal and two more verticals to cut out a square. It wouldn't be possible.

Better to go with what already worked, now the first cut had been made. He edged in close again, pulled the SIG .45, aimed near the gouge at an angle that wouldn't see ricochets bouncing right back at him, and fired.

Eight bullets drained the mag, each impact shredding the gouge wider and deeper as if he was swinging a ten-pound hammer into a concrete wall, until at last the window hit some tensile inflection point.

Glass screamed, metal crashed, and the whole shatterproof array finally gave out, calving into three great plates which toppled inward, thumping down hard on the fine Persian rug. The Dhruv bucked and whined in the snow. Likely he'd warped the blades and done permanent damage to the transmission knuckle with that stunt, and every second in the air moved it closer to a fatal malfunction.

He steered sideways as close as he dared then let the machine coast into autorotation, even as he kicked open the passenger door and flung himself through. The downdraft flattened him hard across the gap to land half-in and half-out of the building, chest on the toppled pane of glass and legs dangling. He kicked and slid, scrabbled for purchase and managed to pull himself in as the Dhruv rotated away, blown back by its own backdraft with no hand at the cyclic.

Wren rolled to the side. The Dhruv rolled like a leaping whale, lost purchase on the air as it toppled then slammed to its side on the snowy ground with a clattering shriek.

The rotor blades tore themselves away in the frozen soil and the transmission knuckle screamed; for a few seconds the whole machine danced like a jitterbug. Wren tucked in tight at the side of the office with snow whipping in around him, waiting for the blast he knew would come, but none did. The engine just whined down to silence.

He stood up and retrieved the SIG .45 from his belly flap.

6

SOMCHAI

Wren kicked open the office door, SIG .45 locked in a two-hand grip.

A corridor-walkway led away, strung above a steep drop to a grand lobby below, all winter-lit by the white tinge of Arctic sun. Teak flooring, Persian rugs and chrome railings stretched along the walkway for ten yards. A stunning modernist chandelier hung to his right five tiers deep, made with the life-size alabaster casts of cherub-like children.

He looked down to the lobby below. It was minimalist, massive and open-plan, with a sunken den and sofas, a dining table and a kitchen bar. The air was warm, climate controlled despite the gale whipping snow in behind him

No sign of Somchai.

Wren advanced along the walkway into a bedroom; a four-poster in the middle of a circular space suspended on tensile cables, like a giant hammock. It swayed slightly as he entered; bed, cabinets, empty. He pushed through to another walkway which led into a rec room of some kind, kitted with cameras in the four corners, then onto a circular staircase of rough corrugated iron. Halfway down Wren stopped to listen, but there was no sound at all. No whoosh of recycled air, no faint cries, not a thing.

The open plan kitchen was empty and pristine as a show home; granite worktops, chrome-fronted appliances. The entrance area spiraled brightly with snow shadows through the reinforced glass, heavyset metal door lodged with triple inch-thick bolt locks. A real fortress. Wren scanned the windows, sunken dining area with twelve-foot table laid for a feast, through the glossy black-tiled lounge with a three-sided chaise longue, until finally he saw Somchai.

His heart rate leaped to ninety easily. Obscured from above by the thick tiers of plaster cast children, there'd been a recent addition to the chandelier. Suspended beneath the cherubs hung an adult male body. Naked, the light tan skin of a wintering Thai, strung from a black metal crossbar. Arms stretched forward as if begging, threaded with taut cables that ended in strapped him to the crossbar. His elbows were threaded the same way, as were his feet and his knees.

Somchai Theeravit. Pythagoras. Left like a Pinocchio puppet, hanging on his strings.

Wren stared.

Dried blood below him. Looked like death by blood loss. No sign of anyone else. No sign of a fight.

It didn't make any sense. Somchai was a Pinocchio leader, right at the top of the Blue Fairy. His local team had been loyal to the last, willing to die to keep his existence a secret. So who had done this? And when?

They could still be here.

Wren moved on without thinking, SIG .45 up and fully operational. Back through the open kitchen he went, found stairs leading down and took them fast. A concrete corridor stretched away and Wren cleared it quickly, past open cells in Pythagoras' gaudy hell: bright yellow walls, padded flooring, oversized soft toys, murals painted with colorful trains and teddy bears.

At the end of the corridor lay a room all in black, cameras studding the ceilings and mounted on tripods, ready for livestreaming to the Blue Fairy, but no people. No Pinocchios. No children.

He swept back up, from the bowels to the lobby to the dizzy heights of floating offices and bedrooms, but found nothing. No sign of the killers. He stood on the smashed window in Theeravit's office looking out into a thickening snowstorm. The jetty onto the Arctic Ocean was obscured by whipping walls of snow.

Most likely they'd come by ship, docked in the jetty and walked right over. Wren doubted they'd come up through Deadhorse. The record would be too easy to track back. But the record here?

Just a snow-coated jetty with no evidence of their passage. No sign of anything in this ice-blasted wilderness.

Standing in the lobby before Theeravit again, Wren gazed at the strange diorama. The dried blood from his threading wounds suggested he'd died more than twelve hours ago. The killers had at least a twelve-hour start on Wren, maybe more.

A dead Pinocchio. The man deserved no better, Wren had no doubt about that, but who would have done this? Not the Blue Fairy, surely. Not to one of their own. Yet all signs pointed to this murder being committed by someone Somchai had known, even trusted. There were no signs of forced entry. Whoever it was, Theeravit had let them in.

Wren stepped closer, looking up into Somchai's blindly staring eyes, and noticed a thin leather cord pulled tight around his neck. He walked around and saw something dangling down Theeravit's back, a glint of metal like a pendulum. Wren jumped up and grabbed it, snapping the leather cord with a sharp snick.

It was an aluminum flash memory drive. Words had been engraved into the shell, words that flipped everything on its head.

I THINK YOU'LL ENJOY THIS ONE, PEQUEÑO 3

The world narrowed down. Wren's heart began to race.

Only one person had ever called him Pequeño 3. The reason he'd been hunting the Blue Fairy to begin with. The man he'd been hunting for twenty years since the Pyramid burned, whose existence was a threat to everything Wren held dear.

His long-dead father, the Apex.

7

ENJOY

drenaline dumped into Wren's system, preparing him for a fight or flight reaction; but there was no place to run and no one to fight. Instead the chemicals left him trembling with an emotion he'd barely felt for twenty-plus years.

Fear.

Fear turned into a weapon, bending his own mind upon itself. The same way Simon must have felt at the end, and Hartright, and countless other Pinocchios when Wren found them. Not since the end days of the Pyramid had Wren felt anything quite like it, but you never really forgot.

How it made you small. Made you weak.

He hadn't forgotten how to fight it either. Fear was a fuel you could burn, and he was working on that already. Pumping his fists in the cold air. Tensing every muscle in his body to fight back the chills. The anger came surging like an old friend, swamping the cold fear with red hot rage.

This wasn't just a message. This was the sign he'd been searching for.

He read the words engraved on the flash drive again, so clearly designed as a provocation.

It sounded like something his father would have said, right before beginning another one of his life and death 'experiments'; maybe Pyramid members pitted against each other in the deserts of Arizona, testing their faith in grand battles of stamina beneath the hot sun, waiting for the first to surrender and beg for water.

Sometimes nobody surrendered, their faith won out, and they all died. The Pyramid had cheered extra hard whenever that happened.

Wren had survived every one of the Apex's games as a child, learning to judge just how far to go to appease his father, without dying. He'd even survived the final 'experiment', where all thousand members of the Pyramid had burned themselves alive.

He'd survive this one too.

He uncapped the drive and plugged its micro-port into his phone. A screen popped up showing one icon in a menu, an mpeg file titled REPARATION. It didn't mean anything to him. He tapped it to open.

The video full-screened across his phone, darkness resolving to a high, fish-eye view of a shadowy, dank prison of some kind. Long narrow pens of wire mesh stretched away, barely two yards across, maybe ten long, with raw concrete floors. Naked men paced inside them and close-ups danced across their faces. It took Wren a second to recognize them.

All famous billionaires.

Dead ahead of the camera was Handel Quanse, CEO of a top finance company, well-known for the enormous profits he'd wrung from the housing crisis. While every other financier had still been buying into the bubble, he'd jumped the gun and spiked it with a crack needle, dumping hundreds of billions in garbage investments everywhere he could.

Those companies failed. He came out richer than ever. Now he was striding up and down the confined space, unashamed in his nakedness, a silver fox in his fifties looking toned, tanned and tall.

Merriot Raine, the inheritor of the Raine diamond fortune, was next to him, though he cut a very different picture. A trust-fund inheritor in his mid-twenties, he didn't have the killer gaze of Quanse or Joes, rather he was huddled limp and terrified in the corner of his cell. All he'd done with his life, as far as Wren was aware of him from the occasional news story, was gamble in the world's top casinos, date the world's top glamor models and open high-end restaurant after restaurant that all went belly up within months.

Wren scanned the rest, six more in total arrayed to the left of Handel Quanse's cell. Wren didn't recognize them all, couldn't pick some out for the distance, but there was Cem Babak the arms trader; an Iranian mob boss in his thirties who'd made an art form of inciting African inter-tribal wars. Next to him was Inigo De Luca, the Italian social media maven who'd sold all his user data to the Russian government in a multi-billion dollar windfall, then turned himself around as a champion of green energy. It was thanks to him that Wren was seeing countless electric charging stations popping up across the country.

Others lay beyond De Luca; one looked like Geert Fothers, another Saul-to-Paul Damascus Road conversion. Until he was fifty years old Fothers had been a tobacco man; to Wren's knowledge he'd played a pivotal role in pushing for fake medical assessments claiming certain cigarettes were not harmful, and perhaps even healthful. In his fifties though, after he was struck down by lung cancer, he'd had a complete change of heart; and lungs too, with implanted organs that kept him alive.

34

He'd turned his prodigious fortune to the fight against cancer, and that involved battling the industry he'd helped to grow. He'd already spent hundreds of millions on the fight.

Wren watched the group of billionaires as they paced. All men, he noted. He wondered what it meant, whether any of this was real or just some deepfake computer graphics fantasy, concocted to serve as propaganda. He was about to scroll the video forward when the camera panned to the right, revealing one more billionaire, taking the total number to ten.

The breath in Wren's throat stopped.

In the cell to Handel Quanse's right was the enormously fat Damalin Joes III, naked belly jutting out and proud a good two feet. He stood in the middle of his cell, so pale and immense he almost filled it side-to-side, staring up at the camera as if he knew what all this was. The look in his eyes made Wren think this wasn't a deepfake. This looked like the real Damalin Joes III.

Once a successful corporate raider, he'd infamously bought up the debts of thousands of Midwest family farmers during the '08 housing crisis, then bankrupted and evicted them all in one swelling roll of human misery that, by some accounts, had set the national economic recovery back by six months.

He was one of the most hated men in America, for the way he'd profited off the pain of the common man. At least he had been.

Now he was a Foundation member.

Wren's jaw dropped open. He thought of the message on the flash drive.

I THINK YOU'LL ENJOY THIS ONE, PEQUEÑO 3

Bullshit, he thought. No way these people, whoever had jailed Damalin Joes, could have known Joes was in the Foundation. Nobody but Wren knew that. He had records, sure, but they were secured. But then here was Joes staring up at the camera, like he knew who the intended audience was.

Wren.

Like some half of the other billionaires present, Joes had experienced his come-to-Jesus moment. Unlike them, his had come at Wren's hands.

8

DAMALIN JOES III

Wren hadn't meant for any of it to happen. Damalin Joes III wasn't even a blip on his radar when he'd gone into the mission; black-ops for the DoD's US Special Operations Command in Cuba. The mission had entailed complete deniability, only Wren and a small insertion team two years back.

They'd set up as darknet drug dealers for La eMe, the Mexican Mafia. Their surface 'goal' had been to score a new Atlantic 'Silk Road' for shipping raw Afghan opium to Cuba, the Pearl of the Antilles. Their deep goal was to uncover and destroy a suspected underworld of opium processing factories somewhere on the island, preventing the forward transit of lab-grade opiates up through Mexico into the US.

He'd had a full work-up done on his cover story, using his Qotl cartel hookups to build out his new identity; a crooked CIA agent looking to cash in on some dark connections after twenty years on the job. It was a story almost too close to reality for comfort.

Damalin Joes III had come into the picture entirely by accident. Turned out he was holidaymaking in Cuba aboard his luxury 400-foot superyacht, hunting an infamous painting by the Uruguayan artist, Joaquín Torres-García. It was pure coincidence that Wren's black-ops mission ended on a superyacht docked in Havana Harbor directly next to Joes'.

The entrepreneurial criminal who'd set up the heroin labs, Herman de Guz, closed out his career with a black bag over his head, looking forward to a five-hundred-mile aerial commute to Guantanamo Bay on the other side of the island. Wren oversaw it all, from the gung-ho clearance of seven private security operators on the yacht to cracking de Guz' panic room to pulling down the black bag over his head, walking the hollering man off his yacht and into the secret flatbed of a waiting pick up truck.

Mission accomplished.

Wren had taken one last look around before climbing into the truck with his squad, rifle poised, all in tactical black gear splashed with enemy blood, and that's when he saw Damalin Joes III.

An enormously fat man standing high up on the upper deck of his neighboring superyacht. 'In Excelsis' was the yacht's name, written in curlicued gold leaf on the side. Bigger than de Guz' ship. It had a bowling alley, two swimming pools, a helipad and a total of 24 bathrooms, Wren would later learn.

Joes looked down at him, dressed in only a white terrycloth dressing gown, and raised a cocktail glass as if in a toast. As if to say, 'Nice job.'

Wren slapped the side of the pickup truck, sending his team on. The engine started and the truck rolled away. Wren stood there for a long moment, looking up at Damalin Joes. An American billionaire, far out of his comfort zone.

"Are you not riding with your team?" he called down. His deep voice carried over the distance easily, but casually, like this was small talk at a cocktail party, not the tail end of a noisy, violent rendition.

Wren debated swiftly. There'd been no mention of an American involved in the drug labs. Certainly not a high-profile billionaire. At the same time, it seemed too much of a coincidence to overlook. He raised his rifle.

"Lower the gangway," he commanded. "I'm coming aboard."

If anything, Joes seemed rather pleased about the prospect. He gave a signal, and within seconds a hatch in the side of the yacht opened.

"I do hope you like a mojito," Joes called as Wren stalked toward the entrance. His second yacht infiltration of the night. "The rum's Havana Maximo 25 Anos, Special Blend. It costs ten thousand a bottle."

Wren ignored him and entered the yacht with his rifle raised. An astonished young man in service whites raised his hands and backed away. Wren ascended up a set of stairs to the top deck, where Damalin Joes was waiting.

For a long moment the two looked at each other. Joes in his fluffy white gown, cocktail held high, Wren in his coarse black strike suit with the rifle.

"Can I tempt you to a drink?" Joes asked. As if a guest like Wren was perfectly commonplace.

Wren almost laughed. Kept his rifle at the ready throughout. "Two things," he said. "With a foreword. Foreword is, you get this yacht moving right now. Out of the harbor. On the way back to the good old USA."

Joes looked at him a long moment. "I haven't retrieved my painting yet."

Later on, Wren would laugh about that phrasing with his team. 'Retrieved', like finding and purchasing a famous painting was not a question of reaching an agreement with the current owner. No, it was more a question of prizing free something that had always belonged to him, with money as the crowbar.

"First thing then," Wren went on smoothly. "You just witnessed a hit that's going to bring half of Havana down on our heads within the hour. There's no covering that up. They see you here, you're going to get tangled up in it. Bad for you, bad for the USA, bad for me. That's reason one."

Joes seemed unphased. Like he dealt with this kind of thing all the time, and it mostly bored him. He took a sip of his mojito. Wren became aware of armed men behind him from the click of a safety switching over. Sounded like two of them, making noises they didn't have to make, but they clearly wanted him to hear. One to his right, one to his left, pretty close judging the layout of the yacht.

"And reason two?" Joes asked. Same easy confidence.

"You were here next to him. That makes you a suspect in my book. So, if you don't order this yacht to move right now, I'll take that as resistance and put a black bag on your head too, requisition your ship and steer it out of the harbor myself."

Joes took another sip, seemed to think about this for a moment. Made a show of looking over to the yacht Wren had busted, to the pier below where his pick-up truck had left from, then back up at Wren. "What do you weigh, maybe two hundred pounds?"

"Two-fifty."

"Then I'm twice the man you are. Put the gun down and let's see how you wrestle."

"Not going to happen," Wren said. "Easy way or hard way, Sir, and-"

"Boring," Joes said, then in one beguilingly smooth movement tossed his drink over the side, slid out of his gown and started at a run toward Wren.

Wren barely restrained his laughter. With the robe gone Joes' pasty white body looked like an uncooked turducken, a chicken stuffed inside a duck stuffed inside a turkey, ready to be basted. But massive. Not the kind of man you'd want to get crushed beneath, same way Wren felt about giant redwoods. When timber was called, you got out of the way.

Ten steps across the deck, maybe, for Joes to reach him.

Wren spun, jogging his right elbow up and out. Far and fast enough to catch the rifle barrel of the guy standing to his right. He wasn't ready, and Wren followed through with a fast step, managed to shoulder barge him square in the sternum. The guy, no slouch himself, maybe two hundred pounds of meat and bone at six foot even, was lifted off his feet and sent backward, leaving his rifle behind.

Wren spun and flung the weapon hard to the right, straight into the face of another security guy in a blue uniform, pistol raised. It took him a second to deal with the incoming rifle, still log-jammed on Wren's sudden attack, then Wren hit him with a flying dropkick in the upper chest.

The guy somersaulted on the spot like a little man on a foosball table, rotating around some hidden axis, almost a full three-sixty before he came down on his face, knees slamming into the deck like the trailing edge of a whip.

Then Damalin Joes hit Wren like a wrecking ball.

Wren was swept immediately off his feet and driven hard into a wall, blasting the wind from his lungs. Before he could get his feet underneath him, Joes swept one meatball hand up between his legs, hoisted Wren bodily by the crotch and hurled him like a human javelin.

Wren flew, saw the bright lights of Havana from the air, then hit the pure white deck and slid on his chest. Already there was the thunder of Damalin Joes charging; each mighty footfall beating the deck like it was a big bass drum. He thought about barking some kind of order, a warning about interfering with the work of a CIA operative about his country's business, but decided to save his wind.

Instead, he rolled and opened his arms wide for what he

anticipated next. Joes didn't disappoint. He flung himself right at Wren, likely hoping to crush the smaller man beneath his immense weight, too high or drunk or arrogant to really think through what he was doing.

Wren braced and Joes hit like a falling redwood, crushing his ribs between a rock and hard place so powerfully Wren almost blacked out.

But he didn't.

As Joes hit, Wren wrapped his hands around Joes' neck, trapping his thick right arm upright beside his face. Joes huffed and tried to tumble free, but Wren had him then. Didn't matter how much mass the big man had; everybody's carotid artery beat near the surface, and Wren squeezed, using Damalin Joes' own arm to block the flow of blood to his brain.

"Don't..." Joes murmured as unconsciousness crept over him, "drink all my rum."

Then he was out.

Wren stood up. His crotch hurt like the devil. Ribs too. He pulled four zip-ties from his belt and hog-tied Joes before he could wake up. Then he looked over at Joes' security contingent, now beading their rifles on his head.

"He's a rich idiot," Wren said. Staring them down. "What's your excuse?"

They put their rifles down.

After that it was just a matter of time.

9

ARENA

Wren refocused on his phone screen, strange memories of his time with Damalin Joes on the yacht blending uneasily with the vision of the man on the screen before him. During their one-week trip back to the USA, they'd become something like friends. After close interrogation, Wren concluded that Joes was guilty of nothing more heinous than coincidentally being alongside a criminal's yacht, and the colossal arrogance that he could take down a Force Recon operator with impunity.

They'd talked. At some point Wren mentioned the Foundation, and Joes asked to join on a dime. Not as a financier, but as a member.

Wren had thought about that hard. By then Joes was an ultra-billionaire, but bored and acting out. The world had opened up for him, and he still wasn't satisfied. In Wren he thought maybe he saw a way to scratch an unseen itch.

Wren made one condition of Joes' acceptance to the Foundation; that he find a way to do something good to make up for the way he'd hoovered up his enormous wealth. He'd steadfastly refused to engage with any of Joes' pointblank arguments about the ultimate benefits of capitalism. Wren was no politician and didn't care either way. For him the calculation was much simpler.

"You want some meaning in this life? You help people."

In the years since, Wren watched Joes take that simple creed further than he'd ever expected. He bought out several entire counties along with great swathes of farming land, then suspended all rent payments from the tenants, while also providing them with a universal basic income.

He called these areas his 'Damalin Incubation Zones'. The idea was to foster local development and fuel ingenuity by freeing up people's time. No more endless exhaustion from working three minimum wage jobs, no more farming dawn 'til dusk just to pay for the rented equipment that pushed conglomerates to ask for more acreage to be covered by a single farmer.

He'd just gotten started in all that, though, and it was only some fifty thousand people affected so far. A pilot program. Not the hundreds of thousands he'd hurt. The renovation of his image, not that he cared too much about that, was a long time coming.

As if to reflect that, Damalin Joes III's name was currently at the top of a game show-like ranking bar down the screen's side. All the billionaires' names were listed there, along with their industry and their net worth, and what looked like a shifting vote tally. The vote numbers were in the tens of thousands already and rising constantly. As far as Wren could tell, it looked like a hate-vote situation, with the worst of the worst at the top.

That was Damalin Joes. Handel Quanse came in second.

Wren watched the phone screen, rapt. Apart from a few guesses, he didn't know what he was looking at. Some kind of reality TV show? But why would any of these men agree to be trapped naked in a cell? So was it a deepfake, imagery created in a computer and rendered to look ultra-realistic? Or was it exactly what it looked like; ten men who'd been kidnapped and imprisoned?

After several minutes of the ten men pacing in their cells, a montage followed. It seemed as if many days had been compressed in the editing suite: the billionaires being fed in their cages; being hosed down with jet spray like animals in a pen; being herded into corners by figures in white haz-mat suits wielding long sparking cattle prods.

The cattle prods changed Wren's calculation significantly. This didn't look like any reality TV show he'd ever seen. That left incredibly realistic deepfake or genuine kidnap scenario. Both would have cost millions to prepare.

After the montage the screen brightened abruptly, and Wren found himself looking down from above at some kind of arena. At first he thought he was looking at a close-up of a strange, unblinking golden eye. Then he realized what it actually was; an oval of sand surrounded by five full tiers of stadium seating. An arena.

Wren's heart skipped a beat and he peered closer at the screen. It looked like stone walls, like a Roman amphitheater where gladiators would fight, skirted outside by a hint of more sand and green scrub. The tiers of seating looked to be full, with brightly colored figures packed in tight. Judging from the scale of their bodies, the arena had to be some two hundred feet on the long axis, around half as big as a football field.

The image sharply crosscut to a close-up in the midst of the tiered seating. A diverse, modern-looking American audience filled up the stands, drinking beer, eating popcorn, waving foam hands like they'd come to watch a football game. Big screens around the walls rose up ten feet high, showing the current ranking of billionaires. Many of the spectators were holding phones with that same ranking on their screens.

The camera briefly closed in. On each phone was the ranking bar with the ten billionaire's names, ten buttons by each of their names. A finger came into the shot, hit a button, and the vote tally shifted. They were voting right now. But voting for what?

The camera zoomed back out, way out like the camera operator was standing on the building's walls, and Wren found himself wowed by the scale of it, even seen on his small phone screen in the dark of Somchai's house. There were men, women, children in face paint. Thousands of them. Wren felt a sickness building in his gut. Something awful was coming.

It came.

Doors around the top of the stands opened, and the billionaires were brought out. They were naked still, steered by the guards in their white haz-mats with their cattle prods. Camera-wielding film crews tracked each one of them, and the big screens on the walls shifted to showing close-ups of their faces. Some were terrified and sobbing, like Merriot Raine, needing to be dragged every step of the way. Others were defiant, heads held high, like Handel Quanse and Damalin Joes III. Joes in particular looked arrogant, walking proud as a bride down the stone steps, his giant naked belly bulging; much as he had when he'd charged Wren on his yacht.

Wren's pulse raced. If this was an anti-popularity contest, Damalin Joes wasn't helping himself. The thought crossed Wren's mind that whatever this was, it wasn't live. The outcome was on a flash stick and had already happened. He could scroll ahead to find out what happened, but he couldn't bring himself to touch the screen.

Joes was on a coin wo. He'd made incredible progress on himself and his footprint in the world, since he'd started with the Foundation. Wren gave him no more attention than anyone else, didn't coddle him, and if anything Joes had responded positively. He was turning his life around. To look at him now, you'd never know it.

"Cut the act," Wren muttered to himself, reading the audience as they cheered or booed accordingly as each billionaire's face appeared on the big screens. They booed loudest for Quanse, Joes and Merriot Raine. They cheered for Geert Fothers; his turnaround had been well in place for a decade now, and his expression was not one of arrogance. If anything, he looked contrite. The crowd loved it.

The ranking bar on the side spun up to a frenzy as the billionaires descended toward the oval arena, names swapping positions rapidly as the audience bent over their phones, tapping the app to cast their votes. Some kind of violent game show, Wren wondered, though the production values were through the roof.

Handel Quanse was first to step out onto the sand, head up and spine erect. This was met with a resounding boo. One of the haz-mats pointed at a mark in the sand and Quanse strode confidently toward it, taking up a position near the center. The others followed suit, Joes arriving second to flank Quanse. Staring out at the crowd.

"Read the room, Damalin," Wren urged, but it was no use. Joes was an arrogant man, not about to kowtow to a rabble like this. Swiftly the billionaires formed up in a neat circle at the center of the arena, maybe thirty yards across.

Abruptly wooden gates in the arena wall opened and the camera crews swarmed. Nine horses were led out, beautiful dark mustangs, easily sixteen hands tall and built like tanks. Their handlers brought them up one to a billionaire, positioned facing away from the center of the circle. The handlers hooked long leather ropes into harnesses mounted around the horses' powerful shoulders.

Maybe some kind of race? Wren scanned the arena,

47

picturing the stampeding chariots of Ben-Hur, but there hardly seemed enough space. He imagined the billionaires getting strapped in armor and given a sword to fight from horseback, but that made no sense; who amongst these pampered men knew how to fight like that? It would be an amateurish, drawn-out joke.

The feed switched back to the shot from above, showing the haz-mat attendants stretched the rope from each horse's harness toward the center of the circle, like spokes in a wheel. There was a damp patch under Merriot Raine where he'd pissed himself. The crowd loved it. On big screens atop the fifth tier Raine's tear-stricken face was blown up large.

Only Handel Quanse didn't have a horse. Wren scanned the ranking; Quanse's name was locked at the top of the vote tally now, his name highlighted in red. Quanse looked around, trying to figure out what this meant, but still he didn't see it coming.

Four haz-mats peeled away from the horses and closed in on Quanse from behind. The camera cut with a crash back to ground level, on the sand and watching Quanse's figure from behind as the haz-mats approached. They leveled their cattle prods and hit him with an almighty electric shock.

Handel Quanse stiffened, his nervous system instantly and overwhelmingly overridden. Not all the money in the world could do a thing to protect him. One of the haz-mats gave him a shove and he toppled, hitting the sand with a thud.

The crowd fell silent.

The four haz-mats dropped their rods and descended on Quanse's jerking body, dragging him to the center of the circle of horses, where they strapped him wrist and ankle with the long harness ropes. Damalin Joes and the eight other billionaires were being guided up into their saddles. Joes was red-faced now, eyes bugging on Quanse, shouting and battling with four haz-mats of his own until they cattle-prodded to rigid silence atop his horse.

Nothing anyone could do about this now. Wren stared mutely, already seeing ahead to where this was going.

The crowd fell silent. Soon the only sound was of Handel Quanse's limbs thrashing out the aftershocks, and the herky-jerky suck of his breathing. One camera operator pushed in on his face and splashed it across the big screen. His eyes were wide and staring, locked within a body temporarily out of his control.

A voice boomed out across the arena. It was female, accented slightly, the words so loud that even Quanse seemed to comprehend them, his eyes twitching.

"Finish him and live!"

The camera feed switched to a split screen of the other billionaires; their faces blown up large. Wren focused on Damalin Joes. Waiting for him to grasp what was required, for the calculation to take place just like it had atop his yacht. Arrogance bordering on mania. An ability to take advantage of the temporary weakness of others. It was a skillset he'd taken from rags to the billionaire rich list.

It didn't take long now. Wren watched the shift in his eyes, the fresh set of his jaw as the decision was made. Grasping that there were no rules anymore. That survival was everything.

Damalin Joes kicked his horse hard in the flanks, yanked on the reins and shouted, "Yaaa!"

His Mustang took off.

The camera tracked him as he tore away. In the background the other billionaires responded, whipping their reins and geeing their horses to run, but they were out of focus and unimportant. Joes' harness rope leading back to Handel Quanse's right arm was first to pull taut; briefly dragging him after Quanse's horse across the sand. Then he hit tension as the other horses bolted away and was pulled apart.

The rope whiplashed clear.

The cameras didn't show the catastrophic damage done, at least not until Joes' horse neared the wall and veered left, leading a frantic spiral of all nine horses galloping around the oval arena, each trailing pieces of Handel Quanse behind them.

Torn to pieces by wild horses.

Wren let out a horrified breath. The crowd roared their approval. After maybe a minute Damalin Joes slowed his horse, fighting for breath and composure. Someone pushed a microphone into his face.

"How does it feel?" they asked. "How does it feel to finally do something good?"

Joes had no answer. Neither did Wren. The screen flashed to black, and a single line of block-capital text appeared that brought some measure of clarity.

YOU ARE OWED REPARATIONS

A moment passed, then another line replaced it.

CLAIM THEM IN BLOOD

10

EVERY LAST DROP

W ren stared as the video ended. The phone returned to just being a phone. He turned the flash drive over and read the inscription again.

I THINK YOU'LL ENJOY THIS ONE, PEQUEÑO 3

Handel Quanse was either dead, executed in the most gruesome display Wren had ever seen, or that was an incredibly persuasive deepfake video. He didn't know what to feel. Stunned. Confused. Enraged.

He brought up his phone and ran an Internet search, looking for instances of the arena film online. He found none. That cleared up nothing. He ran another search for stories publicizing the kidnap of Joes or Quanse or the other billionaires and found nothing either.

What the...?

He rubbed his weary eyes, trying to put Damalin Joes' sickened final expression out of his mind and jumpstart the search for answers. Neither search result made any sense. These 'Reparations', the people who'd gone to all the trouble of making this video, hadn't done it just for Wren's benefit.

So what was it for?

He tried to imagine the effect the death of medieval-level

death of Handel Quanse would have, if released to the public through a streaming app like WeStream. Destructive, was the word that came to mind. After the Saints and the Blue Fairy had caused such chaos, America stood at a precipice. There was anger out there in spades, and fear, and people were primed to turn on each other. Now a billionaire was dead, and the audience had cheered themselves red in the face.

They wouldn't be the only ones.

But the video wasn't online. At least not yet. Which could mean only one thing: the Reparations wanted Wren to see the video first. They wanted this to be personal. They wanted him to think his father was involved.

That pissed him off.

Wren jerked to action, striding back through the grotesque home; now just a set with Somchai Theeravit's dead body as a prop. Stamping up the stairs, he spun up a spider search algorithm to ping him when the Reparations video appeared online, then tapped out a swift message to his top-level Foundation members via Megaphone app: calling, texting and messaging them every minute until they acknowledged receipt.

JUST RECEIVED THE ATTACHED SNUFF FILM, STRAPPED TO PYTHAGORAS' CORPSE. COULD BE A DEEPFAKE, CHECK THAT, BUT I DON'T THINK SO. DAMALIN JOES IS A FOUNDATION MEMBER, TURNING HIS LIFE AROUND. NOW HE'S A CAPTIVE IN A REPUGNANT REALITY TV SHOW. THIS IS PERSONAL.

Wren sent the message, thought for a moment, tapped out more.

FIND OUT WHO CAME TO DEADHORSE BEFORE ME TO KILL PYTHAGORAS, AND WHERE THEY WENT AFTER. FIND OUT WHERE THEY FILMED THIS ARENA. FIND OUT HOW THE BILLIONAIRES WERE

TAKEN, IF THEY WERE TAKEN. FIND OUT WHO THE AUDIENCE ARE, EVERYTHING YOU CAN. LINE UP SOME SUSPECTS WITH THE MEANS, MOTIVE AND OPPORTUNITY TO PULL OFF SOMETHING OF THIS SCALE.

He sent that, wrote one more line, deleted it, then wrote it again and sent.

MY FATHER MAY OR MAY NOT BE INVOLVED. BE CAREFUL.

Standing in an incoming gale of snow blowing through the shattered window of Theeravit's third-floor office, Wren dialed a number from memory. 4:45 a.m. in Alaska, that was 8:45 in New York, and his old boss Gerald Humphreys, Director of US Special Operations Command, answered in moments. In his mid-fifties, Humphreys' deep voice was measured, careful, emotionless.

"Christopher. I've been trying to contact you. Where are you?"

Wren was surprised how little anger he felt upon hearing Humphreys' voice. The man had played both sides in the battle with the Blue Fairy, even trying to have Wren's plane shot out of the sky, but right now Wren didn't care. They weren't friends. The man was an asset to be exploited.

He stopped at the top of the stairs. "I'm out hunting Pinocchios, Gerald. There are some dead ones here. I'll let you know the location soon, but that's not why I'm calling now. There's-"

"The killing, Christopher," Humphreys interrupted, a hint of anger showing now. "You have to stop. You-"

"Damalin Joes III," Wren said, cutting straight to the chase. "Handel Quanse. Merriot Raine. Some of the richest billionaires there are. Tell me they're safe and sound on their superyachts, they haven't been kidnapped, there have been no demands."

53

There was a long silence on Humphreys' end. There was only one reason for that.

"I can neither confirm or deny the pre-"

"That's a yes then," Wren interrupted, feeling his heart plummet in his chest. The video wasn't a deepfake. Handel Quanse was really dead. Damalin Joes' life was on the line.

"... changes here, Christopher," Humphreys was saying, though Wren barely heard. "We have new protocols, new systems to better protect us. Fact is, you're not just a wanted person anymore, you're on a catch/kill list, emphasis on the kill."

He left that hanging. It took a second for Wren to re-engage, putting Quanse's actual death to the side. "What?"

"You've been executing American citizens, man! Pinocchios, but with no due process. We've got hit teams ready to go across the country, waiting for you to show up. Agent Sally Rogers is leading them. You killed," he took a moment, "one in Seattle, one in Idaho, one in Cincinnati, one in Las Vegas, and at least a dozen more. I don't even know where you got their data."

Now Wren's anger began to stir. "I got it from Pleasure Island. I shared it with you. You didn't do anything with it!"

"You mean we didn't swoop in extra-legally and assassinate them? Christopher, you're on a killing spree unlike anything in American history. It places you up there with Dahmer and Bundy. Right now we're focused on catching or killing *you*, not some missing billionaires."

Wren gritted his teeth. It figured, but he'd deal with that later. "Listen to me very carefully, Gerald. I've just come into possession of a snuff film like nothing I've seen before, with all your missing billionaires in it, and one of them's dead already. Handel Quanse, executed through some Dark Age torture, in front of a crowd of roaring Americans who voted for him to die." He took a breath. "Maybe it's the French revolution redux, the beginning of some anti-rich pogrom in the name of income equality; I don't know and I don't much care, but it needs to be stopped." He paused a moment, squaring everything in the balance. "There's a hint my father may be involved, so I'm going after them hard. I need you to pull whatever strings you have left at the Department of Defense and help me this time."

Humphreys took a long moment. "That does sound serious. And your father? If you're right about any of this, the Department will take action. There's something you should know before we proceed any further, however."

Wren snorted. "What, they fired you? Who do I call to-"

"Not exactly. You're not going to like this, Christopher. Rather than bumping me down, they promoted me." A pause. "They made me Director."

It took a second. Wren had to turn the word around once in his head before it hit him. "Overall Director? Not just Director of Special Activities?"

"Director," Humphreys confirmed.

Wren laughed. Was there anyone less fitting to be the top dog in charge of the CIA? "You're kidding me."

"I can guarantee this is not a joke. Check it online."

Wren did; opened his phone and checked the news. It was all there. After the previous Director had been asked to step down for her failures against the Blue Fairy, the baton had been handed to Humphreys for his perceived success.

"You took the credit," Wren said.

"No," Humphreys answered sharply, "I did not. I gave it to you and Rogers, to everyone who lost their lives in the operation, but you've squandered that. You could've come in a hero, but you're too wedded to your purist vigilante morality!"

Only one thing to say to that. "So be purer."

"Be purer?" Humphreys fumed. "Do you really think I

liked having the Blue Fairy harness between my teeth? It was disgusting, repugnant, but sometimes..."

Wren tuned him out. He didn't need a moralizing lecture from Gerald Humphreys of all people, whether he was Director or not. There was only one thing he'd said so far that mattered.

"Sally Rogers is hunting me?" Wren interrupted.

It took Humphreys a second to climb down from his high horse. "Yes. She's been arguing for you at every stage, but you're committing murders." Some of the heat faded from his voice. "She's been asking for leniency, but she's dogged. She will find you."

Wren considered. Gazed out into the driving snow, where the Dhruv helicopter was just a white mound now, secrets buried beneath the surface.

Sally Rogers. Getting hunted by her was only going to make this harder. He didn't want to think about how things would go, if it came down to him and her in the dark, guns pointing at each other.

"Call her off. No more catch/kill order."

Humphreys laughed. "Are you being serious? You're public enemy number one. I can't just call that off. What are you going to give me in return?"

Wren gritted his teeth. Everything had a price.

"I'm going after my father. If I happen to save your billionaires into the bargain, even put down these anti-rich idiots before they cause real damage, that's to your benefit. You want me inside the tent for this, Gerald, not on the outside pissing in." He took a breath, kept on before the other man could speak. "This thing could go bigger than the Blue Fairy, and if my father is involved? We all need to start singing from the same hymn sheet, sharpish."

Humphreys took his time. "Perhaps there's a deal to be done here. It depends-"

"How long have they been missing for?" Wren interrupted. Take the deal as read and start at the beginning. "The billionaires."

Humphreys took his time. Getting on the same page, sweeping the past aside, for now at least. "Three weeks. That's the longest of them. Merriot Raine, he was taken first. He had minimal security forces at the time; they were all killed. The others have been taken in stages, three a night, with warnings to the FBI not to publicize them." Wren heard keys clattering. Humphreys starting the ball rolling. "You said Handel Quanse is dead. You mentioned 'anti-rich'. Do you know why they killed him?"

"Some nonsense about claiming reparations in blood. It's grim stuff, high production values, a video designed to go viral by pitting the rich against the poor. They voted for him to die, it seems. And their ultimate goal? I've got no idea. It's-" Wren stopped as a ping chimed on his phone. The spider coming back with something. He clicked the link through to the streaming app WeScreen, where a new video had just started to play. It began with the spiraling shot of a familiar golden arena, seen from the top down, with the gameshow voting box in the top right. Wren copied the link and sent it to Humphreys.

"The video's just been uploaded. See for yourself."

11

QUESTIONS

Questions churned in Wren's mind as he tore back through the storm on his stolen snowmobile. Four dead Pinocchios and a snuff film featuring a billionaire Foundation member, all laid out for him to see first. There had to be a reason why these 'Reparations' wanted him involved in their schemes, but he had no idea what it was.

He'd never been rich. Other than Joes, he didn't know any rich people. He wasn't a natural target, and neither was his family. Living in a duplex in Delaware with some guy who installed surround sound speaker systems for a living, nobody was going to target them.

So why try to drag him into this? Why include Damalin Joes? Why reference his father?

The snowmobile revved hard. There was almost zero visibility in the storm, and Wren steered with his thighs more than the handles, feeling the verve and flow of the snowcapped land as it punched up through the skids. Flurries of snow crusted over the goggles, an endless curtain of white that kept on unpeeling to nowhere. At least the lay of the land beneath the machine didn't lie.

Or maybe it did.

This whole thing felt like that, a snow screen masking some deeper plot.

He'd checked Theeravit's house over one last time before he left, a fifteen-minute final sweep, but the killers had done a clean job. The Reparations. He even rode out to the jetty to check they hadn't left a trail, but there was no evidence. Not only of their passage through those spaces, but of Theeravit's too. No sign of the cryptography laptop he'd shipped up here. No hard drives at all. No notes, no papers, no clear onward steps left, as if they wanted Wren to have only one lead to follow.

The video.

The snowmobile jolted then hit a downward slope, pulling Wren's attention back to the present. His speed increased, no way to know it from the empty surroundings, but he felt it in the wild revving of the engine. Dangerously fast, the handles hammering into his palms. Any second he could hit the stump of a desiccated tree, the flank of a wandering polar bear, the Jurassic blade of some ancient crag shooting up through the ice.

Hit and be sent flying. Soar through the air then strike Earth head-first, crumple his neck, shatter his collarbones, maybe tear his arms and legs off like poor old Handel Quanse, left as a red spot in the snow soon to be covered over.

Fear raced through his heart and out into his arteries and veins, telling him to slow down. Protect yourself.

Wren pushed the pedal harder and leaned into it.

Faster.

Harder.

The wind ripped at his face. Snow blinded him. His feet went numb with the thumping vibrations punching up from below as the snowmobile bounced like a skier over moguls, faster and faster.

Fear would only hurt you and make you small; that knowledge was branded onto his soul. Uncertainty was a rock to founder on. Faith and self-confidence were everything.

Wren pushed the engine to the max and leaned into the storm. There was no better defense than an overwhelming offense, every time. He'd watched Damalin Joes come to the same realization, sitting atop his horse and listening to the cries of the dying Quanse. You either killed or got killed, and he had no intention of getting killed. If that meant getting used as a cog in some diabolical plot, Wren figured he could ride that horse just as far as he needed to before wrestling it to the ground.

No other thing for it but leap first, plan the landing later.

Fine by Wren. He'd have it no other way.

12

EXTRA-LEGAL

Wren stopped at the depot, checking in on his dead friends. Nobody had moved them. Simon was still there, Hartright laid out beside him, the unnamed second cop lying flat on his back, like he was sleeping off a five-day drunk.

Wren stood in the doorway with his back to them, looking out over the frozen lake. The storm was ebbing now, like a tidal movement draining from an estuary. That was good. Hopefully he could catch the dawn flight out, get a jump on his investigation of the Reparations. He still had a couple of hours until then.

He brought up his phone, powered it on and was inundated with a rush of chimes as notifications poured in. Top of the screen were the latest; reports from the spider algorithm he'd set up to search for fresh instances of the snuff film. In the last hour it looked like hundreds of new versions had gone up.

They were everywhere.

He'd predicted as much to Humphreys. The video was going viral, and he understood why viewers were sharing it. It was horrific viewing, but people liked that kind of thing.

They stopped to rubberneck at a car crash, they searched for video of the aid worker who'd had his head cut off by jihadis, they couldn't help themselves.

It helped that this guy, Handel Quanse, was near-universally despised. Wren only had to scan a few headlines on major news sites to see how they were reporting his death. There was outrage at the murder, but there was also an undercurrent of glee. Why else would they list in the first or second paragraph all the reasons people had to hate him?

Handel Quanse's predatory investment activities had put tens of thousands of people out of work, apparently. Then to add insult to injury, he'd gone on talking head shows to call it tough love. Trickle-down economics, he'd said, only works if you're willing to work as hard as me. Slack off and you deserve to starve by the side of the road.

Comments were already trending toward sympathy with the Reparations. How could they be bad, people were saying, when they took trash like Joes to task? A fair point.

Wren checked into his darknet, where his hackers and the inner Foundation team were putting together lists of potential suspects, beginning with protest groups focused on income inequality: the 99%, Anti-Ca, SST. Wren knew a little about them from the mainstream media, but there wasn't much to know; they were all loose conglomerations of reformers, socialists and marginal communists.

The 99% were named after the percentage of people in society who owned less than 10% of the wealth. Anti-Ca was short for Anti-Capitalist. SST took their name from the Latin phrase favored by John Wilkes Booth, 'Sic Semper Tyrannis', meaning 'Thus Always to Tyrants.' According to the research, some of these groups had greater financing, some less, but none had perpetrated any protest action nearly as massive or as brazen as the Reparations video. None were considered a terrorist threat by Homeland Security, and Wren had received no briefings about any of them. At worst, all they did was turn up at rallies and try to throw red paint on the 'symbols of capitalism', like coffee shop chains and fast-food joints.

Wren scrolled through some photos of past protests the various groups had attended. Mostly they were family-friendly crowds, parents with little kids in tow holding up signs like:

YOUR YACHT OUR DEBT

MONEY COSTS TOO MUCH

COULD YOU PASS THROUGH THE EYE OF THE NEEDLE?

A few members wore black tactical gear with helmets and masks, tried to start fights with the police, but they never achieved the critical mass they were hoping for. The families never joined them in punching through the windows of sneaker shops and designer gyms.

Ani-rich rage. Income inequality. Maybe there was plenty of injustice there, but nothing acute enough for Wren to get involved with. That was for the lawmakers to resolve, not a black-ops operator.

That left him nothing much to go on. He checked his mailbox, found a message from Hellion, his genius hacker.

THE VIDEO IS GUARANTEED NOT DEEPFAKE, CHRISTOPHER. NO METADATA SIGNATURES IN THE VIDEO APPEAR, HOWEVER, NOTHING WE CAN TRACK. WE ARE SEARCHING FOR MANY LINKS: GEOGRAPHICAL, FINANCIAL, DEMOGRAPHIC, BUT NOTHING YET. RECOMMEND YOU EXTRACT INFORMATION FROM SOCIAL MEDIA COMPANIES, WHERE THIS FILM IS POSTED. WE CANNOT HACK THEM FROM HERE. THEY WILL HAVE BETTER METADATA.

Wren grunted. Extract information from social media companies? He didn't pay too close an eye to tech news, but even he knew Internet content companies like WeStream, NameCheck and Iota were locked in battle with the US government over issues of content moderation. The companies wanted the advertising money that disinformation and violent content generated, and the government was tiptoeing around that just trying not to trip over freedom of speech issues.

Inserting himself into the middle of that didn't sound feasible or productive, but maybe it was the best lead he had.

The phone started chiming again as more notifications came in from the spider, and Wren squeezed it silent. Across the way an old guy in a yellow parka walked along the road, pulling a sled loaded with low wooden crates. Wren raised a hand in greeting. The guy waved back.

"The wife calling you?" he shouted.

"You got me," Wren answered with a neighborly grin. "Out all night."

The guy gave him a thumbs up. "Depot open then?"

"Fixing it up," Wren shouted back. "Gas leak. It'll take a few hours."

"Good man," the guy answered, and turned his attention back to pulling his sled.

Wren checked the time. Still two hours to the next flight out. He had to get out of here. Better use that time productively, so he placed the call he'd been putting off. It took minutes, and Wren listened and watched as the old guy trudged on, pulling his load toward the wilderness. Wren wondered what he had in those crates. He was two hundred yards away when the phone finally clicked.

"Agent Rogers."

It was Sally Rogers' voice, but it came through flat and emotionless like he'd never heard it before.

"It's me, Sally," he said. "Have you seen the billionaire video?"

She said nothing. A moment passed and Wren stepped back into the depot and out of the wind, pressing the phone tight to his ear. Sally Rogers had been with him at every stage in their battle against the Blue Fairy. He'd handpicked her to lead his digital team months before that, an ambitious and brilliant analyst looking to move into field operations. Together they'd mutinied against Humphreys, leading to her helping him execute a tanker full of Pinocchios off the New Jersey coast. Making her complicit in all those deaths.

Where did that leave her now? Angry, he figured.

"Turn yourself in, Christopher."

There it was. She did sound angry. Burning cold with anger, in fact.

"I'm sorry, Sally. For how things went. For how that might have affected you. But I think my father's involved with the death of Handel Quanse." He paused a moment. "At least somebody wants me to think that he is. The Reparations, I'm calling them. I need your help to-"

"I don't work for you anymore," she interrupted. "And I can't make any promises, if you force me to hunt you down. I don't want to kill you, but I will."

That was a little stronger than he'd expected. "Let's avoid that outcome, agreed. So can we call a truce? Humphreys is on board if you are. Stop the hunt." A pause. "Even help me."

The wind rushed by sharp and stinging. Rogers breathed low on the other end.

"Killing Pinocchios on the tanker was one thing," she said. "I didn't know about it at the time, but I understand it, I thought maybe it was the right thing. But this? CIA don't even act within the Continental US, Wren. We certainly don't execute citizens without a trial. You're on the hook for all of that, and that means I am too, because I'm an accomplice. So come in. The law has to apply to you too, or none of this is worth anything."

Wren grunted. She was right, he did owe her for that. It surprised him how easily his answer came.

"Fine. When this is done, I'll come in. Peacefully."

He felt a mental milestone ticking over. Once in Rogers' hands, he might go to jail for the rest of his life. He wouldn't see his kids, his wife, his Foundation again. Caught in the moment with the Apex in the wind, though, none of that mattered. Better that he never saw them again, but they were safe, than any other outcome.

"Deal," she said swiftly. "What do you need?"

"I need you to corral the social media companies. The search engines. We need to find out who planted this video. Crack them open with subpoenas, smash in their doors in a dawn raid, censure the CEOs or repossess their infrastructure, I don't care. Get that data and use it to track the Reparations back."

She barely let a beat go by before answering. "Not possible, Christopher."

"Why not?"

She sighed. "You've been out of the loop. We went through all this after the Blue Fairy. The government suspended free speech and censored the press, social media, much of the Internet? We had that power then, but now it's long gone. The big companies have slipped the leash, incorporating overseas, placing their decisions outside the remit of American law. It'll take a year before any of it comes up before the Supreme Court. We can't shut these companies down even if we raid their offices on American soil. Ask your hackers if you don't believe me. We'd have to slap a firewall around the coasts and a dome across the sky to prevent information getting though, and that's an isolationism we can't afford, not after the damage we took from the Blue Fairy." She took a breath. "The world hates us right now. For our excesses, our selfishness, our cruelty. This video capitalizes on that hate perfectly."

Wren cursed under his breath. Of course, she was right. If billionaires were a symbol of anything, it was America. Rags to riches. Make your fortune. Capitalism on speed.

He started pacing in front of the depot, each footstep a crunch through snow, thinking it through. "They're not American companies anymore," he said. "Outside your jurisdiction."

"Exactly," Sally confirmed. "They're colonizers in a new Wild West, the global information landscape, and there are no laws out there, while we're hamstrung by the Constitution. It gives them all the power with none of the accountability, so they do what they want, and what's best for their bottom line."

All that made sense. Wren spun the issue. "It's free to ask. Persuade them helping us is better than siding with these Reparations."

Rogers snorted. "We're asking. We ask all day, Christopher, every day. But they're corporations, their only loyalty is to their bottom line, which means serving exactly what their users want. If their users want disinformation and violence, so be it. So what do you think their answer is, when we ask nicely for their help to shut down and investigate their biggest current revenue stream?"

Wren took that on board and dialed the lens back a step. Big picture. "OK. So give me your read. My hackers say I need metadata on the video from the big companies; how do I get that if the government can't help and the companies won't volunteer it?"

"No legally-mandated force can compel what you're asking," Rogers said. Sounded like she was carefully choosing her words. And did she emphasize 'legally'? Maybe. "That's all she wrote."

Wren took a second, reading between the lines. "Nothing you can do legally. But extra-legally?"

He heard the hint of a smile in her voice. A little of the old Rogers shining through. "What can I say? People break the law all the time."

There it was. A hole in the State apparatus through which he could slip. "People do. But people would never get in if the government had eyes on these companies. Do you have any federal overwatch in place?"

She was right there with him. "Why would we?"

And that was the rest of it. Everything he needed to know. An assault on the Internet companies wasn't going to bring down an immediate federal response. If he was going to jail already, may as well add a few more crimes to the list.

"I'll be in touch," he said, killed the call, then started walking away from the depot, back to where his Jeep was waiting.

13

DASH 8

At 07:32 Wren boarded a passenger turboprop plane out of Deadhorse, capacity thirty-seven, occupancy twelve, all pallid pipeline workers drained of color and life by their stint in the far north. In three hours he hit Anchorage International, where he took a runway shuttle to a private HA-420 HondaJet, capacity six, occupancy one. Flight time to San Francisco International Airport was five hours, scheduled to touch down by 16:14.

He drank coffee, ate a microwave meal of Kobe beef brisket and asparagus, and dug into the Internet.

It frothed with celebration and condemnation both. On streaming site WeScreen there were already hundreds of video responses to Handel Quanse's death: shock-faced teens making O-faces; comedy trolls running play-by-plays like they were commentating a sporting event; talking heads snipped out of network newscasts saying how this was the dawn of some dark new Internet age: post-law, post-decency, heading toward an era of politics by gladiatorial combat.

No one lamented his death. Handel Quanse was a hated man, and as far as most were concerned, these were the just desserts he'd earned. Pegged against that, the Reparations came off as a modern-day kind of Robin Hood.

On social media site NameCheck a spray of hashtags were battling for dominance: #splittherich, #99rising, #stormthebastille, #handelthat! and the clear winner, #REPARATIONS. Trending feeds ticked over constantly in swells of alternating excitement and fear. A little-known Congressman went on record saying it was perhaps a a necessary reckoning. A mega church preacher claimed it was the onset of the Revelation. Video re-mixers on WeScreen auto tuned their comments and turned them into rap battles laid over the scene of Handel Quanse's death.

With every passing hour in the air, Wren watched the tone darken like a scab hardening around a wound, making the message real by reflecting, digesting and amplifying it. Billionaires were not untouchable. The rich could be brought down. The masses liked what they were seeing, and they wanted more.

YOU ARE OWED REPARATIONS
CLAIM THEM IN BLOOD

Already there were instances of real-life mimicry. Sometime around noon the copycat videos began. They started off soft, with a twenty-second clip of kids in ski masks spray-painting WHERE ARE OUR REPARATIONS? on the drive of a wealthy neighbor. That video went viral under the hashtag #REPARATIONS, and opened the floodgates for more.

A fast-food worker in a drive-thru made a fire-in-the-hole video, tossing a full milkshake into the waiting open window of a Ferrari, mostly hitting the driver's young daughter. Another group of teens, this time in mustached Anonymous masks, walked along a marina firing red paintball pellets at the hulls of yachts. #REPARATIONS again. A pool cleaner filmed a fluffy Pomeranian repeatedly trying to climb out of a marble swimming pool, and laughing. #REPARATIONS.

It was beginning with minor property damage and pranks, but those were catalysts only. With the people already on edge, and social media providing virality to videos that offered dopamine satisfaction for strikes back at the wealthy, Wren believed it'd soon lead to real violence. Call it mass self-radicalization on an accelerated timescale. He'd seen it happen in the Pyramid, a thousand people stampeding themselves toward self-immolation. Without anyone able to stop it, the anger would only build.

Wren didn't care. Mobs always did. Made up of people who thought they were righteously redressing some injustice; they became an echo chamber that drove their members to commit fresh and worse injustices.

Injustices to what end? Wren didn't care.

What mattered was digging through their anti-rich bullshit to the core. If that meant destroying the mob before it could mobilize, he would. With an online mob that meant shutting down their Internet access, and it just so happened Wren already had the social media companies in his sights for their metadata on the video.

Two birds with one stone.

He'd already selected his prime target. Housed in an expansive campus along the south coast of San Francisco Bay, the beating heart of Silicon Valley. NameCheck, the biggest social media behemoth and owner of WeScreen, the largest video streaming site. Between the two NameCheck had a near monopoly on the Internet eyeballs of America. They were the prime vector by which this video was spreading.

"It cannot be done," his elite hacker Hellion said, on the jet headed south toward San Francisco, after he'd explained the plan. "No, Christopher, impossible."

Her accent sounded unusually harsh through the scratchy connection; Wren mid-air on the satellite phone, Hellion answering from a convoy somewhere in the ex-Soviet sphere, probably Moldova or Ukraine, two of her favorite haunts.

Hellion was a twenty-one-year-old genius, a Bulgarian wunderkind who'd taken up hacking as a fun thing to do after conquering the world of real-time strategy game StarCraft. Her incredible APM, or Actions Per Minute ratio, meant she could execute up to 400 meaningful keystrokes every sixty seconds, which was faster than most concert pianists.

She'd leveraged that awesome speed into taking down one of the biggest black hat hackers in the world, known only as B4cksl4cker. Now her partner-in-crime, his specialism was corralling vast 'botnets' of remotely slaved computers to do his bidding, whether that was to build deepfake videos, hack into bank vaults or bring down government infrastructure via Trojan-like 'cryptoworms'.

For the past two years they'd been working for Wren through the Foundation, his rehab group for ex-cons, disgraced soldiers and white-collar criminals. For the past three months they'd been hunting Wren's father using the Blue Fairy's stolen infrastructure, a kind of 'second skin' on the Internet, and getting nowhere.

"Why not?" he answered.

Hellion let out a long sigh. "Christopher. Where do I begin? Let me guess, you think this company, NameCheck, it is playground, yes? Children's slide in office, theme park rooms, ping pong in break room? It will be easy to infiltrate and find CEO, you think, force him to help you, correct?"

Wren shrugged. She couldn't see it, but that didn't matter. "I'm sure they've got security. I just need you to hack it and buy me a way through."

Another sigh. "There is no way to 'hack' them,

Christopher. These corporate campuses are digitally air-gapped. Do you know what this means?"

"I can guess."

"Do not guess, please, you will hurt yourself."

Wren smiled. A little bit of Hellion was refreshing. "Enlighten me."

"It means there is no outside Internet line leading into security, personnel, anything," she went on. "Air gap, like digital moat. There is no way to remotely create ID or fake 'fast pass' to CEO's office. And it is CEO you wish to see, correct?"

She was correct. Wren was after Lars Mecklarin, the late-twenties inventor and CEO of NameCheck, famous for still wearing one brand of cheap red sneakers despite being the third-richest person on the planet.

"So phish me an identity. Socially hack him. You have-" Wren checked the time. Already it was past midday, and there were three hours left in the flight. "Four hours until I'm at their door. Find a worker, steal his ID, give it to me."

Hellion chuckled. "You are sweet. NameCheck has impressive biometric analysis, such as retinal scans, fingerprint scans, and so on. Let me send you illustration."

His phone chimed, and images popped up. Maps of the NameCheck campus as seen from above, overlaid with security notation. A cursor appeared and moved to highlight certain parts of the map.

"Look here, only two or three entrances to this campus, guarded by dual guard posts. B4cksl4cker is running background observation for intel. B4cksl4cker?"

A moment passed, then the big Armenian came on the line, his voice husky like a bear. "Christopher, yes, Hellion is correct. I see four elite security force members running biometric ID pass approval. I have leads on screening, also. There is automated detection CCTV on all approach roads, linked to best facial recognition and gait analysis algorithms in existence. You know this, gait recognition?"

"I wouldn't want to guess and hurt myself," Wren countered.

Now B4cksl4cker sighed. Wren's smile broadened. His hackers were always so put-upon. "This means the way you walk, Christopher. It is unique, like fingerprint. If you, Christopher Wren, walk up to their gate with your face and your walk, they will know. You are not in records. You will not pass."

Wren took a moment. "OK. So we're onto forceful insertion. I won't need a pass, then."

B4cksl4cker was ready for that. "Come in by vehicle, try to ram through security gates, they are ready. Hidden blast barricades everywhere. These will rise instantly if you leave the road, capable of stopping military vehicle. Security teams from special forces will meet you, with permission to fire. If you somehow breach past them, there are multiple panic rooms in missile-proof bunkers underground, capable to fit entire command team." He took a breath. "You will never get near CEO."

Wren nodded along. All that certainly limited his attack paths. He couldn't hope to mount any kind of brute-force assault. A parachute drop onto the roof would be spotted by CCTV and lead to campus lockdown. Entry on foot with a paramilitary team would have the same result. Neither could he attempt a covert digital insertion; there were no ways to mount a hack across an air gap.

He was going to have to get creative. He had Hellion and B4cksl4cker, after all, as well as a guy in LA who could fly in to help out, and a wider Foundation filled with all kinds of skillsets.

He explained the plan as it came to him, looking down

through the clouds to the land far below. Maybe beginning to see the shape of things.

"Not possible," Hellion insisted, after he finished. "You are talking about 'God Mode', Christopher. This is dream. Impossible coordination. Many moving parts. We do not have time. I have tried this before, and never succeeded."

Wren just smiled. 'God Mode' was a nice name for what he was suggesting. "You never tried it with me."

14

GRUBER

The jet soared in over San Francisco around 4 p.m., and as it banked Wren saw the NameCheck campus lying below like a brightly colored theme park. Large adult trampolines, a full volleyball court, whimsical designs written out in various pathways through the green inner courtyard.

The jet landed within minutes at San Francisco Airport and taxied to a private stair car, where Wren was shuttled to the customs building and ushered through at pace.

As planned, his LA Foundation member had flown in ahead and was now waiting for him in short-stay parking. Steven Gruber was a slim, tousle-headed 33-year-old NSA analyst, dressed in board shorts and a Hawaiian shirt, sitting in a rented yellow Prius. Wren gave him a nod and strode over, carrying no baggage, and climbed into the back like it was a taxi.

"Good to see you, Steven. Let's drive."

"Man says drive," Gruber said and pulled away, into the spaghetti network of feeder roads out of the airport. "Man says fly up from LA, I get it done. Everything you need's in back."

Wren grunted thanks, unzipping the Day-Glo pink and green backpack on the seat beside him. Steven Gruber had this curious habit of starting his sentences about Wren as 'Man says-' or 'Man does-'. Maybe they'd address it in a coin meeting sometime soon; issues with authority, probably. When had their last coin meeting been?

The Prius cleared the overhanging access roads and rolled onto the open 101. Gruber rolled the windows down and warm, salty air rushed in; a relief after being cooped up on planes for nine hours. Wren took a moment to just breathe. It was a beautiful afternoon in the Bay Area, an azure sky streaked with hair-thin cirrus clouds like a balding old man's well-combed head. Hot, low 90s. A total shift after the snowstorm in Deadhorse, and he shrugged off his woolen jacket.

"Sixteen months," Gruber said, conversationally, like they didn't know each other all that well and Wren hadn't once broken into a mass orgy with him at the center, sweaty and pink-assed, "since I heard direct from you."

"That's my bad," Wren said, turning his attention to the backpack. "I've been busy."

"I know that," Gruber said, smiling and glancing at Wren in the rearview. "Taking out the Saints. The Pinocchios. You're a national hero."

Wren tipped out the backpack. Pink short shorts came first. That was ridiculous. He pushed them to one side. A yellow string vest followed. What the…? He looked up at Gruber. Dressed like a normal person. He looked at the pink and yellow outfit.

"You said light and bright," Gruber said, watching Wren in the mirror. "I didn't have time to keep looking; that's what they had."

"Were you in a strip club?" Wren retorted.

"The airport. A sports clothing store, that's what they had."

Wren held up the yellow vest. 'Skimpy', was one way to describe it. "There wasn't a GAP?"

"Man said come fast. I came fast. And it wasn't the only thing on your shopping list. Does it really matter?"

Wren sighed. No, he supposed it didn't. He'd certainly look non-threatening, dressed in the shorts and vest, and that was the point. He rummaged through the rest of the backpack's contents while the Prius weaved gently through traffic, with the Bay peeling and unpeeling to his left behind layers of industrial buildings, housing, parks.

4:25, time rushing by.

There was the earpiece he'd asked for, and a clippable bodycam to wear on his chest. It was light enough, but looking at the flimsy yellow shirt he figured it wouldn't hold up the weight. A camera wasn't much good that drooped to the floor.

"There's a strap, shoulder-holster thing," Gruber said, trying to point while driving.

"Look at the road," Wren said. "I'm not getting pulled over."

"Yeah," Gruber said, then continued softly to himself, "man says look at the road, look at the road."

Wren found the strap.

"You wear it like a Go-Pro," Gruber said encouragingly. "Life-streaming, the kids are calling it."

Wren looked at the strap, an elasticized band in hot pink. He was going to look like a clown. "Which kids?"

"In the shop. They showed me some clips. It's the new big thing. Life-streaming with commentary, the only way to vlog."

Vlog? Of course, that's what these #REPARATION posts were about. Wren sighed and kept looking through

Gruber's shopping. Big sunglasses, check. At least these were black. Blue flip-flops, because why not add blue to the mix? A burner cell phone: he booted it. There was a welcome message from Hellion and B4cksl4cker waiting for him, along with twin icons. The first he pushed, and it synced the phone with the earpiece and the bodycam; footage of the car seat began streaming on the screen. He inserted the earpiece and heard a low testing hum, then Hellion's voice.

"Getting signal," she said. "Lift me up."

Wren lifted the bodycam.

"Good," Hellion said. "Checking levels. Precision. Contours. Excellent, your boy bought nice lens." There was a pause, then, "Christopher, are you wearing that?"

He put the bodycam back down. She'd seen the shorts and top laid out on the seat. "Not your department."

"You have figure for this, I am sure, but-"

Wren tapped the earpiece and her voice cut out. Everything was here, except...

"Where's the board?" he asked Gruber.

"In the trunk," Gruber said enthusiastically. "You're going to love it. I got you the top model, glides smooth as a lunar rover."

Wren frowned. Was that an expression? "All right."

"Man says all right," Gruber muttered.

Wren opened his mouth to address the 'Man says...', briefly thought better of it, then went ahead anyway. "You realize I can hear you, every time you say, 'Man says' something?"

"Hmm?" Gruber asked, looking at Wren in the mirror.

"I'm saying, when you repeat what I said and add 'Man says' before it, there's no need."

Gruber looked puzzled, like he had no idea what Wren was talking about. "How's that?"

Wren opened his mouth to continue, then gave up. "Never mind."

"Man says never mind," Gruber muttered to himself.

Wren let it go, and pulled his shirt off, shrugged on the yellow vest. It had to be several sizes too small for him: tight to his broad shoulders, snug on his ripped stomach. The tattoos on his chest were showing; his wife's name, Loralei, his kids Quinn and Jake.

"Suits you," said Gruber.

Wren ignored him and swapped his pants for the pink short shorts. They were really short. He hadn't dressed like this since, well, his Pyramid days? Running in the desert, a few minutes of stolen fun from all the cultish pain and nonsensical BS.

He snapped back to attention. His heavy-duty boots came off, replaced with the flip-flops. The bodycam clipped onto his chest and the harness went around his shoulder. He tapped the earpiece again, bringing Hellion back online.

She sounded amused. "I'm not saying anything."

"What?" Wren asked.

"B4cksl4cker says this is good look for you. I'm waiting to see effect when you stand."

Wren frowned down at the bodycam. How had she-?

"Traffic cams," Hellion said. "Hacked. We are tracking you, with good angles through windows. You arrive in five minutes. Get out in four. You will need to approach via board; this is common practice. All feeds show NameCheck CEO is in position, we think building three, but campus also has underground facilities, these may link many buildings. He may not be there-"

"He's there," Wren said.

"Are you talking to me?" Gruber asked, confused.

Wren ignored him, looking now at his pink pants. There

wasn't even a pocket to put the cell phone in. He'd just have to hold it.

"There's an arm strap," Gruber said, pointing helpfully.

Wren found it. Orange; he'd mistaken it for part of the backpack. He was going to look like Jackson Pollack had vomited up a rainbow. He tucked the cell phone into the strap and cinched it around his left bicep; it barely fit.

"Christopher," Gruber said from up front. Wren looked up. In the mirror, it looked like uncertain emotions were playing across his face. "I know this is not the time, and like you said, you've been busy, but I could really use a coin meeting. Not now of course, but I mean, just…"

He trailed off.

Wren nodded. This was his fault; sixteen months was too long without a check-in. Losing his family, then hunting down the Saints and the Blue Fairy had distracted him, but that was no excuse. He had a responsibility to his members, and maybe Gruber had already fallen off the wagon. Gone back to the orgies that had been his addiction. There wasn't anything necessarily wrong with 'free love', but Gruber was an addict and couldn't handle it, plus the groups and cults who ran the events were generally self-destructive.

He softened his voice. "You're right, Steven, we're overdue. We'll do it as soon as this is finished, I promise. Thank you again for coming today. I couldn't do this without you."

That puffed Gruber up a little.

"And I'm sorry I haven't been there. The coin system's a promise and I've been breaking it. I'll do better." Gruber nodded along. Wren thought he saw the glimmer of tears forming in the young man's eyes. "But for these clothes, I think I have to penalize you a coin."

Gruber laughed. The moment broke. Wren smiled too. This was what it was all about, why he had hunted down the

Blue Fairy, why all this mattered. Not just his family, but the Foundation too. That brought the thought of Damalin Joes III to mind, out there somewhere facing a gruesome death, and the smile faded from his face.

They approached NameCheck.

Wren pictured Hellion and B4cksl4cker poised like spiders over their computers, half a world away. His other Foundation members somewhere out there, crunching video on the biggest servers B4cksl4cker could steal. Hunting for leads. It all came down to this.

"Here is your spot," came Hellion's voice in his ear. "Outside surveillance range. Get out."

Wren tapped Gruber's shoulder, and he pulled off the freeway onto a quiet side road with a big palm tree and a view over parked cars to the calm green-blue waters of the Bay. The NameCheck campus was less than a mile away. Wren got out, leaving the backpack and his old clothes behind. The Bay breeze blew a warm wind around his bare legs.

Would he pass? Probably. With no bag, not even any pockets, he wouldn't look like anyone's idea of a threat. A big guy still, bearded and tattooed, but beards and tattoos were commonplace in Silicon Valley. And pièce de résistance? He popped the trunk and took out his hoverboard. 4:32. Time to get moving.

15

NAMECHECK

Wren had never ridden a hoverboard before. It was small, sturdy, white and felt like a motorized bathroom scale; just enough space to fit his feet then a five-inch wheel either side. Like a Segway, it responded to the way he balanced his bodyweight; slightly forward, slightly backward, left to right, steering as he leaned.

He leaned forward and it picked up some speed. He whipped past a few pedestrians, leaving them in his dust. It was quite exhilarating, more so even than riding a snowmobile with a flashing blue light; something about the power of just 'leaning' ever so slightly and having the world respond accordingly.

He whipped past the end of the parking lot then was out onto an exposed strip by the Bay; winds buffeted him and made for their own challenges. Easily 15mph now, half of the 100m record sprint speed, like a superhero gliding in for a dramatic landing. One bump in the sidewalk would send him flying, almost naked, without any of the protective leathers a motorcyclist would wear.

God Mode.

He whizzed onto Veterans Boulevard and slid off the

sidewalk into a cycle lane. New-build residential lots flew by either side. Soon the warehouse bulk of the NameCheck campus rose up ahead like a cluster of colorful cruise liners.

He drew in.

"They have eyes on the road from here," Hellion said in his ear. "You're already in their early warning system, so don't step off the hoverboard here. Remember, gait analysis of the way you walk. Also, do not take off your sunglasses. Facial analysis."

Wren grunted. In moments he'd be there, hopefully categorized under the security algorithms as a STATUS UNKNOWN. Hellion had been emphatic about the importance of achieving that status. By withholding his facial and gait data, the NameCheck system wouldn't have enough data to categorize him as either AUTHORISED or UNAUTHORISED, and would therefore kick him over to the gate security team to run a direct ID check on.

Wren slowed as he passed the familiar NameCheck logo, a twenty-foot sign on the campus' grassy corner, rising out of a bed of plastic flowers. The buildings were angular and modernist, off-setting the fortress-like look of their construction with playful colors and plasticky flair. His target was the north end access road, a broad avenue with a low gate.

A steady stream of millennials was trickling out through the gate. Closing time. There were two guard-boxes made up to look like ice-cream vendors, left and right.

"Left," Hellion said as Wren rolled up, scanning the scene through the bodycam. Wren veered over then Hellion corrected with a snappy, "No, right!"

He played it off as a trick. Almost threw himself off the hoverboard, then spun up to the desk. A glass window, two guards behind it, neither looking so cheerful. Decals in the window of different ice creams. It made a mockery of their job, really. How often did punk kids come up asking for a Mister Softee, raspberry sauce, thinking it was some great joke?

"Angle up," Hellion said, and Wren leaned back slightly, giving the bodycam the view it needed of the guards' faces. "Now buy us a minute."

"You see that, brah?" Wren asked the guard, adopting a California surfer accent. "Sick twists. You ride?"

The security guard eyed him dispassionately. Probably Wren's age, mid-thirties, half-jealous at how much money Wren must make, half-dismayed at what a dumbass he looked on his hoverboard in his stripper costume.

"The system can't log you when you ride up," the guard said tiredly. His colleague in back looked on. "You have to walk. The memos have gone out many times."

"Ah, sorry brother," Wren said, "I'm just an addict, you know? I can't get enough of the air, shooting down the boulevard riding the wind, there's nothing like the lean, do you-"

"Pass," the guard said, holding out a hand.

"Fifty seconds yet," Hellion said, keys clacking wildly through the earpiece.

"Pass, I feel that," said Wren smoothly, "I got it right here." He went for his pockets, then made a show of discovering he had none. He patted his hips. Patted his shirt. "Shoot."

"Forty seconds," Hellion said.

The guard's expression locked. 'You're all children,' that expression said. Wren leaned into it.

"I forgot," he said.

"So go home and get it," the guard said. "Ride the wind." Hellion laughed.

"Nah, I think I got it here," Wren said, and went for his phone. "Got a special leave."

The guard sighed.

"Longer," Hellion said.

Wren unzipped his shoulder holster and took out his phone, then fumbled it on purpose. It hit the cement walk-up and he leaned over to get it. The hoverboard responded to his shift in weight, banging against the guard post's cement plinth. Wren rocked back and turned, then bent over again.

"Step down, sir," the guard said, with the infinite patience of a parent with a toddler.

Wren looked up at him, playing confused.

"Off the board. To get your phone."

Wren smiled and laughed "Right on."

"Don't walk," Hellion said. "One step. Almost there."

Wren put one foot down, fished for the phone with the other.

"Twenty seconds," Hellion said.

The guards were waiting. Starting to lose the edge of patience, maybe getting suspicious.

"Here you go, brah," Wren said, and held out the phone. The guy took it and sighed.

"It's locked. PIN."

"Ready," Hellion said.

Wren took the phone, tapped in the PIN and handed it back.

The guard squinted. If everything had gone well, Hellion had near-field hacked the guard's computer, built Wren a pass by overwriting a legitimate employee, then backloaded it onto Wren's phone.

The guard squinted. The moment stretched out. If something went wrong here, that was it. NameCheck security would be alerted, and he'd never get close to the CEO. The guard turned to his colleague, pointed at the screen, and the guy looked, smiled, looked up at Wren.

"You really like the hoverboard, huh?" he asked.

Wren didn't know what that was about. "Sure do, brah."

The front guard handed the phone back. "In you go, Mr. Rider. Like the wind."

Wren grinned like an idiot and rolled away from the guard booth, through the gate, looking at his phone. There was a pass with his photo, time-slotted for that hour, but it wasn't under his name. Where his name was supposed to be, it now read AIR RIDER.

"You're kidding me," he muttered. "Hellion."

"What?" she answered, clearly restraining her laughter. "This is good strong American name."

"Hardly God Mode as I envisioned it."

That made her burst out laughing.

"You are in," B4cksl4cker reasoned. "This is very good cover. Now, proceed to building 3, Christopher."

He knew better than to argue it in the moment. In the aftermath, it'd just be too ridiculous. Better to roll with the punches.

"That's Mr. Rider to you."

They both laughed as he rolled into the campus.

16

GOD MODE

W ren rolled along a rubberized red asphalt path through an inner green space of spruce trees and grass, workers out picnicking on the grass. On the right lay a trampoline pod with two teenagers, no doubt coding prodigies, bouncing merrily. The interior building façades were coated in shades of garish neon orange, yellow and pink that matched Wren's clothes.

"Building 3 is to your left," Hellion said.

Wren veered left, passing the sculpture of a dinosaur, twenty feet high. It had giant rainbow feathers and a placard scrawled at its feet: RETHINK THE PAST. A pod of employees passed him, playing some kind of Augmented Reality Game that saw them swiping at invisible enemies in the air.

"Here," Hellion said. "Left at Narnia."

The path forked whimsically at a lamppost jeweled with fake snow, and Wren followed it. His pass scanned at the entrance to building 3, a violet affair with diagonally slanted windows. Finally he dismounted the hoverboard, took his first step into the building, where the gait analysis cameras should no longer be filming.

A security guard inside gave him a wave, and Wren headed up stairs decorated with child-like artwork on the walls, along a corridor beside a sports hall where people wearing giant inflatable plastic ball-suits were trying to play soccer, bouncing off each other.

Lars Mecklarin, CEO of NameCheck, was in his office on the third floor running a meeting around a standing conference desk. Wren strode up alongside the room's all-glass wall, surveying the five people inside: two in suits, three in colorful shorts and T-shirts boasting punk hairstyles, extreme body modification, tattoos. The atmosphere seemed intense.

Wren opened the glass door and stepped in. All eyes turned to him.

"Who the hell are you?" a guy asked, short-sleeve suit jacket, wireframe spectacles and a topknot with shaved sides. Not Lars. Lars wasn't even looking at them, focused on something on a tablet before him.

"Rider," Hellion said dramatically in Wren's ear. "Air Rider." He ignored her.

"My name is Christopher Wren," he said calmly and confidently, projecting strength. These people before him were not weak. Each ran a division that dwarfed his Foundation, each managed budgets that made his slush fund look like the dregs in a beggar's cup, each influenced the daily thoughts of millions, far more than the reach of his Megaphone app. Next to them Wren was just an ant stumbling into a magpie's nest. "I'm here about the Reparations videos." He let that hang. "About what you're going to do about them."

The topknot guy frowned. "Are you even supposed to be here? What's your clearance level?"

"I'm new," Wren said. "Lars Mecklarin, it's about the Reparations videos. You'll want to hear what I've got to say."

Lars looked up.

Next to the others, he appeared normal. Wren had seen him on magazine covers: lily-white, slender, nondescript T-shirt and cargo pants, large nose and limpid eyes with a shaving rash on his throat; just another billionaire, though he hadn't made the Reparations cut. Yet there was an intense focus in those pale, wet eyes to match any stone-cold killer Wren had met. You didn't get to where he'd risen without crushing plenty of people along the way.

He gazed at Wren for a moment, and his wet eyes shifted. Now there was curiosity alongside the intensity, maybe even something close to excitement. "It's OK. You can go, Alec."

The topknot guy, Alec, frowned. "Are you for real, Lars? This guy's a nobody. I'm calling sec-"

"Don't call security," Lars said firmly, and Alec froze. "I know who he is. It'll be all right."

Alec looked confused.

"Go, all of you," Lars said. "We'll pick this up later."

It took a few seconds for the others to register it. They obviously had questions. They'd ask each other as soon as they stepped out. Probably one of them would call security anyway. It didn't matter. Wren had reached the inner sanctum.

They shuffled out.

A few seconds passed as Lars Mecklarin studied him.

"Christopher Wren," he said at last. Like he was amused. "You're famous. I heard the FBI are hunting you?" He let that hang. It made sense to Wren. The head of a globe-spanning corporation would get security briefings direct from the government. "I didn't recognize you, dressed like that."

"I'm undercover," Wren answered, not missing a beat. "This is what your employees wear."

Lars almost cracked a smile. They stared at each other.

"A call just went out to the police," Hellion said in his ear. "I couldn't block it. Do this quickly."

There was no such thing as quickly. Wren just stood. The message had already been delivered; his presence here alone said it all, and Lars was smart enough to receive it.

"You're making a point," he said. "That you can break into my company? Get in a room with me. I don't know how you did it; I'm told our security is triple-layered and uncrackable, best in the world. But here you are."

"I've got some of the best hackers in the world. You'd be amazed what a hoverboard and sunglasses can achieve."

Lars' eyes narrowed, parsing that out. "So you're here. It won't make a difference. I can imagine what you want: for me to block the Reparations videos. Am I right?"

Wren just stared. Lars looked like a nice enough guy, as far as billionaires went. Better than Handel Quanse, that was for sure. Don't be evil, all that. An idealist, after a fashion, but unwilling to take responsibility for the dangers his tool of mass communication could cause.

"Think of it as an opportunity," Wren said. "Not a setback."

Lars angled his head slightly. "Before you make your pitch, let me give you the answer. It's no. Under no circumstances, as I said to the CIA, the FBI, the President herself. We fought them all off already, after they suspended habeas corpus with the Blue Fairy. That was you too, correct?" A long pause. "I understand your fears, but you don't know what this place is. NameCheck. It's more than just a company; it's the next stage in human connection. Nothing you can say, nothing you can do, is going to change that. I won't put hard locks on the Reparations videos. Free speech is at stake, and that's just the start."

Wren didn't break eye contact. "Now can I make the pitch?"

Lars laughed. "By all means."

"The campus is going into lockdown," Hellion said in

Wren's ear. "Satellite feeds show security sweeping the grounds. There's an armed squad coming your way; police cars scrambling down 101. They'll be outside the office in minutes."

He ignored her. "Two sides to the pitch, Lars. First side, you're going to get great press if you cooperate with me. Open your servers and let us find the origin of the execution video, there may be metadata attached that'll leapfrog me to the source. You think I took risks to get in here? I'll do anything to find the people who made this video. Anything." He took a breath. "Thus far, wins all around. The public will love you for arresting the slide into violence. So we move onto the flip side, and this is just gravy now, you shut down the copycats. We both know these videos are not in the public interest. You flip your model right now, start human vetting of every new uploaded video, it shuts this thing down before it gets too dangerous."

A moment passed.

"We have vetting procedures already," Mecklarin said. "The execution video clearly contravenes our standards, and it comes down every time it's re-posted. As for the copycats, who are you to say they're not in the public interest? Plus what you suggest, human vetting on this kind of scale, is an impossible task."

"Not impossible," Wren countered. He was no expert, but he'd had a thorough briefing from his hackers. "Outsource human judgment for pennies per video, set up a system of trusted vendors who require less frequent oversight, you'll cut down the BS massively within minutes of setting it up. It'll dig into your profits, but that's the cost of doing business."

Mecklarin snorted. "Outsourced human judgment for every video? Even with a trusted vendor scheme, that'll take months to set up."

"So get started now. Now what about server access, the video metadata? That's what I want most."

"Absolute non-starter," Mecklarin said. Face flat and implacable. "I'm sorry, but it's impossible. If we believe in privacy, which we do, I can't just hand data over to you whenever you ask."

He stared at Wren. Wren stared back.

"You want to hear the third side of the pitch?" Wren asked.

Mecklarin smiled. "Is it a threat?"

Wren took a step forward, held up his phone so Lars could see a video just beginning to roll. "Let's find out."

17

DEEPFAKE

I t was a familiar video, but altered.

Hellion ran the new feed and Lars Mecklarin watched. In seconds he realized what he was seeing and leaned in. After ten seconds he looked up at Wren.

"You think that's going to compel me? Nobody's going to believe it."

Wren killed the video. There were hundreds of copycat Reparations videos now. People vandalizing the property of the wealthy, spitting in their faces, running them out of restaurants. It was an easy thing to digitally cut out the faces of the attackers and put Lars Mecklarin's face in their place. Deepfake technology had come a long way. The way Hellion and B4cksl4cker had rigged it, it looked real. Lars Mecklarin tearing the brand name sneakers off a child's feet. Lars Mecklarin punching an old man in the chest, then relieving him of his watch.

"This is a proof of concept," Wren said. "Exposing the flaws of the NameCheck system. I upload this video, or something like it but very much worse, and it goes live right away, right? There's no advance moderation across your whole network. How long will it be up there, drawing views, before you get around to bringing it down?"

Lars snorted. "Not up for long. As I said, we have moderation. And very much worse, like what?"

Wren leaned in, spoke more quietly. "You know I took down the Blue Fairy. You'll also know what kind of footage those sick men were collecting. That I now have. I could put your face into a thousand videos like that in seconds. Would that get your attention?"

It did. Lars visibly winced, as if he'd been punched in the gut. Starting to imagine what that could mean, spread across his social media empire. Videos that were poison, even if they only surfaced briefly, could do irreparable damage to his brand. To his company.

"You wouldn't do that."

Wren smiled. "Wouldn't I? Who's to say I haven't already? Who's to say the first video of many isn't cued up and ready to go out right now?"

Lars' eyes widened, his skin paling further. Wren recognized the onset of shock, heart racing, breath shortening. "It won't matter. People will know it's not me. And in any case, that kind of video already contravenes our standards. It'll be crushed swiftly. The algorithms will flag it, dial it down and nobody will ever see it."

"Nobody," Wren said, considering. "Hours. Shall we put that to the test?"

Lars paled harder. "No. Don't-"

"It's already done." In the background Hellion worked her keyboard. "Use that tablet. Bring up your page."

Lars licked his lips. Wren knew the pattern of fear well: dry mouth, shortness of breath, clenched jaw. You couldn't prevent automatic responses no matter how hardened you were. "My page?"

"On NameCheck. A billion friends, that's you, right? Never mind, I'll do it for you."

Wren leaned over, tapped Mecklarin's tablet and brought up the NameCheck site. A simple search revealed Mecklarin's front page. Oddly, he hadn't posted anything for years.

"Security response are entering the building," Hellion said in Wren's ear. Mecklarin scrolled, hit refresh, then the video was there. Now there was footage of a group of men led by a deepfaked version of Lars Mecklarin, hounding a young woman carrying a Versace bag.

"This is nothing," he said.

"Keep watching," Wren advised.

"Security are right behind you," Hellion said. Mecklarin's eyes briefly darted to the side, confirming it. Wren turned. An armed private security squad stood beyond the glass wall, five figures with rifles trained on him.

Wren turned back to Lars. "You better hope they don't shoot me."

Lars nodded, held out a hand to ward the squad team off. Watching the video on his feed.

"B4cksl4cker is amplifying now," Hellion said.

"There," said Wren, pointing.

Lars eyes widened as the share count on the video suddenly rocketed. In seconds it was past a thousand, two thousand, three thousand. For a second the count froze, then jumped to ten thousand and climbing.

"We can do this with any footage," Wren said. "Force virality. Share it again and again, too fast for you to respond. Millions of people will see what we want them to see, splashed all over your front page. We will do that, if you don't help me. I'm asking only for server access to track that video back. Advance human moderation of all uploads will go a long way as a gesture of goodwill, also."

Lars looked up at Wren. This was a man abruptly on the

edge, seeing an end he'd never envisioned closing in. "How are you doing this?"

Wren shrugged. "It's easy enough, the same way the Reparations videos are doing it. A few botnets to drive up shares and force it to go viral. Gaming your system as it currently exists, Lars. Look at the trending table."

Twenty thousand shares in less than a minute, and the video had already hit the top of the trending table on the right. All the fight went out of Lars at once, like he'd been knocked out standing up. Seeing control of his life's work snatched out of his hands.

"You can't do this with pornographic material. Not with my face. You wouldn't."

"I'm already doing it," Wren answered firmly. "As long as you're letting the copycat videos through, you'll be letting whatever deepfake videos I put up through as well. A hundred every second, as soon as I say the word. Horrific stuff, Lars. Nobody should ever see it, spread across your network, using your tools. So do something to stop it."

Lars looked distraught. "I-"

"The digital Wild West is over, Lars. Think of me as the sheriff riding into town. You follow a law of common decency or I will destroy you personally, using your network as the weapon. Tell me you'll give me what I need."

Lars stared, running through the ramifications. The same face Damalin Joes had made on horseback, right before he led the execution of Handel Quanse. Already thinking of ways to turn this to his benefit and get the first-mover advantage in a new era of ethical communication. You didn't become a billionaire without being able to take advantage of a crisis.

"Lars," Wren barked.

"I'll do it," the man answered. "It'll cost billions. Backlog the entire Internet. But we'll do it."

"Then make the calls. Get me that video ready." Wren

pointed through the glass. "And wave them off, too. I'm leaving now. You'll hear from my team; we'll want everything you've got. Get it ready. Goodbye, Lars. Be grateful it's not you in one of the Reparations' cages."

Lars squared his shoulders. There was that visionary resilience coming through now. He picked up his phone and met Wren's eyes, then waved off the squad behind the glass.

Wren walked out. The squad tracked him with their muzzles but made no move to intercept. Down the stairs Wren went, past the bobble-bodied soccer game and out into the balmy afternoon light. Sirens screeched closer.

"That is fast," said Hellion in his ear. "It is happening already."

"They provided the video?"

"Yes, also all video on NameCheck is going dark. Their child companies too; WeScreen is showing a blank! It looks like every single one. We begin analysis of original video for metadata, Christopher. This is great win."

She hooted. Another record-setting hack.

It was a beginning.

18

BFFS

Wren rode off on his hoverboard. More security rushed past him. Who would think a near-naked man on a hoverboard was a threat? Running ahead of the descriptions. Wren gritted his teeth and leaned forward, speeding up. By the exit his legs were trembling.

"What is wrong, Christopher?" Hellion asked. "Your heart is racing."

He tapped the earpiece to mute it, pocketed the bodycam and rode through the exit barrier. Police were rushing up. A yellow Prius pulled up at the sidewalk and Wren jumped off the hoverboard, opened the backseat and tumbled in.

"Christopher," Steven Gruber said.

"Drive," Wren said. "Back North."

"Drive," said Gruber, not bothering with the 'Man says' this time, and pulled into traffic.

Wren opened the window wide and leaned out into the breeze, feeling the pop of sweat evaporating off his forehead. God Mode came with its own stresses.

"Water," Gruber said, holding out a bottle. Wren took a

long pull, turned to watch the sirens outside Namecheck recede, then looked ahead to where Gruber was watching him worriedly in the rearview mirror. Time to pull himself together.

"Lars Mecklarin liked my outfit," he said.

Gruber just stared.

"I got comments on the hoverboard too. Vintage, they said."

"It is a classic," Gruber answered, off-balance. "So did you-?"

Wren nodded. "We have the video. In the meantime, all video feeds are coming down across NameCheck and WeScreen."

"Wow," Gruber whispered. "How much data is that?"

"I don't know," Wren said. "A few hundred exabytes. Uncountable, probably. It'll get better."

Gruber whistled low. "Remind me never to get on your bad side."

"Never going to happen," Wren said. "We're BFFs."

Gruber beamed happily. Best Friends Forever. Wren looked out the window, then tapped the earpiece and heard Hellion's concerned voice.

"Christopher, what happened?"

"Post-God Mode jitters," he said. "Better done without a voice in my head."

She snorted. "Do you regret this, now? It is difficult, yes?"

"You told me so," Wren answered. "But we managed. Now, where are we up to with the metadata?"

Keys clattered from her end. "Working. We have NameCheck access now, B4cksl4cker is reconstructing the upload path for the execution video."

Wren sat up straight. "You have access?"

"Yes, Mecklarin opened data port for us. His system is very poorly organized, Christopher. He is like a hoarder."

He laughed. Of course she would criticize Lars Mecklarin. "So what have you got?"

"Nothing yet. This will take time, building matrix for analysis, enforcing structure, managing 'Big Data'. Good immediate news is, I sent your bodycam footage to other social media companies. Their videos are coming down. Moderation will begin."

Wren grunted. "We slowed the copycats down."

"It would appear so. This is good, yes?" She paused a moment. "Christopher, I have monitor on your heart rate, and it is erratic. This is not normal for you."

He grunted. Contemplated switching off the earpiece again, but that would only rile her up worse. Besides, she wasn't wrong. His pulse was a reedy, too-fast thrum in his temples. Riding the knife edge of exhaustion.

"I haven't been sleeping so well."

"When did you last sleep?"

He ran a quick calculation. "Properly? Four days ago."

In the background came B4cksl4cker's baritone laugh. His voice joined the line. "This is close to my record. Christopher, when I was hacking Northern Korea Republic, I did not sleep for one-hundred and fourteen hours. This is long time, yes? Long enough for hallucinations."

"I'm not hallucinating. I caught a few hours here and there."

"Few hours is not sleep, Christopher. You must sleep now. Hellion and I will extract data from NameCheck database. Trust us with this."

Wren looked out the window. San Francisco Bay whipped by to the side, but filmed with a gray fuzz, now that the adrenaline high was pulling back. It left a throb in his head and a strange lightness to the world around him. Looking down he saw faint red stains on his palms.

The same blood he'd shown to Hartright, way up in the Arctic ice of Deadhorse. He was dead now, along with so many Pinocchios.

"I do trust you," he said. "And I'll sleep soon. For now I've got something else in mind."

"What?" Hellion asked.

Wren didn't say anything for a long moment. Always plunging into the past. He looked ahead to Gruber.

"Steven, you're on the line with Hellion and B4cksl4cker?"

"Yes, Christopher. I, uh, honestly I think they're right." He chanced a look around. "You don't look so great."

"I don't feel so great, but I can leverage that, where we're going. There's more in San Francisco than Silicon Valley." He took a breath, considering if this was a path he really wanted to take. Of course, there was no avoiding it. Call it karma. Not all data existed within the silos of the social media companies. "Take us to San Quentin."

Nobody said anything for a moment, until Gruber broke the silence. "San Quentin Prison?"

"The very same. Keep heading north, cross the Golden Gate Bridge, you can't miss it."

Gruber chuckled uncomfortably. "Are we, uh, going in?"

"I am. Hellion, get me Rogers or Humphreys, whoever answers first. We need a visitor pass for a very particular inmate."

A moment passed before she answered. "This does not sound wise, Christopher. What are you seeking?"

"Something to round out our profile of the Reparations. Unless you're confident the metadata will give us everything we need?"

There was a silence. "Metadata will be useful. It is one data point."

"Exactly. More data is always better. I think Shakespeare himself said that."

Hellion said nothing.

"We'll be there in an hour."

19

SAN QUENTIN

San Quentin State Prison lay on a stubby, snout-like promontory stretching a mile and a half into the blue-green waters San Rafael Bay. Wren and Gruber pulled around on the John T. Knox Freeway in the mellow early-evening light, warm winds blowing through the open windows. At the Richmond-San Rafael Bridge, stretching six miles low and level across the water, they turned right onto the prison road.

It ran half a mile along a row of handsome wooden residences, each with incredible bay views and excellent prison visitation opportunities. Wren adjusted his shirt, tight as a Twaron vest against his skin, as they drew into San Quentin's small visitor lot. On the right stood a US Post Office in gleaming white stucco, on the left was a shuttered HANDICRAFT SHOP, where the prisoners could sell their wares.

Wren briefly admired the many clumps of abstract-shaped clay on shelves in the window, a series of brightly colored busts, some watercolors in back. Arts programs were some of the most popular in any prison, he knew. They offered an escape from the gray reality.

The Prius rocked to a gentle halt a few yards from the black grille gate, manned by two armed guards. Wren had been to San Quentin several times before and knew the layout well: the four main blocks watched over by the large white and red lighthouse-looking gun tower; condemned men to the north, with east, south and west for gen. pop.; the open grass yard, the six closed concrete yards, the long warehouse-like 'factories' where prisoners were put to work dry-cleaning sheets for local businesses.

Giving back to their new community, at incredibly cheap hourly rates.

Steven Gruber cleared his throat, was looking back at him. "Do I, uh, let you out here?"

"Here's good," Wren said, and opened the door. Standing too fast made him briefly dizzy, and he held briefly to the Prius' frame.

"Um, do I wait here?" Gruber asked.

"Visitor parking," Wren said, and pointed to the side. "This shouldn't take long."

He walked toward the gate. There were familiar signs describing prohibited apparel, their colors faded behind glass in the relentless California sun. Nothing that the guards or the prisoners might wear was allowed: not the blue jeans or shirts of the inmates, not the tan shirts and forest green khakis of the guards, not the orange jumpsuits of prisoners in transit. Nothing metal, no stud buttons, no underwire bras. Wren couldn't help a smile as he approached the black grille gate. Still wearing his skimpy NameCheck gear, there was no way they could find fault.

Laugh, maybe.

The guard at the gate stared at him like he was an alien exiting the dropship. The guy had a barrel chest with porkchop arms and wore a black beanie with the prison's gold star brand on his head, pulled low so the brim blocked the sun.

"Help you, Sir?"

He didn't sound like he wanted to help.

"I'm in the system," Wren said. "Christopher Wren. It should be marked expedited."

His call to Director Humphreys thirty minutes back had been combative but effective. Humphreys had agreed to pull some strings, gaining urgent visitation rights if Wren 'promised to behave himself'.

"You owe me one for NameCheck," Wren had said, as the Prius had glided across the red glory of the Golden Gate Bridge. "You've been trying to crack that data lockbox for a decade."

"And we'll pay for that access," Humphreys had countered. "You just opened up a Pandora's Box of First Amendment chaos. But I won't argue the toss with you now. Rogers tells me you're coming in when all this is done. I'm going to hold you to that."

The guard appraised Wren like he didn't believe he could possibly have expedited status. Not in that outfit. He held up a finger slowly, said, "One moment," then headed into the guard box, leaving his colleague to watch Wren and smirk. It took a few minutes, Wren squinting against the sun.

"What's with the get-up?" the other guard asked, gesturing with his rifle. A slim guy with a thousand-yard stare.

"I'm on vacation," Wren answered.

Barrel chest came back out, and now his demeanor had changed significantly. On the ball, doing things by the book. Wren didn't know for sure, but he assumed his visitation request had been marked with a level red anti-terrorism flag. Nobody wanted to get in the way of that.

"I'll need some identification, Sir."

"Got it here," Wren said, and pulled his Agent Without Portfolio CIA ID from the hot pink shoulder band he'd used for the Go Pro, held it up for the guard to inspect. The guy leaned in, nodded once then signaled for the gate. It opened and he led Wren through.

Visitor parking lay to the left, behind a tall wire fence. Wren glimpsed Steven Gruber gazing through the wires at him, looking as lost as Merriot Raine. Wren gave him a reassuring wink then looked ahead, thinking about the man he'd come to see.

Rick Cherney, brother of Terry Cherney, who together had led the Sons of SAM in the early aughties. The Sons of Sam were a pseudoscientific finance cult that looked to set up a private fiefdom on a series of pleasure yachts moored off the California coast. Both brothers had been Wall Street bankers for a time, had lived wild and crazy lives in New York running investment scams on penny dollar stocks and pyramid trades, all while building up a network of Success-And-Money groupies, or SAMs for short.

Wren had been brought in early in his CIA career, as a cult expert on secondment to the FBI. The Cherneys had metastasized by then, turning their SAM followers, worshippers of all-things money, loose on any vulnerable people in their lives. On orders from Rick and Terry, the SAMs had drained numerous life savings accounts into their yacht-fund coffers, often on pain of death. Their reign of homicidal fraud only drew to a close when a couple of retirees managed to hit a silent panic button before getting executed in their Malibu beach house for refusing to open their private safe to a pair of success-addled SAM acolytes.

Wren was brought in for late-stage interrogations. The Cherney brothers had effectively taken a Manson defense, updated for the 21st Century. They claimed to have no knowledge that their followers were breaking laws to make the kind of money they'd brought in; certainly not that they were killing people for their cash. They'd never ordered any of it. All they'd done was inspire their SAMs to embrace the American dream. How could they be held responsible for what they'd done to achieve it?

They didn't crack under questioning. Wren was brought in as a last resort.

He entered the interrogation room armed only with a manila briefcase that contained three photographs, which one-by-one he laid out. Three of their SAMs who'd never been arraigned. That the FBI didn't even know about. That Wren had found on his own, through the Foundation. Three killers who'd helped jumpstart the brothers' rush to illegal acquisition.

They were posed in ashes. Laid on scrap heaps with junk yard backdrops. Burned down to the bone everywhere except their faces.

Rick had looked at the pictures and swiftly looked away. Clearly, he recognized the bodies. The younger of the two brothers, he followed his brother's lead in all things. Terry though was cocky, thick-lipped and full of New York swagger, clearly certain he was going to get away with it all.

"Whatever these are, they're over-exposed," he'd said, appraising the photos with a faint sneer. "Next time use a light meter."

Wren was unphased. Didn't matter that the photographs were deepfake mockups, created by a Hollywood creative Wren had just brought into the Foundation. They were convincing fakes.

"You think the system is the prison," Wren had said, gesturing around at the white walls of their interrogation room in a downtown LA jail. "Boys, you are dead wrong. Truth is, as of this moment, the system is the only place you're safe from me. The day you walk out of court free as birds, that's the day you put on an invisible orange jumpsuit you'll never take off again." He paused a moment, watching their reaction. There was none. "Every day you'll spend waiting for another set of SAM photos to come in the mail. I'll pose them real nice next time, get the lighting just so." He looked at Rick. "Might be Terry in the ashes, first. Might be you, Rick. Would you like that?" Terry snorted. "Might not come for a few months, even a year, but you'll know that any day, any moment, it will come. I'm not big on mercy, boys."

He leaned back in the chair. Terry sat there like a log, unperturbed. Rick though was starting to doubt. Eyes flickering to the photos, to his brother, maybe imagining what he'd look like burned up like the rest.

"You can't do that," Rick said.

"Look at those pictures and tell me what I can't do."

"It's bullshit," Terry said. "Those are fakes. Don't listen to him."

Wren had Rick separated out. Worked on him alone in a confession booth, watching closely as his eyes roved like he was looking for a way out. Wren afforded none. Kept talking about how it would look to see Terry all burned up. Offering a cushy life behind bars, maybe out on appeal after ten years, if he just cooperated. It was better than certain death at Wren's hands.

Within an hour he cracked. Gave the FBI everything they needed to put him and his brother safely behind the bars of San Quentin.

Now the Visitor Center loomed large before Wren in the evening light. It had a crenelated top like some medieval castle, and towered over him three stories tall, with rifle-armed guards patrolling the roof. Long opaque glass strips ran up the structure's sides like elongated church windows, matched by off-yellow shallow buttresses, striping the building like architectural bars.

Brutalist. Eloquent.

An old building. An old history. California's first prison, and only Death Row site.

The guard led him into the cool shadow of the Visitors Entrance, where he stepped through the metal detector, nothing to detect, and they led him right toward the visitation area. Down a long corridor past vending machines boasting jello cups, hot chocolate and packets of chips, until the space opened up in a row of six barred-off pods. No glass here; visitors could sit across from each other, reach through the bars, even be alone in the cage with the prisoner, if they wanted to.

Terry Cherney was waiting. Run to fat since his heyday, bloated like a pig and swelling out of his blue-on-blue outfit. Narrow pebble glasses on his head, a shock of gray hair that looked like a terrible wig, thick cheeks puffing then eyes widening as he saw Wren, as he recognized him.

"No," he said, standing up. Started shaking his head. "Not a chance. No way I'm talking to him."

Wren wasn't surprised.

Two months after the brothers had been locked up, Rick had tried to kill himself by driving plastic ball pens into both of his eyes. The shame of flipping on his brother, was how they told it. He'd survived, but blinded and with permanent brain damage. They still kept him in San Quentin, where Wren had heard he often wailed late into the night. Awaiting a death he'd tried to hasten, and failed.

"Terry," Wren said, as the fat man climbed to his feet, staring with mounting alarm.

"I've got nothing to say to this fool," Terry shouted at the guard. "Don't let him in!"

The guard opened the cell gate and admitted Wren, then

locked the door after him and walked away. A cage barely seven feet on a side.

Wren studied Terry. He didn't look good. A decade of listening to your brother wail through the nights would do that to you. "It's your lucky day, Terry. I'm here to break you out."

20

SAMS

Terry Cherney just stared, gimlet eyes intent like a bug, searching for whatever trick Wren was going to pull. "You're going to get me out of San Quentin?"

Wren just smiled. Sat down. "There's no getting out of San Quentin. Nobody in the world's got the pull to do that. But there are other prisons, and other ways to escape." He tapped his temple.

"You're a whack job," Terry said. "I'm not listening to this. Guard."

The guard was on the other side of the room.

"Last night a billionaire died in a televised execution," Wren said, taking his time. "In an arena, before millions of viewers. Did you hear about that?"

Terry stared at him like Wren's mouth was a nest and the words spilling out were poisonous spiders.

"I'll guess you did. The victim was Handel Quanse, one of your contemporaries. Heyday of conspicuous consumption, greed is good, all that, though he turned a corner in recent years. They strapped his limbs up to nine horses, then pulled him apart." Wren let that hang. "That's one heck of a margin call, right? I'm here because I think you know something about it. I know you're still in touch with your SAMs. If anyone's got their ear to the ground on financial extremism, it's you."

Terry looked away. "Guard."

"I can help you, Terry," Wren pressed. "Tell me what you know, I make things better for you here."

"Better?" Terry scoffed. "Like you made things better for my brother?"

Wren was ready for that. "Let's talk about your brother. The way I understand it, you hear from him plenty. He wails through the night, they say. Now, maybe that's just the brain damage talking, or maybe he's in real pain. Physical, sure, it can't feel good to have busted eyes, no tear ducts left after they took them out, but I'd guess it's more than that. The spiritual cost, Terry. It's gotta claw at him. Knowing he let you down. Thought he was protecting you from me, thought his death would get rid of the shame, but none of it worked."

"Shut up," Terry said.

"You ever try calling that out to him, in the night? Maybe soothe him at first, until you get sick of the wailing, and you just tell him to shut up?"

Terry was getting hot. "You did that to him. You made that happen."

Wren shook his head. "Not me. I'd say it was your choices, Terry, all the way down the line. You damned your own brother when you started exploiting people to death. You carried him with you on that journey. I just held you both accountable. Though I'm pretty sure this is hell for him. Every day, every night." Wren paused a moment. "Now I'm offering him a way out."

Terry's throat pulsed visibly; his jaw tight. "I'll crush you."

"Don't talk nonsense. If you could do that, you'd have done it ten years back, and-"

Terry chose that moment to charge. Thick ham legs shooting him into a two-step stampede, which Wren turned like a matador turns a bull. On his feet and off-line before Terry had taken his first step, giving him a little shove on the way by. The big man's grasping hands shot through the bars and did nothing to halt his momentum, so he hit the cage wall full tilt down the left side of his face and bounced.

Back he went, staggering into the bars on the other side, and Wren was there to catch him. Kicked the man's feet out so he couldn't get them under him, sliding him down the bars fast and gentle to the ground.

Then he stood back. Sat down again like nothing had happened.

"We can do this all night, Terry. You won't lay a hand on me. Talk, though, and I'll open the door, set both you and Rick free."

Terry swore, rocking to get back to his feet, to the seat. Panting. A long vertical welt showed up down his face. Maybe he was thinking about mounting another charge, but this time thought better of it.

"What have you got to offer me, you psycho?"

"Arts and crafts classes."

Terry laughed. The first peal came like a cannon blasting off, the others followed like a fusillade off the bow, echoing loud and long.

"Your brother's blind," Wren plowed on, "but he can feel clay. I checked up on the facilities here; they've got potter's wheels, kilns, the capacity to fire anything between a thimble and a full-size toilet, should he want to. Something to do, Terry, other than think about killing himself. A way out."

"You call that a way out? You really are a psycho."

"The therapeutic benefits of pottery have been well-researched. It'll help with-"

"Rick hates art," Terry said. "With a passion. I guess you didn't do your research very well, or you'd remember he once burned an original Matisse just because he could. And you think pottery might be an *escape* for him? He broke his brain trying to kill himself, and I've lived with what's left of him for ten years now. Wailing, you call it?" He leaned in. "It's one wail. Two words. 'Kill me', he says. Again and again. And you think pottery's going to solve that?"

Wren set his jaw. "So you won't give me anything for pottery classes?"

Terry gave a brittle birdshot laugh. "Not a single dime. Handel Quanse is dead? Good. Kill them all."

Wren nodded. There was always a back up plan.

"All right. Second option, I get him removed from the prison on compassionate grounds. I've got it pre-approved. Put him in a secure psych ward somewhere, they'll keep him sedated, give him some counseling, try to ease his pain. How does that sound?"

Terry stood up. "You don't get it. Rick wants to die. That's it. Not some drug-addled coma. Not arts and crafts. He wants to die, and it's your fault. I will never help you. Never."

Wren took a breath. Saw in Terry the same stubbornness he'd seen before. Back then he'd used Rick to get justice, take the Cherney brothers out of circulation before they could hurt other people. That didn't mean there wasn't a cost. Justice often came with its own pain, even for the one administering it.

In a smooth movement, Wren unzipped the pocket in his armband and pulled out a plastic blister pack of pills. They were full-strength generic opioids, enough for permanent blast-off. No problem getting through the prison's metal detector. No need for a pat down, given his CIA credentials.

A single stop-off on the 101 north at a pharmacy, using a doctor's scrip hacked through the remote ordering system.

Terry's eyes flashed wide.

"Third option," Wren said. "A final way out of the prison. Easy overdose, he'll go out in his sleep. It's a way out for you, too. Peace, at nights."

Terry's eyes sharpened. "You f-"

"Limited time deal," Wren interjected. "Once in a lifetime, and it's coming at you this minute, Terry. You give me everything you've heard from your SAMs, help me hunt down these Reparations, and I take this pack to Rick right now. I'll sit there and wait. Hell, I'll even hold his hand, say a prayer. No man deserves to be tied to this life when all he wants is to leave, am I right?"

Terry's eyes blazed. Fury blending with a strange kind of hope. "What are you doing? Who the hell do you think you are?"

Wren smiled, sad. "I'm not a monster, Terry. The man wants to die, and he's wanted it for a decade." He leaned back. "If clay's no good, and a mental health ward's no good, then this is what I've got." He paused. "You just say the word. His fate's in your hands."

Terry stared. In that moment he looked for all the world like Damalin Joes, the moment before he gee'd his horse on. Wren saw the decision click over.

"What do you want to know?"

Twenty minutes later, getting into Rick's cell was easy enough. Wren's status gave him the run of the place. By then the warden was involved, but Wren brushed him off, refused to see the injured Cherney brother in visitation, so they escorted him to the cell. On Wren's orders, the guard walked away.

Rick Cherney was sitting on his bed, vacant eyes staring at the wall. A gaunt, sallow version of his brother, like a dark mirror. Wren knew Rick heard his approach, but he didn't so much as flinch as the cell doors clanked shut. Hands flat on his lap like a good Catholic boy, just staring into the darkness.

"Terry sent me," Wren said.

At that Rick turned. Whatever was left of his brain after the pens had done their vicious work recognized that name.

"I hear you've been calling for him. Every night, right? He's come through."

Wren pulled out the blister pack, popped the pills one by one, then folded them into Rick's hands. His palms were pale as milk. Apparently, he never went out in the yard. Just sat on his bed day in and day out, staring through the wall like it might any minute open up and admit him through.

Rick's fingers sifted the pills. Slowly at first, then getting faster. His blind eyes looked to Wren.

"Terry says he loves you," Wren said. "He'll see you on the other side. The rest is up to you."

Rick took a second longer, then put the pills in his mouth and dry-swallowed. It took a few gulps. Wren waited as the pills took effect. He held Rick's hand, as the weight he'd been carrying for years began to lift. As he sagged to the side. He even said a prayer, as promised.

It didn't take long for Rick to slip under. The overdose came fast and silent. When his pulse stopped, Wren lifted his legs tenderly, laid his thin, wasted body out on the cot.

"Goodbye, Rick," he said, and brushed his empty eyelids closed.

21

ANTI-CA

The walk out from the Visitor Center felt like Wren was lumbering along the bottom of the sea. Exhausted. Maybe finally hallucinating. Feeling sick.

"Did you get what you wanted?" the warden asked eagerly, a watercolor smear somewhere to Wren's side.

Wren just nodded mutely. Didn't trust himself to speak. It felt like the words would come out inflected by Rick Cherney, a keening in his throat rising to a wail...

The sun was bright outside still, filtering down through dapples of seaweed-like cirrus clouds. A man was dead, and he couldn't call that anything but a mercy, but the death weighed him down. Coming on the heels of Handel Quanse, it left him wrung out.

Steven Gruber was waiting for him in the visitor lot outside. Standing outside the bright yellow Prius, both of them like facets from a forgotten world.

"Everything OK, Christopher?"

"I'll be OK," he said, sounded like a drunk in his own ears. "Let's go."

Wren fell into the back seat. Gruber started the soundless

electric engine. They pulled out of the lot, bay on the right, fancy houses on the right.

"Where are we going?"

Wren blinked up, already drifting under. He couldn't sleep yet. "East," he said, "take the bridge." He fumbled against the seat until he found the earpiece, tapped it securely in, and dialed through to Hellion and B4cksl4cker.

"Christopher." Hellion's voice jolted him up above the surface one more time. He blinked, saw they were halfway across the San Rafael Bridge, so low to the water it felt like they were skimming right over the placid surface.

"Hellion," he said, taking a second to sync up his thoughts with everything he'd learned. "I got a lot from Terry Cherney. He has dozens of SAMs out there, all of them active in various financial pseudo-cults, some anti-rich, some pro."

He floated for a moment, lining up what was to come next.

"Yes?" Hellion prompted.

"He thinks Anti-Ca are our best target. He's heard about incredible dark money flows in the last two years, pouring into their coffers. A concerted effort to build out their infrastructure, setting up secret training compounds around the country." He paused, swallowed, went on. "He didn't know what for, but he knew they were buying in weapons, bomb-making gear, maybe potassium-cyanide."

There was silence for a moment. "Potassium-cyanide, this is suicide drug, yes?"

"Yes," Wren confirmed. "Same as they used at Jonestown. One of Cherney's SAMs is an Anti-Ca member, and she's been writing to him about that, whether she should stay or go." His head spun and he took a few careful breaths. "Apparently every one of their compounds has standing suicide orders, should it ever come to the end. Should federal forces attempt a raid, should the end of days come about, you know how it goes. Fight back as far as they can, then take all life to erase the record. Whoosh their way to heaven."

"Whoosh?" Hellion asked, her keys clacking distantly.

Wren was having trouble focusing.

"Where are compounds, Christopher?" came B4cksl4cker's bass voice.

"Cherney only knew about one compound. Northern Nevada somewhere, not even the SAM knew the exact location. They took her out blindfolded. She said there were families there, children, all kinds. She saw the gallon jugs of potassium-cyanide."

"Yes," came Hellion's voice again. "We will find this place. If there is synchrony with NameCheck metadata, this will help narrow a location."

Wren gulped agreement. "It could be the arena site. Set up the, uh…" He couldn't find the word.

"Search algorithms," B4cksl4cker supplied.

"Exactly. Top down, satellite, drone. Find the sand. Find the arena, the compound. Um." He was drifting now, caught himself swaying in the seat. Hellion said something but he didn't catch it. "I think we're going to have to hit it fast and hard," he went on, pushing the words out as fast as he could, barely outrunning the mounting waves of gray lapping at his thoughts. "I'll need a strike team, but discreet. Fast and hard enough to prevent a mass suicide."

"Strike team. You wish me to prepare this?"

"As best you can. Foundation operators only." He thought of something more. "And Rogers. We're going to need her help with this, if only to keep the feds out long enough to make sense of it. I'd call her, but I'm…"

He drifted.

"Christopher. You have done enough. You must sleep now, yes?"

The world was gray. He saw Rick Cherney's body lying

there like Somchai Theeravit's back in Deadhorse. Cherney was a killer too, but it hadn't felt like that, in his last moments. Justice took a toll on everyone.

"Yeah," he said, "thanks," then took the earpiece out, closed his eyes and fell into darkness immediately.

22

SUICIDE ORDER

Wren was back in the Pyramid. It was the last day again, and all around him lay smoking bodies. A thousand dead, burned alive in the Apex's suicide order. Wren's friends, his family, the people he'd known all his young life. There was a terrible stench, and a heat, and he realized that in one hand he held a lit match, burning down to his fingers. In the other he held a paintbrush, sopping with acrid-smelling napalm.

He'd burned them all.

Wren jerked awake, panting hard. He looked around and the world swirled. Dizziness like a bad hangover filled his head. It was dark but bright white lights arced by, like the off wash of headlights from a highway. He tried to control himself, turn the fear to anger or something he could use, but control didn't come easily.

He rolled, fell off the seat into the footwell of a vehicle. The Prius? He pushed himself up, ignoring the mounting nausea, and scrabbled for the door handle. He had to get out. Away from the dream, away from the past. At last his hand found the lever, the door swung outward and he flung himself through.

The sandy roadside shale was chill beneath his bare arms. Still wearing his scanty NameCheck gear. He pushed himself to his feet and turned, taking in the unfamiliar surroundings.

Off to his left a highway spun like the CERN Hadron collider, shooting cars like atoms through the darkness. An Interstate highway. To the right was some kind of unmanned gas station; pumps but no shop to pay at, a canopy roof but no sign showing the price at the pump. A few lights shone from tall poles, marking an island of white in the darkness, beyond which lay gravel, scrub reeds rising out of desert sand, then darkness. There was a faint humming in the air.

Wren felt his pulse settling, the nightmare pulling away. He worked on his breathing. He hadn't had that dream in years. The end days of the Pyramid. It took him back to the interrogation cell with Terry Cherney, listening to the big man talk about suicide orders in Anti-Ca cells. Gallon jugs of potassium-cyanide. A suicide order ready to roll down, crushing families beneath it. Friends. Children, just like all of Wren's brothers and sisters who'd died for the Apex's mad dreams.

He took hold of the Prius' roof, breathing deep and even, and counted the pumps. There were six in total. Each of them was occupied by a vehicle, and all of them were unusual, which helped banish the dream further. One was tiny, barely nine feet long, like a roofed chair on wheels. There was a glossy sedan, and some kind of low-slung supercar, then a bizarre gray truck thing with six wheels that was all harsh angles and looked like a cyber tank, and there, cherry on the cake, was a NameCheck-branded mapping vehicle. Wren blinked, checking he wasn't hallucinating. A tall pole stuck out of its roof like a lollipop, gumball red at the top and equipped with multiple dark camera eyes, used for making street-level 3D maps of the real world.

What was going on?

Wren circled the Prius, saw the charging cable leading from its battery cap and back to one of the six pumps, just like the five other cables. He put the pieces together. A fast-charging station for electric vehicles. But there were no drivers in sight. Which meant...

There was a clank nearby as the trunk of the supercar slammed down, then Gruber appeared. He did a double take when he saw Wren. "You're awake?"

"I am. What's going on here?"

"Oh," said Gruber, looking around at the vehicles. "A lot, I guess. Um..." He paused a minute. "Do you want water?" He didn't wait for an answer, instead hurried over and leaned into the Prius' front seat, coming back with a bottle. "Here."

Wren drained the bottle in one go, head back and looking to the stars. A full sky of them. Past midnight, he figured, by Orion's position. He'd slept for around seven hours; far more than he'd intended. A hunger pang suddenly bit at his stomach. He scrunched the bottle and dropped it into the footwell.

"Tell me."

"Sure, but, uh..." He tilted his head to one side, the way people who weren't accustomed to an in-ear device often did, as if it would give them some distance from the voice abruptly in their head. "I'm talking to Hellion. Well, listening is more accurate." His eyes defocused. "OK, yes. I got it." He refocused. "She wants to speak to you."

Wren held out a hand.

"First she says you eat, though," Gruber said, and leaned back into the Prius, came back with a strawberry milkshake and a ham and cheese sandwich. He put them in Wren's hand.

"Give me the earpiece," Wren said.

"Eat first, Hellion says," said Gruber. He looked uncomfortable. "I'm not sure what the hierarchy is here, but she's right. You haven't eaten in most of a day. You should."

Wren glowered but opened up the sandwich's plastic bag and took a bite. The soft white bread filled his dry mouth like a stodgy, comforting blanket. He took a glug of the milkshake, and the sweetness lit up his palate. When *had* he last eaten? Too long. Gradually the swirling in his head began to recede.

"Hand her over," Wren said, around a mouthful of sandwich. "No debating the hierarchy."

Gruber nodded sharply, then tilted his head and banged on the side like he was trying to shake out water after swimming, catching the earpiece when it dropped free. He gave it a rough rub down and handed it over. Wren took it and looked at it for a moment.

"Thanks."

"De nada," Gruber said. "I'll take a nap now too, I think. I'm shattered."

He wandered off. Where? Wren had no idea. He gave the earpiece another rub then inserted it, and swiftly heard Hellion's familiar tones. Not only Hellion: she was talking quietly with B4cksl4cker in Russian.

"I'm here," he said. "I need a full sit-rep."

"Christopher!" B4cksl4cker said, like he was welcoming him late to a party. "It is good you are alive."

Wren snorted.

"We thought it was best to let you sleep," Hellion said. "There is a lot to process right now, both good news and bad."

"Tell me there's been no suicide order."

That took her a moment. "Of Anti-Ca? Why would there be?"

Wren had no good answer for that. Because he'd seen it in a dream? His pulse pounded noisily in his temples. "Because that's what Cherney said. They've drilled for it. If they think we're coming for them, I believe they'll carry it out. Women, children, whether they want it or not. I can't allow that to happen."

"Then this is also good news," Hellion said. "There is no suicide order we can detect. We are on their communications. We have location for this strike."

That woke him up. "Where? And how did you get it?"

"How is by combination of Cherney eyewitness and Namecheck metadata. This is Anti-Ca compound, dark money, North Nevada, on edge of Duck Valley Reservation," Hellion took a breath. "One hundred miles north of place called Battle Mountain. Do you know this place?"

Wren racked his memory. "The reservation, not the town."

"It is remote. Wild everywhere. Except for compound."

Wren's mind began spinning. Thinking about children holding cups full of poison cut with grape-flavored soda. Thinking about the young Christopher Wren, then known only as Pequeño 3, forced to burn everyone he knew alive. "Is the arena there, too?"

"Not that we can see. We have scanned all surrounding land for several thousand square miles. If it was there, it is not there now."

Wren played that out. "Then how certain are we this place is connected to the Reparations? What's the link?"

"Metadata from NameCheck confirms video upload first came from this compound," B4cksl4cker said. "Secret Anti-Ca facility. Many weapons stockpiled, bombmaking equipment. This is just beginning for them, we think."

Wren considered. Thinking about past raids on cults that had gone bad, like Waco. He had to be sure, and do it right. "You have eyes on the compound?"

"Yes," said Hellion, and Wren's phone pinged from inside the Prius. He had to lean in through the back window to fish it out. An image had autoloaded, looked to be the heat map of a large compound.

"This is infrared image of Anti-Ca from drone we have circling," Hellion said. "Look at top right."

At the top of the map a couple dozen individual heat signatures were pressed in a building closely together, looked like a bunker of some kind.

"We believe this is holding cell. Many ages in this room; perhaps waiting for suicide."

Wren studied the map. "You think they have a sense we're coming?"

"Social media is down, Christopher, because of you. There is footage of you on hoverboard, Mr. Air Rider, on nightly news. Everybody knows you are coming."

He grunted, looked down at his pink and yellow outfit. Not his most elegant debut on the national media. "Anything else? If we hit this place hard, people are going to die. We need to be sure."

"We are sure," Hellion said. "There is more, from Foundation research. Anti-Ca belief system has changed sharply in last two years."

Wren looked out at the dark sky, finished the milkshake with a big glug. "Changed how?"

"Two years ago they had one. Reparations, they wanted. Redistribution of wealth from rich to poor. Nobody was listening. Then two years ago they went silent. We can see dark money flows coming in. This is like incubation period, yes? Now there is arena video, and calls for Reparation in blood."

"They've radicalized. Become extreme."

"Yes. Perhaps under guiding hand of one man with very particular set of skills."

Wren frowned. That was one way to reference his father. He looked over to the road.

"How far out are we?"

"Currently one hour from Duck Valley. We have been

driving you this direction for last seven hours. Rogers took flight, she is there now, waiting in desert. We also picked up things along the way. Some vehicles."

Wren looked at the pumps. "I count five. Who's driving them?"

A beat passed. "Steven Gruber is driving the Prius."

That was half an answer at best. "And the others?"

"I am driving the others."

For a moment Wren thought he'd misheard. Then he realized he hadn't. Of course. That explained how strange the vehicles looked. Each one was a prototype for a new range. "These are self-driving cars?"

"Remotely enabled," Hellion said. "It is simple hack to control via wireless protocol."

Wren held in a sigh. This is what you got when you fell asleep and left the hackers in charge. "You're driving five cars at once?"

"This is easy matter. In gaming I would control hundreds."

"This is not a game."

She just laughed.

"Where did you get them?"

"You were in San Francisco, Christopher. Silicon Valley, there are many such cars with road approval. I only hacked five. I could have taken many more."

Wren looked out over the desert. Hackers were like children with toys. "Why?"

"There is very practical application. For fast strike on Anti-Ca compound. It is reinforced heavily, metal walls. These vehicles will be foot soldiers for our assault. Battering ram, cannon fodder for absorb incoming fire. Many uses."

Wren sighed. So they had several remote-controlled vehicles to play with. That was good, he guessed. It only took them halfway, though.

"Who's on my strike team?"

"Yes. Let me see." Keys clacked. "We have an ex-Qotl cartel member you took across the border, Alejandro. He is very nice man, a Scorpio I think, but dark past. Many drug mule crossings across Mexico border, before he changed mind. There is also Doona, she was child soldier in South Sudan before you rescued her, eighteen but excellent shot with AK-47, she says. Last, there is Chuck Metzler. I do not really know much about Chuck, but he was very interested, and he says he was in Afghanistan, so..."

Wren tilted his head slightly, not sure if he was hearing correctly. Alejandro and Doona were trained operatives, each trustworthy and capable. Alejandro was a solid, squat Mexican who'd changed his life dramatically since joining the Foundation, starting a non-profit to help addicts turn their lives around. Doona had been handling weapons since she was twelve years old, had killed her first man at thirteen, and Wren wasn't keen to throw her into combat again. He'd send her back home, if she would go. As for Chuck?

Chuck was a pathological liar. Just putting himself forward for this expedition was enough to get him coin zeroed. He'd have to be sent back for sure; as far as Wren knew he'd never even fired a gun. Wren had caught him swindling old folks out of their social security checks in an elaborate, circular Ponzi scheme in the Florida Panhandle. It had been a holiday for Wren, with his family to see the alligators. Chuck had been working the coaches. Fast-talking hadn't saved him from Wren; a new member joined up within twenty minutes.

"You put an open call out on the boards? And Chuck answered?"

"Yes. Your Foundation members exist behind firewall from each other, Christopher. Your purposeful design, yes?

We do not know these people; they do not know each other. This makes them difficult to vet. Why do you ask?"

"Chuck's a conman. Maybe he has a death wish? More likely he just wants to go where the 'fun' is." He sighed. At least there was Rogers and Alejandro, Doona at a push. "OK. Are they all in position?"

"Five miles out from compound. Waiting for you."

"All right." He took a breath. Getting everything lined up, tracking back along their conversation. "So what's the bad news?"

There was a brief silence before Hellion spoke again. "There has been another Reparations video."

23

HATCHET

Wren brought up his phone, and as before the video full-screened to darkness. On the right hung the gameshow-like box with the names of all nine remaining billionaires, vote tallies spinning beside them like slot machine wheels. Millions of votes and growing fast. Now trust-fund inheritor Merriot Raine was at the top, with billionaire financier Damalin Joes in second.

"This happened live four hours ago," Hellion said in Wren's ear. "The vote counts reflect real votes cast through websites and apps via the darknet."

"Why didn't you wake me?"

"What would you have done, Christopher? On three hours sleep, in transit to strike location? You would not sleep again, after seeing this. It is better we let you rest."

Wren was about to grumble, point out that he didn't need much sleep, then a strobe lit the darkness on his phone's screen. Electric-blue lights flashed like scalpel blades through the black, briefly revealing the same long, narrow cages as before. Dead ahead on the concrete floor, naked and pale, lay Damalin Joes, just now shuddering awake.

The flashes sped up, freezing images of the big man like

stop-motion animation. Joes rubbing his face. Rolling up to a seated position. Fingers touching some kind of thick collar around his neck. Wren squinted closer to try and pick it out, but it was dark and Joes kept moving, then gasped as he saw something ahead of him. The camera panned slightly as Joes scrabbled backward, heels hammering on the floor until his back struck a pole in the fencing. A haz-mat figure was standing some ten paces away, near the entrance of his cage.

The strobe lights flashed faster. The figure looked like a butcher in a slaughterhouse apron, splattered red. A large camera rested on his shoulder, a bulbous microphone projecting like a distended forehead above its one dark eye, red light blinking.

The feed cut to that camera, on a level with and close up to Damalin Joes.

"What do you want?" Joes asked, pressed back against the cage wall. He was clearly straining for bass, to sound powerful and commanding, but it came through reedy.

The camera inclined slightly to the side, focusing on a rough wooden block a few feet from Joes, with a wicked-looking hatchet buried in the middle. Joes's eyes bugged. The sleek silver blade glinted in the flashing light. The camera refocused on Joes, who looked at the blade, the camera, then beyond to the cell gate. The camera swiveled to follow his gaze.

The gate stood ajar.

By the time the camera swung back, Joes had gotten to his feet and was reaching for the hatchet. The second his fingers closed around the grip, a chime sounded through the cells and a light flashed on the strange collar around his neck.

Joes let go of the hatchet at once and reached up to his neck as if stung. The camera zoomed in as Joes ran his fingers over the device hesitantly. He tugged on it several times, worked it between his fingers, but failed to find a release catch. A thick band of metal, looked to be barely room to get one finger between it and his skin. Cautiously he tried to bend the metal, but it didn't flex. For a long moment his eyes fixed on the hatchet, putting the pieces together.

As if to help him along, the strobes began flashing brighter, illuminating all the cages. To his right the eight remaining occupants of the Forbes list were starting to rouse. They each had a collar around their necks and a haz-mat camera operator standing over them. No one else had a hatchet, though.

Looking into Joes' eyes, Wren saw the decision happen; another moment just like the death of Handel Quanse. Maybe one of a long string of such decisions Damalin Joes III had taken all his life, to exploit the opportunity before him. When life handed you lemons…

Joes took hold of the hatchet once more. Again there was a chime, a flash from his neck, and now also a display on the side of the blade that lit up bright red. Joes pried the blade from the wooden block and held it up to study the display; the camera pushed in alongside him. There was some kind of digital LED readout slotted into the blade itself, displaying a single name in block capitals.

RAINE

Wren glanced at the voting tally. Raine's name was at the top by a close margin, with Cem Babak the arms dealer just below him. Raine's name was also on the hatchet. It seemed pretty clear.

Joes wasted no time thinking through the morals of it. He strode past his camera operator and out of the cell, swishing the hatchet experimentally through the air. Flashing strobes illuminated his path. Merriot Raine was in the cell next door. The gate hung open. Joes stepped in.

Raine was already on his knees, wide eyes flickering from Joes' face to the blade.

"No," he said. "Please, Damalin, don't. I can pay you. Whatever you want. I can pay."

Joes lifted one finger to his lips, strode closer and pulled back the blade. Raine started to scream. It was all happening so fast. Joes brought the hatchet down.

The blow didn't land. What happened instead was intense and stunning: a blinding light filled the cells, Joes' collar lit up an electric blue and he jerked, unable to finish the downward sweep. Raine screamed and Joes lurched to the side, barely catching himself on the chain-link cell wall.

Wren recognized the sudden shift. Joes had just been hit by an incredible electric shock, presumably delivered by the collar around his neck. Like the cattle prods they'd used to level Handel Quanse. As if to confirm it, Joes' left hand shot up to the collar, his breaths came in a painful wheeze, but he didn't waste time recovering. Instead he took a shaky step over to the screaming Merriot Raine, lifted the hatchet again and tried to bring it down a second time.

This time Wren's phone screen turned wholly white, so dazzling he had to look away, before returning to darkness lit by occasional strobes. Now Damalin Joes lay slumped across the body of Merriot Raine, who was crying out for help and struggling to get free. The hatchet lay on the floor beside them both, the display screen glowing red.

"What's going on?" Wren muttered.

"The vote changed," Hellion explained in Wren's ear. "See the side tally?"

Wren looked at the vote bar on the right, where the number one slot had shifted. Now Cem Babak's name was at the top. As if to confirm it, the camera focused in on the blade of the hatchet, where the same name was highlighted in red.

BABAK

"It's updated live," Wren said. "Nominated by the popular vote?"

"Exactly," Hellion said. "Millions of people were voting when this went live."

Wren nodded along. "So Joes gets punished if he tries to use the hatchet against the wrong man?"

"Precisely. It is ingenious, yes? Like video game without tutorial, where you..."

Wren tuned her out and focused on the footage. The image of Joes atop the wriggling Raine cut away, replaced by a shot of social-media-sellout turned green-energy-ecowarrior Inigo De Luca running down the side passage, also wearing a thick shock collar. He looked like he'd been chiseled from marble, muscular and so pale he was vampiric in the flashing lights.

De Luca entered Raine's cell, smoothly swept up the hatchet, swung it above his head without once looking at the display and brought it down-

His shock came synced to another long flash. Wren turned away until the screen resolved back to darkness broken only by the strobe. Now two bodies lay slumped atop Merriot Raine, and Raine was still wriggling frantically to get free. The hatchet lay off to the side, the blade display shifting rapidly name as the vote tallies spun.

RAINE

BABAK

JOES

"They are slow learners," Hellion said.

Wren grunted, watching as other dim bodies closed in like ghosts from the dark, coming toward Joes and De Luca on the floor. Merriot Raine finally escaped past them. Cem Babak the arms dealer stood at the entrance to Raine's cell now, thick and solid with the swollen trapezoids of a powerlifter, eyeing the hatchet until a foot suddenly lashed out into his knee. Damalin Joes had regained consciousness. There was a yelp and Babak went down.

Joes rose swiftly to his feet, sent a sharp heel kick into Babak's face. Seemed like he'd had some fight training; was pretty handy with his limbs. Voices clamored in the bristling dark, calling for Joes to stop and think, but he was clearly beyond that now. The camera caught the mad flare in his red eyes; probably half-blind from the flashes of light and half-mad from the shocks, driven now by animal instinct alone.

Babak and De Luca both lay on the ground. The hatchet lay to the side. Joes lunged over and swept it up, raised the weapon high to strike Babak and-

-stopped.

"Finally he understands," Hellion said.

Wren glanced at the vote tallies, his own heart thumping. This wasn't live right now, but still he felt the surging excitement, the illicit thrill of watching something real. Like gladiatorial combat in the days of Ancient Rome. At least one of these billionaires was going to die, and it was hard not to pick a favorite and root behind them.

Merriot Raine topped the ranking again. A man who'd never done nothing with his inherited money but squander it on himself. An easy man to hate, and a coward to boot. His vote totals had shot up again, after he'd fled and left the hatchet behind.

Now the hatchet display showed his name.

RAINE

Joes strode out of the cell, over Babak's unconscious body, and broke into a run. The screen split into two to show Joes charging on the left, Merriot cowering on the right in some other cell. Joes reached the end of the row of cages in seconds and plunged through the open cell gate. Raine had dropped to his knees in the corner, arms up and begging.

"Please, Damalin!" he shouted, raising his arms as Joes raised the hatchet back. "I can make it worth your while, everything I have I can-"

"It's not about the money, Raine," Joes replied, then brought the blade arcing down. There was no flash this time, no electric shock. The hatchet blade cleaved through Merriot Raine's soft palm like a cord of wood, slicing deep into his wrist. He screamed, blood sprayed out over Damalin Joes, but he just raised the hatchet and brought it down again, this time into Merriot Raine's skull.

Now he fell silent. His body dropped. His name fell off the listing.

Damalin Joes stood in the cell, chest heaving, vote tallies spiraling up, the name on his hatchet shifting rapidly. Out in the darkness, the other billionaires clustered and stared. Wren anticipated the feed cutting away, the game ending, but it didn't. Perhaps Joes had expected the same thing, but after a minute or two, he seemed to realize, and brought the blade up slowly to his eyes.

BABAK, read the display.

"It goes on like this," Hellion interrupted. "Another five minutes. One more dies."

Wren watched it through to the end, when the action faded to black with the same stark end titles as before.

YOU ARE OWED REPARATIONS

CLAIM THEM IN BLOOD

For a long moment Wren stood leaning against the Prius, trying to come to grips with what he'd just seen. Afterglow from the flashes in that sick prison still spotted his retinas.

He didn't want to watch any more videos like it. Who would? At the same time, it was no more gory than mainstream movies and TV shows. It had been filmed like them; high production levels somehow made the violence more palatable, as if you could watch and pretend it was just another piece of bingeable entertainment.

It made you root for the billionaires to die.

Through it the Reparations were training their audience to

cheer on real deaths. It helped that these were some of the most despised men on the planet, but not all deservedly so. Damalin Joes III had been turning himself around. Inigo De Luca, Geert Fothers, a handful of others had ramped up their charitable giving to incredible levels.

Killing them was no answer to the fear and anger people were feeling, after the Saints and the Blue Fairy. Though in the heat of the moment, Wren knew it would feel like it. Violence was a contagion. Show people the way and they'd follow.

Then something struck him.

"How did this get out," he asked. "We killed social media. We added moderation on all videos going live. How is anyone seeing this or voting on it without NameCheck and the rest to distribute it?"

Hellion took a breath. "Yes. You are not going to like this, Christopher. It looks like they played us from beginning. Played you, really. You see..."

24

HOW?

Wren stamped away from the road and into the nearby desert, fury burning through his veins and Hellion's words reverberating in his ears.

"First execution film had tiny piece of code attached, virus," Hellion explained. "This virus installed new app on every device. Phone, computer, tablet, whatever. App replaces NameCheck, Iota, WeStream, all Internet companies. Reparations video plays through new app, and app allows all content. No moderation." She took a breath then piled on. "There are many copycat videos, now. Such video uploads passed one per second one hour ago, and it is not just children damaging property. It is worse. Hatchets, Christopher. People are being assaulted. Some are dying."

Wren kicked up dust and clenched his knuckles, staring out at the stars then the flashing cars racing by on the highway.

"Reason this has worked so well, Christopher," Hellion went on, "there is no other streaming site. No other place to upload, watch video. No entertainment except Reparations." A pause. "We did this."

Wren frowned. Felt understanding coming on but wasn't ready for it. "What do you mean?"

"We shut down many companies after WeStream. These companies followed some rules. Now there is nothing. True Wild West, Christopher. No law at all. Worse, video through this app is untraceable. We cannot hack them. This is game, and they win."

They win. The words rang in Wren's head and chimed with the message carved in the flash drive, wrapped around Somchai Theeravit's neck.

I THINK YOU'LL ENJOY THIS ONE, PEQUEÑO 3.

Like some kind of game.

"This is why they wanted me," he said softly.

"What?"

Now the pieces were coming together. Finally starting to see the land beneath the thick layer of snow. Pythagoras strung up and waiting for his attention. Damalin Joes III staring at the cameras. He'd known back in Deadhorse that there was some reason the Reparations wanted him personally involved.

Here it was.

"They set me up," he said. "They knew I'd go after social media. Knew I'd break laws to clear cut the Internet in ways nobody else could."

Hellion had sucked in a breath. "Yes, this may be true. You are wrecking ball."

Wren snorted. Wrecking ball was putting it lightly. He'd always leaped before he looked. But Rogers had made it very clear how difficult the Internet companies were to rein in. Nothing could control them, not government laws, not military force, not hackers on the darknet. The change had to come from within, and getting within organizations and bringing them down was Wren's specialty.

Hellion was right. He'd been played.

"No other video sources to watch," he murmured. "No way to bring them down."

"Yes. App is now only supplier of unmoderated video content." A pause. "No competition. Reparations own eyes of the world."

Wren shook his head, trying to kickstart a lead. "How many people have the app?"

A second passed as keys clacked. "Hard to be certain, but at least one hundred million subscribers."

That was an immense number. One hundred million people feeding off this darkness. Feeding into it. Uploading videos in this new violence economy. Killing people for kicks and fame, with Damalin Joes' life on the line.

All Wren's responsibility.

"How many dead, in the copycat attacks?"

"Best guess? Dozen, perhaps. Hatchet attacks, Christopher. Very messy."

Wren stamped a tight arc around the recharging station's white glow, feeling the world flipping around him. When laws cracked with no accountability, new permissions were granted; not just to him but to everyone. People would watch the app like an addiction. Not all, but many. Some would be sick already, wouldn't need much to push them over the edge. Others needed a few more shoves.

There were seven billionaires left. Enough material for six more 'episodes', assuming one death per episode and a single winner. All with the goal of ripping the US apart. Wren's mind raced. The government couldn't move fast enough to stop this thing. His hackers hadn't even seen it coming. That left only one path.

Swift, unrelenting justice.

He stopped in his tracks. They'd wanted it personal. Now it was.

"Hellion?"

"Yes, Christopher."

"Tell the Foundation to hunt the killer copycats," he said through gritted teeth. "Use clues from the videos to locate them. All of them."

A moment passed. "We can do this. Hunt them and hen do what, Christopher?"

The words catch/kill floated through his head. The same order Humphreys had laid against him, but the first half of that equation wasn't going to get the job done, and the Foundation didn't have the resources to imprison people anyway. When you were in the Wild West, justice came at the barrel of a gun.

"Kill them."

There was silence for a moment.

"Are you sure?"

"I'm sure. Relay the order. Kill them and film it. We need to put up some warning flags. Enforce some accountability." He paused, spinning the next few hours forward. "This movement has to die at all costs. We'll all pay our reparations when it's over."

25

ROGERS

The convoy went dark five miles out from the Anti-Ca compound, silent electric engines whirring. Wren's pulse rate rose, sixty to seventy, in anticipation.

A phone alarm went off, and it took him a minute to realize what it was. Not Hellion or the Foundation, but the alarm he'd set every night for the past three months. Time to call his wife back in Delaware.

Gruber was asleep in the passenger seat, now, with Wren driving. The phone was in back, and he let the alarm ring until it gave out.

"Here," Hellion said, on a rise a mile out.

The convoy pulled over ahead, shaping up like an odd low wall in the darkness. Wren parked at the front, looked at Gruber with his head lolled against the window, and decided to let him sleep through. He was intelligence, not combat. Better not to give him the choice.

He opened the door and strode out. The desert air hummed with night life: brown bats swooping on buzzing insects; kit foxes rustling down prey-trails; chuckwalla lizards and woodrats burrowing up from their dens. A dusty wind carried the lush scent of dry sage and the rain-smell of creosote bushes. Off to the left he could just pick out the outline of the compound by moonlight, low on an open brush savannah. A dark ring in the night, no lights.

To his right was Rogers. Standing alone in the dark, alone, half her face lit by the moon, blond hair pulled back tight. Jaw set, eyes gleaming with things unsaid. Beyond her stood his 'team': the slim silhouette of Doona, the short and stocky Alejandro, the office-worker frame of Chuck. They didn't advance to greet him; waiting to let the Wren-Rogers fracas play out.

"There you are," Rogers said. Not loud, but her voice carried in the quiet. "I've been looking for you."

Wren took a few steps closer. For some reason her voice made him sad. Nostalgia for their brief cooperation against the Blue Fairy, maybe; a vision of himself that couldn't last. "Here I am."

Seconds passed. An owl hooted far off. "Our deal stands," she said. "When this is over, you come in."

"That's right. Humphreys knows you're here?"

"In theory, but not specifically. We never found the Blue Fairy mole, so if your father had one then, he still has one now." A pause. It was strange to hear her talking with such certainty about his father. "So I'm off portfolio. Humphreys has given me latitude."

Wren nodded. He knew about going off portfolio. To bring down a cult you had to bend all the rules.

"I'll pay for my part in this, too, when it's done," she added. "Not quite like you, but for my conduct. I've cut corners."

Wren grunted. That was probably on him.

"My team are in Deadhorse," she went on. "They found the bodies in the depot. Bad guys. Lots of evidence in

Somchai Theeravit's bunker linking them to abuse. Not a whisper about his activities anywhere."

"He was a shipping magnate. When you're a millionaire, people look the other way."

Rogers stared. Judging. "That's really the issue now, isn't it? Wealth and privilege."

"Wealth and privilege," Wren agreed. "They're no protections now."

A moment passed. "I met your team. One of them is a copier salesman."

Wren took that on board. Chuck. His new job? That was embarrassing. "He's undercover."

"As a copier salesman? To break open the infamous dark paper cabal?"

Wren said nothing. It didn't seem like jokes between them were possible now.

"He asked me where the safety was on his Glock 17," Rogers said. "His own gun, Christopher."

Wren grimaced; glad Rogers wouldn't see it in the darkness. Glocks didn't have a safety; they had a trigger lock. Everyone knew that.

"He's in training. Don't worry about him, he's here to observe only. Or Doona. It'll be you, me and Alejandro with the cavalry, we'll be good."

Rogers glared, eye whites catching the silvery light. "Cavalry. Call them stolen vehicles. Who's going to pay for that?"

There were some criticisms he wasn't going to entertain right now. "Add them to my tab. Let it go, Rogers. We've got bigger things to deal with right now."

She stared. She let it go. "I've run the circumference." She pointed, beyond the line of silent vehicles to the dusty savannah bowl. "I don't see anything. No lights, nothing. Your hacker's been in touch, her thermal drone confirms they're still in guard positions on the rooftops, with women and children huddled in the main building."

"They know a hit's coming. Or they fear it."

Rogers shrugged. There was plenty of fear to go around. "After you crushed their Internet presence, I'd be surprised if every Anti-Ca compound wasn't on high alert."

It was a good point. "No word on the suicide order?"

"Just that they have the supplies. Potassium-cyanide. Orders smuggled and laundered through various small-time labs in neighboring states. But no death order in the air."

Wren nodded. At least they had that, though it all depended on how far gone the Anti-Ca people were. If they received the order and were willing, they could all be dead within minutes.

"How many?"

"Census says zero. In government records this place doesn't exist. From the drone though, looks like sixty-three."

Wren whistled low. Sixty-three against him, Rogers and Alejandro. Even with three remote-driven vehicles, they weren't good odds. "Armaments?"

"Looks like some heavy munitions. Rifles, a handful of autocannons, grenades, potentially bombs."

Wren grunted. "Entrenched security?"

"There's a wall around the compound, many buildings butting against it. Tin sheeting, it looks like, but still."

"Likely reinforced. Do reports say they're laying in for a siege?"

Rogers just glared. "No. They've got lots of orange juice, though."

It took Wren a second to register that. Hellion hadn't mentioned it; probably she hadn't realized the significance. He flashed on the chemical reactions that accompanied potassium-cyanide when swallowed. Fruit juice sped the fatal reaction. It was how they'd taken their cyanide in Jonestown.

A third of the deaths at Jonestown had been children. Seventy people had received the poison unwillingly, via syringe. Rogers' eyes glowed with that same knowledge.

"How many children?" Wren asked. His throat was tight.

"A dozen, best guess, from the thermal imaging. Gathered in the central bunker."

He saw red. "The drone shows they're alive?"

"Sixty-three are alive. If others are dead, we wouldn't see that."

Wren's mouth went dry. They'd be cold; invisible to infrared. Ready to be buried in their pits. It was hard not to feel the shadow of his father overhanging the dark compound; Apex of the largest suicide cult in American history. Getting people to kill themselves because the power felt good.

"Sentries?"

Rogers held up a tablet, the screen dim but live. Wren took it and scanned the infrared footage from Hellion's drone. There were hot red figures spread around the faint outline of the compound's circular wall. Some proned out like snipers, some clustered tight together, likely behind barricades, perhaps manning the autocannons.

At the center was the main bunker, one room brightly lit with multiple heat signatures. Some small and fragile looking; the children. Kept in a cell. Wren's jaw set. If anyone was going to spill whatever they knew, it was the people in that room. The doubters, who needed to be locked away with the kids.

Wren picked out a route through several of the sniper emplacements, fastest path to the bunker.

He held up the map for Rogers to see. "I'll go right. You go left. Our goal is the bunker."

"To save the kids," she said.

"And dig out what they know."

"Couldn't have said it better myself."

Wren committed the outline to memory. "We go now," he said, felt the urgency shooting adrenaline into his system. "Where's my gear?"

"In the truck."

"Two minutes. I talk to my team and we'll roll."

"Have at it."

He strode past her. His 'team' were waiting. Alejandro was squat and solid, dark wifebeater over dark gang tattoos, tear drops down his cheeks. Doona was as black as jet, only the whites of her eyes gleaming in the night, hair cropped close and clutching a rifle. Chuck did look like a copier salesman in the desert; timid, trying to be brave, way out of place.

"Chuck, you stay here," Wren said in a firm voice, giving no room for argument. "Alejandro, you're mid-convoy, I suggest the mapping car; shoot only if they're shooting at you. Doona, I don't want you in this. You're barely through immediate PTSD."

Doona racked the slide of her AR:15. "I ride with you, or I run there myself. Either way, I am fighting."

Wren considered that, made allowances. She was eighteen, after all. "We do need you. Mid-convoy then, the car behind Alejandro, the saloon. Same directive. Study this outline." He held out the tablet, pointed to the central courtyard area inside the compound walls, in front of the bunker. "I want you both in the middle right here, stirring up as much trouble as possible. Your vehicles will remain in motion at all times. Hellion?"

"Yes," Hellion responded. "I will do this."

Wren refocused on his team. "You keep them busy with noise and fury. Rogers and I will break for the bunker at the center. Any questions?"

Alejandro and Doona stared back at him. Wren nodded.

"What about me?" Chuck asked.

"You shouldn't even be here," Wren said and strode away.

"Are you wearing that?" Doona called after him.

Wren had forgotten his clothes. Still the skimpy gym outfit. "It's tactical," he called over his shoulder. "Get in your vehicles."

Rogers stood at the trailer bed of her Ford pickup, gesturing to the supply cache of boxes inside, lit by the Ford's dim running lights. "You like Twaron armor? Fill your boots."

Looked like she'd brought an armory. Wren opened boxes and grabbed a pair of sturdy combat pants, a tough canvas jacket and proper boots, pulled them on in the dark. A Twaron para-aramid bulletproof vest and thigh-plates came next, then a shoulder-holster for a Colt M1911 with left thigh ammo belt, a Benelli M2 3-gun tactical shotgun with a 24-shell chest bandolier. He sighted down the shotgun, dry-fired it, then twisted it in his right hand to check the loading port, plucking four shells from the bandolier in a quad formation in his left hand. With a clean sweeping movement he speed-loaded two of the shells, two more then spun the shotgun upright again.

"Smooth," Rogers said.

"I've been practicing. Now, shall we?"

"We shall."

Wren strode back to the Prius.

"Ready for this, Hellion?" he asked.

"As ever, Christopher," she answered in his ear. "We take them by surprise. I will punch hole with tank truck. Draw fire. Trust me, I have raided compounds like this thousand times before."

Wren throttled a laugh. "In video games."

"Is same thing. Just do not get shot."

"Amen to that."

He opened the Prius' door, woke Gruber and asked the man to step out.

"Huh?" Gruber asked groggily. "Are we there?"

"Just step out a second," Wren said. "I'll explain."

He stepped out. Wren got in, hit the gas and peeled out with a rush of dirt.

"Taking lead," Hellion said in his ear. "Good luck, Christopher. B4cksl4cker will be your voice operator. I will be occupied with running vehicles."

The convoy woke behind him. The cyber truck pulled into the lead, with Wren, Rogers, Alejandro and Doona following on behind, chased by the tiny silver chair car. Across the desert savannah the vehicle train accelerated to ramming speed.

26

COMPOUND

Three minutes of darkness and dust followed, the Prius rocking and jolting over hummocks in the hardpan desert, then the first crash came from ahead as the huge cyber truck hit the tin sheeting and ruptured a hole straight through.

"No response yet," B4cksl4cker said in his ear, "hit in four."

Three seconds, two, one then the Prius hit the gap, scraping sparks down its bodywork off reinforced joists backing the tin wall. Wren burst through into an interior that was now flooded with a sudden storm of high beams; Hellion's attack truck already starting a spin like Damalin Joes' horse in the Reparations video, headlights blaring. The Prius banked hard to join its mad spiral, and Wren surveyed the compound's interior as they spun around at forty miles an hour.

Tin outer walls, wooden buildings like the Pyramid's fake town in Arizona, now four vehicles spinning tight donuts in the center, wheels spinning, with the final two crashing through in seconds to enter the furious dance.

"Rooftops," B4cksl4cker said sharply. "Snipers are

activating, I see ten, no, eleven on infrared, all around you; they are sniping us, aiming for engine blocks and windshields."

Wren couldn't hear the incoming fire through the roaring of vehicles, couldn't see the snipers through the riotous spill of light.

"Give me a target!" Wren barked as the Prius circled wildly, taking an incoming high caliber round that crumped in through the back window and out through the chassis.

"Main building is heavily guarded, Christopher! I recommend best access is over rooftops; large building due south has two snipers, large wooden bay doors, clear route to main building."

Wren yanked the Prius hard over, cutting through the dance and rerouting Hellion's slaved vehicles, in seconds barreling thirty miles an hour straight into the barred wooden front of what looked to be a motor pit. The Prius hit and the doors ripped off their hinges to fly ahead like a desperately flapping butterfly.

The Prius skidded into a dark interior of vehicle elevators, stacked tires and stripped-back pickups. Wren killed his lights before the butterfly doors landed and flung himself out the door. The car sped on to crash through metal shelving and beyond while Wren rolled into cover behind a tire stack.

From outside the sound of electric vehicles tearing over dirt chewed into the air, pierced now by the deep cracking reports of armor-piercing rounds slotting through metal.

"Two on the walkway ten o'clock," came B4cksl4cker's voice; swift analysis of Wren's body-cam footage. "Rifles trained on the door. Another two possibly three on floor with you, to your-" pause, "-two o'clock, behind shelves. Could be grenade, one of them had arm back and-"

Wren heard the dull skittery clink of metal on the concrete flooring, ringing scant feet to his left, where the roving headlights from Hellion's dance troupe flashed out an epileptic's nightmare.

Grenade. Wren lurched up at once, drawing instant rifle fire that sprayed rubber chunks off the tires and blasted chips from the wooden walls beyond, then dived. A second and a half later the grenade blew.

Light washed out, the percussive bark followed and a blast wind caught the soles of his feet as he flew beyond the edge of the tire stack. The tires erupted and buried him in torn and burning vulcanized rubber.

"Cover me!" he managed to shout, before a second clink landed nearby then thumped up against the blanket of carbon black tire shreds. Wren scrabbled to get under the chunky blanket then the second grenade erupted.

The blast rang out like a wet firework, shredding tires and spraying rubber fragments across his left hip, chest and thigh, pummeling his ears and showering him with a secondary rain of burning black confetti. More clinks landed nearby, then a thud to match them as one grenade landed amongst the tires, and Wren had half a second to shout, "Hellion!" and half a second longer to contemplate his imminent disintegration, when two things happened at once.

The grenades erupted like a string of firecrackers, each blast tremendous and devastating, hurling tires through the air, gouging craters into the concrete floor, sending shrapnel whistling out through the walls and spattering Wren. Shrapnel also ripped through the side panels, dented the chassis, burst the tires, imploded the glass and bent the A and B columns of the cyber tank truck now skidding to a stop directly over Wren's prone body.

Saving his life.

"Cover," came B4cksl4cker's voice, barely audible over the tinnitus ring of the blasts. "Literally. Now get up."

Wren wasn't going to waste the opportunity it presented,

while just tossed more grenades. He rolled through burning tire scraps and out from under the scarred truck as several more blasts rang out nearby, answered now by incoming fire and the roaring of engines.

He raised his head by the driver side door to see a hellish scene of fire, light, smoke and tracer rounds; the sleek red supercar shot across the wreckage-strewn mechanic's pit to collide with a desk by the wall, drawing screams. The snipers above trained their fire on a secondary vehicle incoming, the mapping car with Alejandro leaning out the window and firing up into the gantry, now pulling squealing, smoking donuts through the rubble.

"Every building is rigged like this," B4cksl4cker said, "Hellion is regrouping for another charge."

Wren was already running, taking advantage of the confusion and ignoring the stinging pain down his left side. He vaulted a spray of shattered crates, reached the crumpled desk as the supercar revved its wheels into a hard reverse, then rolled over the top, dropping flush in beside two bearded men with startled faces. They brandished rifles and wore a bandolier of grenades each, even now trying to bring their weapons to bear.

Wren fired twice with the shotgun; twin contact shots, one each in the chest at point blank range. Two shell-loads of bismuth pellet slugs blasted through their bodies like wet cardboard, the immense volley of sound lost within the chaos of squealing wheels and sniper fire.

Two down.

Sniper fire pinged the countertop. Wren slid out flat on his back, aiming upward to put two tightly grouped shots through the underside of the walkway corner; the slugs tore through metal and into the men above, drawing fresh screams.

"Take the rooftops," B4cksl4cker said. "Hellion is coming

in again but snipers are finding our range. If they take out vehicles, all fire will turn on you."

Wren strode three steps over the shotgunned bodies, speed-loaded four more shells and raced up the metal ladder to the gantry. From behind more gunfire came; he spun, saw Alejandro surfing atop the mapping car like a pole dancer now, firing across the burning space at the two injured snipers above. Seemed he had it covered.

Wren reached the gantry and kept climbing, five more rungs to an open chute to the roof, where for a second he paused.

"Get me a distraction," he ordered.

"Ten seconds," Hellion answered, and Wren heard it coming; the roaring of his convoy charging toward the motor pit, probably enough mass and velocity to take out the support walls and bring the whole thing down.

Just as the first vehicle struck below, he surged up the last few rungs into moonlight and the roar of battle.

27

ROOFTOPS

The roof itself lurched a clear foot down with the impact below; the whole corner support blown out with a resounding crunch. Wren felt the backwash wind of a bullet brush his temple then he lurched sideways into a shoulder-punishing roll.

Another shot tore up the tarpaper as he rose to his feet, catching glimpses of twin shooters at the roof's northwest and southeast corners, each silhouetted against the charging headlights of Hellion's dwindling cavalry as they raced a distraction derby below, plowing into more buildings' supports.

A second crunch jolted the roof as Hellion hit it again, a fault line opened down the middle and the structure began to tip. Wren scrambled up the steepening surface chased by gunfire until a third impact came and dropped the southeast corner of the building completely away.

The sniper's scream ended in a thud as he landed below. Wren leveled the shotgun and charged at the northwest corner, speed-firing four slugs in a second flat. Two punched into the roof, one zinged away through the air and the fourth pinged the sniper dead on.

Wren didn't slow, reached the trembling roof at a full sprint and leaped. One second he sailed through the air, vehicles stampeding twenty feet below like the running of the bulls, then his chest slammed into the next roof over. His left foot caught his weight against the wall, the shotgun clattered away to the dirt below, then he was up again and zigzagging, Colt in his hand and picking out targets.

"Take out their supports along my route," he shouted into the night.

"Hellion's on it," B4cksl4cker responded instantly, and five steps along Wren felt the hit come below. The jolt dislodged another sniper and Wren fired three rounds into his center mass, then hit the edge and was airborne again. Alejandro surfed by on his mapping car below, firing calmly. Wren hit the next roof smoothly and ran at two figures in a machine-gun nest circled with sandbags.

One yanked at the oversized weapon, spinning it off its pre-sighted tripod aimed at the courtyard, but took a shoulder and rolled back. The second grasped for the trigger but was thrown off-balance by the tiny silver chair car thudding into the building below.

Wren fired two shots through the guy's chest, heard B4cksl4cker's cry of surprise, then was leaping again. "Report!" he barked.

"Two more and you're there," B4cksl4cker snapped, "central hub is reinforced with concrete, ram proof; they are retreating toward it. I see seven snipers remain, eight down; Alejandro and Doona are picking them off, Rogers is circling to meet you. Only three vehicles left in commission."

Wren jumped another roof, fired on two guys Doona had pinned down, and got his first clear look at the main hub. It had a low rolled aluminum roof, a radio antenna lit up by stray flashes of light, concrete walls and a metal blast door, with two snipers hunkered in a recessed guard tower.

"Suicide order has gone out!" B4cksl4cker shouted abruptly.

He had to get inside that building.

"On my signal hit the wall below the guard tower with everything you've got," Wren answered, unloaded his last two bullets into a lone figure then ducked behind the rain barrel cover he'd been using. He reloaded the Colt with a smooth slam into the handgrip, took a second to breathe while incoming fire fragged musically off the barrel's wooden staves.

"Doona's hit," B4cksl4cker narrated as the prickly sound of gunfire ran out across the compound. Wren peeked over his shoulder; Hellion's three remaining vehicles were pulling into a tight spiral again, spinning up speed like a centrifuge. "Alejandro's securing her."

"Send me the map car and hit the building," Wren answered, working the angles. It would be ugly, but...

"Pick up?" Hellion chimed in.

"Exactly, give me the count."

"Coming in three, two-"

Wren spun out of cover; the map truck was right there and sweeping toward him. The timing was perfect; he leaped and took the elevated camera bulb in his gut, hunched over it with his elbows locking him in position, the Colt out and firing.

"Go!"

Hellion broke the convoy's spiral like a carpet unrolling, unleashing their stored force in a line direct to the hub. Wren clung onto the map car and charged like a medieval knight jousting. The east guard tower unleashed their fire on him, strafing off the camera as they tried to pick him off. He hit one, took a dart of shrapnel off his right elbow, then dropped away the second before collision.

The convoy crashed dead into the concrete hub and momentum rocked it forward; the camera globe dinged the roof of the guard shelter while Wren slapped meatily off the wall and fell to the dust. He saw stars and breathed cordite, too dizzy to think, feeling it through his back as the two remaining vehicles crashed into the reinforced wall.

Then someone was shouting in his ear, pulling him to his feet.

Alejandro. He pressed Wren flat against the wall as bullets sparked off the map car's mangled metalwork.

"Ay, Dios mío, pendejo, what happened to your face?"

Wren ran a hand up to his cheek and felt hot blood. "I'm fine."

"This way," Alejandro shouted, and turned to run for the bunker door, but something zinged in and spun him.

Wren darted in and grabbed him, pulled him into shallow cover behind the map car just as the supercar pulled up. Most of its glass was starred or missing from incoming fire, the bodywork was pocked with hundreds of bullet holes. Lucky the battery was under the chassis, or they would've killed the drive by sheer chance by now. Wren tugged the rear door open, saw Doona laid sprawled and pale in the backseat, but she inched up to make room for Alejandro beside her.

"Get them out of here," he ordered, and the supercar reversed hard across the courtyard toward the hole in the wall, drawing heavy fire. "Get a doctor on the line, talk Chuck through treatment for them both."

"On it," B4ckslacker answered, "end this, Christopher."

He grunted, spun to see Rogers by his side. She gave him a nod, and he pointed to the hub's outer concrete shell. It had broken like an egg under the vehicle's impacts; the concrete walls shearing out of the too-shallow foundations and opening a slim vertical crack.

"Cover me," Wren shouted, then fed himself through the crack into darkness.

28

HUB

Lights sputtered fitfully inside, faintly illuminating dozens of faces spread before him.

Old people. Children. A young pregnant woman, a man in a wheelchair, all staring up at him from the edges of a ten by twelve room. Like a scene from the Pyramid: desperate people driven to an extreme, but still devoted to whatever their cult leader ordained.

Not a fortress. Not a room full of dead bodies yet, reeking with the burned almond fog of potassium cyanide. Just terrified souls staring back at him. He raised his palms and spoke in a calm, authoritative voice.

"I'm not here to hurt you. What I need to know is-"

A large figure lurched suddenly up on the right, leveling a gun, and Wren flung himself to the side. There was a vicious bang, the room lit up for a split second like the Reparation's strobing cells, then Wren was scrabbling on all fours over arms and legs in the darkness, unwilling to take an answering shot and risk innocents with the ricochet.

For five seconds the room was wild with screams, then Wren surged; his shoulder struck the thickset figure in the midriff, the gun discharged behind Wren's back, and they thumped down together amongst squealing bodies. Wren let his momentum propel a crushing elbow into the figure's face.

Teeth cracked. The big guy went limp, and Wren snatched up the weapon; another Colt by the feel and weight, an LW Commander.

"They're alive," came a voice at his back and he whirled, both Colts trained on a figure by the crack in the wall. Rogers. She wasn't even looking at him; she was focused on the people huddled in the flickering shadows.

"These ones are," Wren called over them. "The suicide order went out, and I'll wager their most devoted are already heaped up in the back. I'll dig in; you find out what these people know."

Rogers nodded. The light of gunfire flashes and wheeling headlights washed through the jagged crack beside her like Taser strikes.

"And watch your six. Anyone comes in, shoot them."

He turned without waiting for a response. Answers had to lie deeper inside. He scanned the dark room, saw only one door and he strode toward it, holding his hand to the earpiece.

"Get the vehicles out of here, we'll need them intact for extraction."

"Relaying," B4cksl4cker said.

Wren laid one hand on the door handle and pulled, taking a sharp step to the side.

Light spilled in and gunfire erupted through the opening. Chips spat off the far wall, drawing fresh cries. Rogers shouted something but Wren ignored it, counting bullets. Three weapons, one semi-automatic. The hail of bullets halted for a moment, and Wren dropped low and bobbed around the door, sighted on two shapes leaning at the end of a bright corridor, and fired.

Twin hits.

Wren didn't wait, charging into the corridor full speed. A

rifle muzzle appeared around an open door to the left and he fired to pin it down. It fired in return, blind shots stitching a line across the far wall and up the ceiling, taking out one of the lights in a spray of sparks and glass. Wren hit the opposite wall, ran low and fast under the angle of spray to whip a big right hook through the open door frame.

His fist hit a soft throat and the rifle dropped. The figure groaned and Wren snatched up the weapon, stepped through and launched a headbutt into the sagging guy's forehead. He dropped.

Intermittent fire came from the end of the corridor, and Wren leaned out of the door, shot out the two remaining lights in sprays of glass, then moved. One of the two figures at the end of the corridor was sagged against the corner, gun propped across her chest. Wren fired first, caught her in the shoulder and sent her reeling. The other lay still, flat on his back whispering last words nobody would hear.

"Wren?" Rogers called.

"I have them," he answered, and dropped to retrieve the weapon from the woman and check her pulse. It was erratic, she was breathing weakly now, likely not long left.

"Where is he?" Wren asked.

The woman's eyes stared back in confusion. She'd never died before, didn't know what it meant, what anything meant anymore. Her mouth opened and she tried to frame words, but nothing came out.

"Is he here?" Wren pressed. "The Apex?"

If anything, her last expression was one of puzzlement. Her face froze like that. Wren stood.

Rogers was calling him.

"I'm fine," he said, choking the words out, "three down."

"They're rallying out there, Christopher! B4cksl4cker says we're far outnumbered. We need to get out of here now."

"Soon," he answered, and strode deeper into the dark.

29

DEEPER

Lights guttered throughout the compound. Wren strode on, Colt at the ready and heart racing as he turned every sputtering corner, but no more shots rang out. There were no more people to shoot.

No leader, at least not in here.

In a room decked out with burned down candles, he found bodies. Old people. A few children. Sprawled in their death throes already. He kneeled; they were warm still, with bubbly froth on their lips like shaving foam. There were cups scattered on the floor and the bitter stink of almonds in the air, cut with the sweet zest of orange juice.

Potassium cyanide.

The order had come down. It looked like he'd disturbed them at the beginning of their work, though these didn't look like the most devoted. The most devoted were out on the rooftops fighting. These were the ones who'd had to be compelled. Who weren't able to fight, and couldn't be trusted to take the medicine themselves.

His anger blurred with disgust. Kill the weak first. He had scattershot memories of his long slaughter through the fake town, painting napalm onto unwilling bodies at the Apex's command…

A deep thudding reverberated up through Wren's belly, pulling him back to the present. He looked around. "What's that sound?"

"They are ramming main doors," came B4cksl4cker's scratchy voice in his ear, high and distant. "I think they will hold for now, but. Ah. They are attaching lines to door. Bringing vehicles into position. It will be like Handel Quanse. You have minutes only, Christopher."

Wren left the suicide room with its stink and its memories and hurried on. To his left a long office room had been stripped, the contents of three metal filing cabinets torched in situ, computers pummeled by sledgehammers, nothing that could help him now. In a kitchen he found unmarked chemical kegs stinking of potassium cyanide, alongside half-full cartons of orange juice. In a dormitory hall he rifled through drawers, cabinets, under beds, in desks, but there was nothing: no flash drives, no cameras, no trapdoor leading down to a dungeon holding the billionaires.

This was the right place, but there was nothing he could use. Somewhere far off shots tinkled musically.

"Sun is coming up," Hellion barked in his ear. Wren blinked, realized he was looking at his own face in a bathroom mirror. He looked like a zombie afflicted with a flesh-eating virus. The grenades had spattered fragments of rubber across his cheek and neck, turning him a mottled black. The pain from that was really settling in. His whole body felt hammered.

He moved. The FBI would be here soon to clean up this mess. The site would lock down in a siege. There had to be something of value, and he had to find it now, but what? He staggered back to the corridor where he'd begun. At the end of a blood trail lay the dead woman, she'd managed to drag herself along maybe ten feet.

"Alejandro is in trouble," came Hellion's voice in his ear. "He needs medical attention now."

"Trouble," Wren echoed. Racking his mind for the next move.

"We are waiting for you," she sped on. "Christopher, we have to get out, they are pulling blast doors now. Fourteen men, three vehicles. You cannot fight them."

Wren grunted. Everybody was outside, except for the ones in the cell. The reluctant ones. It gave him an idea. He ran to the kitchen, mixed up a fresh cocktail, then sped back into the cell. A few dozen pairs of eyes widened on him. It was dark and it stank of fear.

"You look like death," Rogers said, white eyes wide as he approached, nodding at the cup in his hand. "What's that you've got?"

Wren ignored her, surveyed these remnants of Anti-Ca. The man whose teeth he'd busted now lay slumped against the wall, his face pale. The rest were a few old folks, the pregnant girl who could barely be twenty years old, the guy in a wheelchair and some kids. To them he had to look like the devil.

Time to stamp that home.

He held out the plastic. Pilfered from the kitchen, now filled to the brim with orange liquid.

"To your health," he said, and held the cup up like a toast.

They stared. An indictment. Every one of them knew what it meant, and Wren trapped that knowledge with a hard stare, looking into their eyes one by one and seeking out the softest touches, those least strong in their faith.

He saw what he was looking for in the pregnant girl's eyes.

He'd seen it a million times before. Shock and awe. A

soul carried along by the tide of her cult, not strong enough to break free, each time taking the next step because all her friends and family were too.

Wren held he cup out toward her. She flinched, though he was ten feet away.

"How about you, sister?" he asked. "Will you toast our good health?"

Her eyes peeled wide, trying to press herself back into the wall. Wren strode toward her. She was blond and string-thin apart from the swell of her belly. Eight months along perhaps, risking her baby just by being here, but what was risk when you expected to die by your own hand?

He dropped to one knee before her, holding the brimming cup right in front of her face. "You want to die for the movement? So die."

Her eyes danced from Wren to Rogers. She didn't understand. She didn't want to drink, but Wren had her isolated, forced to think for herself.

"Don't listen to a word-" someone shouted, and Wren spun, drew his Colt and fired. The bullet hit the wall next to an elderly woman's head. She looked like she'd swallowed her tongue.

He holstered the weapon like nothing had happened. The girl was bug-eyed now.

"Don't be afraid," Wren said hypnotically. "I've been here before. I've done this before. I know you're ready to die and take your baby along with you. Your cause here is just. So prove it."

He pushed the cup against her lips. She tried to pull away but there was nowhere to go. Orange liquid spilled down her chin. "Drink."

"I-I-" she stammered.

"What's the matter? Lost your faith?"

No one spoke. Rogers sucked in a breath.

"That's what I thought," Wren said. "So tell me where the Apex is, or I'll hold your nose and pour this down your throat."

She sucked air in a sharp gasp, eyes dancing side to side, looking for help. None came.

"For God's sake, tell him what you know!" Rogers shouted. "Where are the Reparations? For your baby's sake, tell us!"

Wren ignored her. Nothing needed to be explained. Everything came down to him, this woman, and justice in a cup full of bitter liquid. He tipped the cup further, so the liquid wetted her lips.

"Where's the arena?" Rogers shouted. "Where are the billionaires? Tell us where they are!"

Wren tipped more. The acrid orange liquid poured over the girl's chin and streamed into the hollow of her throat. She shook her head to spray it away, so Wren took hold of her jaw in one hand and squeezed until her mouth popped open.

"Drink," he commanded, and poured the liquid into her mouth.

Something hit Wren from the side, hard enough to send the liquid sloshing to the floor and Wren tumbling. He hit the deck, rolled and came up on his knees, Colt drawn and extended.

Rogers stood there; her own gun trained in on him.

Wren felt the world twisting.

"What the hell are you doing, Chris?" Rogers shouted.

He knew that look in her wild eyes. Always going too far, it said. Permission denied. But you had to go far. If there was one thing he'd learned in the Pyramid, it was that you had to be willing to go right up to the edge, sometimes even jump over.

He turned back to the spluttering girl. She was trying to retch out the liquid. She couldn't know it wasn't potassium cyanide, rather a bitter mix of orange juice and apple cider vinegar. All they'd had in the kitchen.

"Where is he?" Wren asked. "I have the antidote. You need it, or you're going to die a slow and painful death. Tell me. Where is the Apex?"

"Who?" the girl cried, wiping her mouth frantically, spitting and gagging. She was beyond terror now; pale skin, sweat trails running down her cheeks, eyes flared and shaking. She thought she was seconds from death.

"Give her the antidote!" Rogers barked. He looked at her. The gun was still trained on his chest. It gave him the rest of the play. The edge he wasn't supposed to cross; the way to show these people how serious he was.

"She knows something, Rogers."

"Bullshit she does! I put up with you killing the Pinocchios on Pleasure Island, with all your crazy tactics, but this is too far. You're not going to get answers by killing her. Give her the damn antidote!"

She took a step toward him, her weapon trained on his chest, her blond hair pulled loose from its tight bun and clinging to her cheeks. Grit, grime, furious blue eyes. She looked beautiful, really. Standing up for what was right.

"Stand down, Agent Rogers. The bullet will go right through you."

"So let it!" she countered. "I won't let you execute another innocent."

"She's not innocent," he growled. "The Pinocchios weren't innocent. All these people are part of it."

"Part of what, your father's cult?" Rogers eyes were wide with disbelief. "He died twenty-five years ago! Let it go, Chris."

He shook his head.

"That's it. I'm accelerating our timeline. I'm taking you in right now."

Her finger squeezed the trigger. Wren felt it more than he saw it. Reaching boiling point.

He fired first.

Hit her left of center mass.

She was punched back. Colt M1911 at close range, standard issue .45 ACP full metal jacket rounds in the chamber, 230 grain and traveling at a muzzle velocity of 830 feet per second; a relatively large slug, relatively slow out of the barrel, famously ineffective against body armor.

The Twaron vest should take the brunt of it. He hoped so. Either way, Rogers spun and went down.

Screams followed.

Always there was screaming at a transformation. Wren didn't need to see them; their horrified eyes, but this was part of it. To truly break the hold of a cult you had to break its link to the past, go beyond its sense of rules. The Reparations understood that. Take away any semblance of control and drop a nuclear bomb where it had been.

Rogers hit the floor. A voice called in his ear, warning the blast doors were about to breach. Wren spun back to the girl. She was spitting still, wiping her tongue on her sleeve. There were so many things to say, but now he didn't need to say any of them. Actions spoke louder.

He leveled the gun at her face.

"I was there!" she cried abruptly.

There it was. He felt the moment teetering. What did it matter that her people were coming in through the blast doors any second? Wren was here right now.

"I don't know about this 'Apex', but at the arena when they killed the billionaire? I was there! We didn't even think it was real." Tears raced down her cheeks. "I swear, we didn't know. I'll tell you everything, if you-"

There was an almighty crash that resounded through the building. The wall shook and the crack sheared wider.

"They are in, Christopher," B4cksl4cker shouted. "Ten seconds to exfiltration. There is one chance."

Sound rushed back in like air filling a vacuum. Wren heard the remnants of the convoy ripping through the defenses outside, rattled by gunfire. He heard the stamping of feet racing through the building, coming for him. In. Out. Ahead was the girl; pregnant. By his side lay Rogers, unconscious. Life was made of choices.

He chose both. Holstered the Colt and took the girl by the arm, grabbed Rogers by the wrist, and dragged them both up to the crack. Rogers went first, like posting a deadweight sack through a vertical letterbox, then Wren pulled the girl through after him.

She flopped to the earth just as figures stormed the cell in back. Rogers' Ford pickup was waiting for them outside, rocking with stalled momentum, taking bullets off its A-columns and bodywork, all the glass already gone. Gruber was in the driver's seat, looking wild-eyed and terrified. Doona was in the passenger seat, bandaged and returning fire.

She pushed the back door open and Wren bundled the girl in ahead, dragged Rogers after him, and Gruber hit reverse with a jerk. They revved backward through the courtyard of wreckage, away from the hail of gunfire past scattered flames and fallen bodies, to scrape sparks off the gouge in the compound wall and out into the night.

30

COME IN, CHRISTOPHER

Wren woke in a moving vehicle, head fogged with a range of thoughts seeking some kind of completion. He remembered Rogers crumpled on a dark floor, and a girl sobbing, and the blurry, misremembered face of the Apex, and couldn't understand what they meant.

The vehicle jogged side to side. An ambulance? He was lying flat on a gurney, drip bags spooling blood into him, one at his wrist, another leading up to his throat.

"Don't touch that," came a stern voice. He looked and his vision swirled. Rogers?

"You're supposed to be anesthetized. You don't want to be conscious for this."

"Unhh," he managed to say.

"Trust me. That's a lot of tissue damage to your face. Unless you want to lose these good looks, I need you out for this, Christopher. There's a good boy, put your head down."

She was familiar. He couldn't quite grasp who she was. Not Rogers. Matronly. Tough. For some reason the words Munchausen Syndrome-by-proxy came into his mind. Was that…? He smiled, yes, remembering a case. Marissa, the surgical nurse who kept her patients sick for longer than she should. Only a little at first, only a few days, but then lengthening it, enjoying the power, the attention, their neediness.

Who knew, in time, if she would have graduated to killing them? With kindness, with constant care? Attend the funeral, sob along with the rest, enjoy the silent thrill of absolute power. He remembered picking her out by chance from datasets during a hospital opioid drug sting, a side project he'd taken on when the recovery times of patients didn't stack up. He remembered the moment he'd confronted her in the underground parking lot. Put her on a coin.

"Coin… zero…" he managed.

She snorted. Short, sharp. "You're in no state to make threats, young man. Now get back under, you're in my care here. Count down from five."

He laughed, barely a breath, though it wasn't funny. He managed the five, then…

When he woke next the movement had stopped; he wasn't in a vehicle anymore. It was a bedroom. The curtains were drawn, but light glowed through them warm and orange, revealing walls painted pale green, a full-length mirror, pine wardrobes reaching close to the ceiling.

He twisted but it hurt to move. He remembered taking rubber shrapnel from several grenades. Flashes of his own face in a mirror somewhere, black and mottled, came back to him. Names played in his head: Rogers. Gruber. Doona.

He climbed from the bed. Someone had taken his pink shorts off and replaced them with a pair of Hawaiian swimming trunks, red and black with embroidered skulls. Hardly better. His head pulsed and his mouth felt as dry as beef jerky.

With careful fingers he stroked the bandages on his left side. They began at the tip of his elbow and ran along his triceps, filled out his armpit but absent down his ribcage, where the Twaron vest had caught the grenade's spray. They picked up again over his hip then stopped where the thigh plate had been. He touched his jaw tentatively, then his cheek. Bandages too. There was that sensation of numbness that signaled a bad injury, temporarily masked by strong painkillers. Soon they'd wear off, and it wasn't going to be pretty. For now though, he was golden.

He leaned over and drew the curtain.

Light flooded in, momentarily blinding him. He blinked as his eyes teared up and adjusted. A cornfield came into focus outside; fields of green and gold plants standing proud like thousands of soldiers awaiting the sheafer. A red clay yard covered the gap, with a few tattered old pick-ups parked neatly. A barn stood to the right, faded red. It was mid-afternoon, judging by the high sun in the blue sky, around 3 p.m.

The exfiltration from the compound came back to him in flashes, as the Ford had pulled up to where Chuck was waiting in the dark. He'd checked Rogers; her Twaron vest had stopped the bullet, which proved a relief. Alejandro was out cold on the side of the road with a through-and-through shoulder wound, Chuck was dithering, Doona had taken shrapnel in her right thigh, and Gruber was trying to dab at Wren's face.

He'd told Hellion to activate their medical backup. Marissa Brey, his 'Angel of Death' Foundation member, on standby nearby.

They'd lit out. He remembered the thin stream of lights pouring out of the compound, coming for them. The pregnant girl was babbling by then, weepy and terrified. He held her face and looked in her eyes. "It wasn't poison," he said. "Orange juice and apple cider vinegar, that's all. You and your baby are fine."

She'd tried to slap him. He rolled most of it, then they were away. The girl handcuffed in the Ford, Alejandro curled into the pickup bed alongside Rogers, Gruber in the driver's seat, Doona riding shotgun. He sat by the girl and tried to interrogate her, but blood-loss and wooziness got the better of him, making his thoughts wander.

From there it was brief highlights only: the handover to the medical team as they pulled up for a mid-desert meet; him insisting Rogers, Alejandro and Doona all had treatment before him; traveling while Marissa put in stitches, the minibus clanging and jolting; finally his turn on the operating bench, and the anesthetic to put him under...

Then he was here.

Maybe ten hours gone. Half a day, and no time to waste.

A white T-shirt lay on a chair, and he pulled it on. His shoulder and side tightened, but the pain remained muted. Out the door he went, down wooden stairs to a hall hanging heavy with the smell of cinnamon and caramelizing butter, like someone had been baking cookies. There was a sunken den, a dining room, and an open-plan kitchen with a granite-topped island. A beautiful Midwestern farmhouse, right out of a furniture catalog.

"Hello?" he called.

No answer came. He patted his pockets, but his phone was gone. He went to the faucet and poured out a tall glass of lukewarm water, drained it, repeated that three times. Popped the fridge, found a quart of milk and drained half. Took five still-warm cookies from the cooling rack and started eating as he limped out, swinging the screen door onto the front porch. They were delicious.

Outside there was red dirt, balmy air, sharp sun in his eyes. He held up a hand to shield the light and headed for the barn. The corn rustled in the wind. Reedy cirrus clouds drifted like washed-out blood smears. He passed a large tractor then reached the barn doors. They creaked loudly as he pulled, announcing his entrance.

He wasn't at all ready for what lay on the other side.

Eyes turned his way, a dozen? People seated around a cluster of tool-bitten workbenches on the hay-strewn floor, watching some kind of PowerPoint presentation on a rigged-up projector screen. Vehicles crowded around them in the barn's wings; an ambulance, the bullet-scarred Ford, others.

Wren stared. He couldn't make sense of it. Some kind of business meeting, in a barn, in, where? Iowa?

Then he recognized one of them. In the hot dark, sitting at the center of the group, the first one to rise was-

Wren almost took a step back. Not possible.

Chicago Teddy?

He wasn't big like he'd once been, before an assassin for the Order of the Saints had put a bullet in his skull nine months earlier. Last time Wren had seen him he'd been in a coma with no hope of waking any time soon. Extensive risk of brain damage, the doctors had said. Wren had arranged for the best possible care on the Foundation's tab, but feared the worst.

Now he was here. Half-bald on one side where they'd jacked open his skull, buzz cut for the rest. He had a tight goatee beard shot through liberally with gray on a Hollywood-square jaw. He looked like an oversized skeleton wearing Teddy's skin, making him more angular and somehow infused with purpose.

Wren's jaw opened, closed.

Teddy and Cheryl had led a cult of play-acting 'vampires' in Chicago's S&M scene for years, before Wren came along and put a stop to all the fun. Nobody had died by then, as they'd taken it in turns to 'bleed' each other, but that date hadn't been far off.

Wren's eyes roamed, and yes, there was Cheryl too, seated

at Teddy's left like Mary Magdalene at the last supper. Steven Gruber was on the other side, looking unhappy. Doona was there in bandages, even Chuck too, Alejandro in a wheelchair, along with many others: Alli the scrapyard worker from Wyoming, who'd helped him bring down the Order of the Saints; his Montlake professor of film, Raymond Craik, looking severe in a Mandarin-collared shirt; his mpeg analyst, Sonny Leland, out of Houston; Marissa Brey, his Munchausen Syndrome by Proxy surgeon; then two more that were both the cherry and cream on the cake.

Hellion and B4cksl4cker. Wren blinked in disbelief. Right there at the edge, but not actually in person, as he'd first thought. Rather twin large-screen TVs had been set up atop giant cable spools, streaming live video footage of them from the waist up. The effect was uncannily impressive, like they were in the barn.

Altogether, it felt like a dream; one of those teenaged dreams he'd heard about, where you're suddenly naked in school and everybody's looking and laughing. Of course, all his dreams at high school had been nightmares about the Pyramid, but he'd seen enough TV to know the trope.

Except this was real. The sun was hot on his back. The clay was cool underfoot.

"Come in, Christopher," Teddy said, his voice a deep grind. "We're ready for you."

31

BARN

Wren entered. In the gloom he picked out more faces, more names. Members of the Foundation, gathered together. Now he saw the single chair set before them, alone, like the defendant in a kangaroo court.

"Take a seat, Christopher," Teddy said.

Wren stood by the chair. He didn't know what to feel. Anger, maybe. Perhaps pride.

"You're looking better, Teddy," he said, and let that hang for a moment. They were all staring at him. Waiting to see what he would do. Their leader, Christopher Wren, as unpredictable as ever. "Thinner, at least."

"A coma will do that to you," Teddy said. "Please, sit down."

Christopher looked at the chair, back up at his jury. "I'm not sure we have time for this. Whatever this is."

"We insist. Please take a seat."

"I prefer to stand."

Teddy looked a little put out. Wren gazed calmly at him, at the others. Putting the pieces together. Teddy opened his mouth to speak, but Wren beat him to it.

"It's an intervention. I get that, and it makes sense you'd head it up, Teddy. You always wanted a cult of your own."

Teddy looked uncomfortable. "It's not that, Christopher, it's-"

"It's what? You don't like my methods, or you're worried about my mental state?" He paused a moment, thinking both through. "You wouldn't be the first on either. I'm right there with you. I just shot Sally Rogers." He took a breath, remembering the awful moment. It didn't sit well. "That's bad, I agree. I need to pay for it, I agree. But right now, punishment can wait. Damalin Joes' life is at risk. America is at risk. My father is out there, pulling the strings." He took a breath, looking into their eyes. "I need to talk to the girl. Hunt down the Reparations and cut off their head. What else is there to discuss right now?"

Teddy looked more embarrassed than chastised. He glanced side to side; at Cheryl in her leathers, at Alli in her denim dungarees, at the hackers on their screens atop their cable spool like it was the kids' table. None offered him any support, but he didn't let that slow him down. "You *did* shoot Agent Sally Rogers. The Foundation *is* worried about your mental state. We're gathered here less as an intervention and more as a..." Teddy shifted uncomfortably. "Vote of no confidence."

Wren almost laughed. Held it in.

"Vote of no confidence. In my own Foundation?"

"Is it your Foundation, Christopher?" Teddy countered. "You don't communicate, except to make demands. You don't run coin meetings anymore. You just kill without compunction. You shot Sally Rogers." He paused. "Is this who we are? What the Foundation is for?"

Wren let that wash over him. Took a sidetrack. "Is Rogers OK?"

Teddy shifted in his seat. "When last we saw her? Yes."

"What do you mean?"

"You dropped her at a hospital five hours back." A pause. "We couldn't bring her here."

Wren looked around the barn. Farming equipment. Some old bales of cornstalks, maybe useful for composting. Tired old hoes, rakes and shovels. "Because heaven forbid she should see this place. The incredible tech you've got, I can't imagine the secrets she'd uncover."

"Christopher," Hellion said abruptly, her Slavic accent coming loud through the speakers and cutting the cozy barn vibe. "Take this seriously, yes?"

She looked bored, like she had a million better things to be doing.

"So get serious. I'm listening."

She shrugged and gestured half-heartedly off her screen. "We voted. This is Theodore's job. Listen to him."

He turned to Teddy, and Teddy took a moment, then took a breath, puffing his skeletal frame up. "We did take a vote, Christopher. About you. About your role in the Foundation."

That was worth another laugh. He'd built the Foundation with his bare hands. But he didn't laugh. He just waited for Teddy to go on.

"You see, all this began with Dr. Ferat."

That was hardly a surprise. Dr. Grayson Ferat had been one of Wren's earliest members, a professor with a penchant for exploiting the work and life experience of his students, turning them into examples in his many research papers. Wren had refocused his attentions on the Foundation fifteen years back, put him on a coin, and just three months ago Ferat had gone to his death against the Blue Fairy. He was a hero.

"Ferat's dead," he said.

"He is," Teddy allowed. "But you are aware he was

rewriting the Foundation? Setting up committees, hierarchies, buddy programs, buying up properties and formalizing the coin system?"

Wren grunted. Distantly, he was aware of all that. He'd been too busy killing Pinocchios and hunting his father's trail to pay much attention.

"What you're seeing here is a natural outgrowth of that work. You remain the Foundation's head, obviously. The CEO, if you like. Charismatic leader, a man we all owe loyalty to, some of us our lives, but…" he paused. "I'm afraid that's not enough anymore."

"So what do you want?" Wren asked. He'd be more amused than angry, if it weren't for the ticking Reparations clock. "To be off the coins again?"

Teddy blinked. "Off the coins? No! Of course not."

Wren weighed Teddy's loyalty in the balance. He'd always wanted to be free of the Foundation's system of accountability, the coins. Maybe that was even fair, now. Several members of the Foundation had paid with their lives. Teddy and Cheryl had almost died, likewise Doona and Chuck. Dr. Ferat was dead. Abdul was dead. Wren had pressed many of his members into the Foundation, but he didn't want to press them to die.

It didn't leave him with much. Take it with grace, maybe.

"Then what?" he asked,

"Nobody wants off the coin system, Christopher," Teddy said, leaning forward now. "If anything, we want deeper in."

That surprised him. "What do you mean, deeper in?"

"We need training," Teddy said. "We need resources. We need to work together better if we're going to do this properly." His voice swelled. "I don't regret getting shot for you, Christopher. I'm proud of it and I'd do it again. But I want to be better prepared the next time, so I don't need to get shot. I want your skills. We all want them. We want you to train us. We want a school. We want the Foundation to have a thousand members, ten thousand members on different continents, all around the world. We want to take this thing you've built and make it bigger. You can't do that alone. You go it alone, or with untrained members," he glanced briefly toward Chuck, "and Rogers gets shot. People get hurt who shouldn't. We want to avoid that."

Wren took a breath, trying to absorb that. Deeper in. He hadn't expected any of this and didn't know what to think. To make matters worse, his side was beginning to tingle; first sign that the painkiller was wearing off.

"We also want a code of conduct. A moral system to better underlie the coins and everything we do. One that binds you as much as it binds us, because without you the Foundation falls apart." Teddy paused, "We don't want that. This group has the capacity to be a truly beautiful thing. Rehabilitation. A second chance. A way to meaningfully contribute. We simply want higher standards, for us as well as for yourself. Everyone in this barn is ready to fight, even die for this cause, if you can show us it's truly worth dying for."

Wren listened to Teddy, wondering at how fast things could change. Teddy himself was a different man than the lost, desperate soul he'd been in Chicago, living in the past and unable to see any future. Wren was changing too; he could feel it. The hunt for his father had transformed him. The loss of his family. Just moments ago he'd thought the Foundation was falling apart. Now he might be deeper in than ever.

"You want to take the Foundation bigger," he said. "And you want me to be accountable."

Teddy nodded, looking slightly relieved. "Yes, exactly that."

"And you want training," Wren summarized. "Maybe more facilities like this?" he gestured around at the barn.

Teddy smiled encouragingly. In for a penny, in for a pound, Wren figured. It was true that in the last year he'd used the Foundation in ways he'd never really anticipated. It was only fair the Foundation should change too, to accommodate that. That he should change in turn.

"OK," he said, thinking it through as he spoke. "I agree. And let's go further. You've all gathered here already, so let's formalize that by instituting a Board of Directors. Everyone here is now a member. Yes, even Chuck." He looked at Chuck, who instantly reddened. There was the slightest chuckle. "After this it can be a vote system to decide leadership, with contribution weighted by coin status." Wren focused in on the thin, shaven-headed man at the center. "Teddy, they've already elevated you, so why don't you head it up? COO, Chief Operations Officer. I can be President, partially a figurehead role, but with authority in a crisis. That's non-negotiable. I built this thing and I can't let it slip completely. As for the rest, Dr. Ferat's expansion, joint coin meetings, the buddy system? I like your ideas. Work on them."

Teddy had his palms flat on the trestle table now, as if he had to stabilize himself. Probably this was going far better than he'd expected. Maybe worried it was all a dream.

"And the camps?" he asked.

Wren considered. He'd kept a loose eye on Dr. Ferat's purchases. Eight months ago the good doctor had started buying up large, obscure properties across the States using Foundation money. Farms, mostly, but some sections of unplumbed wilderness, still scattered with dinosaur bones left untouched for millennia. They were meant to be training camps, places to learn paramilitary tactics, hacking, Neuro-

Linguistic Programming, cult de-indoctrination and whatever else it took to be a good Foundation member.

Wren didn't much like it, another step taking his Foundation further into the real world, but he'd been pushing for his members to take those steps anyway. His calls to action had put them on the radar of numerous intelligence agencies. Fully establishing the physical properties would be the biggest step yet, giving the FBI a nexus to assault in the future, just like Wren had hit the Anti-Ca compound.

But still...

"Keep them," Wren said. You had to compromise. He needed to train, prep and outfit the Foundation core better if he wanted to keep calling on them. And if their expansion plans came about, taking the Foundation to a thousand members, God forbid as high as ten thousand someday, they would need a physical presence. "But keep them absolutely secret and absolutely above board. We will never have cause for a face-off with the authorities. Hellion, B4cksl4cker," he turned to them, "that's on you. Protect Dr. Ferat's legacy."

"And the coins?"

That was Chuck. Wren looked back at him. The man shouldn't even be here. But he was here. Wren looked at Teddy, playing it all out.

"You want to put me on a coin?"

Teddy glared back at him undeterred. "Coin zero, Christopher. For shooting Sally Rogers. At the edge of our tether."

Wren grimaced. Nodded.

"Coin zero. OK. But we're still in a crisis. Formalization of all these new rules and systems can wait until the immediate threat is over. Does anyone disagree?"

Wren looked around. Nobody spoke. He didn't know what he'd do if they did. Go it alone, maybe. Split the Foundation down the middle, between those loyal to him and those loyal to Teddy. Happily, no one spoke or raised their hand.

Coin zero, then, in his own organization. Wren could live with that.

Time to get back on the clock.

"Now, where's the girl from the compound?"

32

DUCKS IN A ROW

S teven Gruber was first up, handed Wren an earpiece
then led him out of the barn.

"I can't believe you're even standing," he said,
walking alongside as they stepped out into the swirling, dry
air. Wren inserted the earpiece, heard the beep as it paired
him through to Hellion and B4cksl4cker. "The doctor said-"

"Doctors are babies," Wren said, which impressed Gruber
into silence but drew a snort from Hellion in his ear.

"You are baby," Hellion said. "You cannot even walk
properly. Like aliens in human bodies. What movie is this,
B4cksl4cker?"

"Bodysnatchers," came B4cksl4cker's voice without
skipping a beat.

"Exactly, like you do not know how to use your own
legs."

Wren didn't bother to answer. Rather he found himself
smiling. Pain was just weakness leaving the body, after all.

"And your face, Christopher," Hellion went on, "it is
hideous. Leatherface. Mr. Hyde. Yes. You will need cosmetic
surgery, if you wish to be beautiful again."

"Again?" B4cksl4cker asked.

Wren tuned them out. Focused on walking through the gathering pain. Getting his ducks in a row. "Tell me how Rogers is."

"Yes, Agent Rogers," Hellion said. "We are watching her hospital. She will be fine. Soon she will be looking for you again."

Wren grunted. Of course she would. "Doona and Alejandro, are they OK?"

"Yes. Both are healthy. Alejandro lost much blood and is resting now. Doona also."

Wren thought that through. His strike team were out of action, and Rogers was off the game board for now. That brought positives as well as negatives. Director Humphreys would have to send someone else after him; somebody less effective. It bought him latitude.

"And the Reparations?"

Hellion's voice sank. "This is ugly."

He made the leap. "There's been another video, already?"

"One. It is strange. Damalin Joes having angry sex with a woman, but she is pixelated. We cannot see any details. The leader, we suspect. She calls it a reward for what he did."

Wren hadn't expected that. A reward.

"Additional, copycat videos have increased by factor of ten, on Reparations app." Keys clattered. "Highlights are, this morning four high school lacrosse players tied up their coach and pulled him apart in school parking lot. Four SUV vehicles to do this work. Apparently, coach abused two of them years ago. Claiming reparations in blood, Christopher. They filmed this, of course. They are heroes in the app now." She took a breath. "Also, there have been three mass shootings, two on country clubs that killed a dozen total, one that did not make it past lobby of Fortune 500 company. Add this to handful of hatchet attacks, and day is only half over for you. All claim for Reparations."

"Death count?" Wren growled.

"Rising toward one hundred. Your borders are closing. One man in Los Angeles Airport killed five Haitian tourists before guards shot him down, shouting about foreigners. Bomb threats are closing schools and train stations, reports of armed gangs roaming streets, some video. Police are activated but avoiding full pitch battle."

"People are going crazy," Gruber contributed from by Wren's side. "Like hell just opened up."

"America's on the boil," Wren said softly.

"Old crimes," B4cksl4cker said in his ear. "Hashtag Reparations. Up-votes for videos on this app hit ten million within minutes. People around all world are enjoying this and cheering. It is best entertainment yet, 'great Satan' America finally consuming itself."

Wren stepped up onto the porch deck, thinking hard. He'd set a lot of plates spinning before heading into the Anti-Ca compound: likely Hellion had kept on top of the results.

"Anything on a location for the arena?"

"Nothing definitive," she answered. "We are constructing data ghosts. Models of potentials, but this is all guesswork. We need more hard details."

Wren worked the possibilities. Data ghosts and details. "How many prospective targets have you got?"

"Based on an oval space, tiered seating, filled with sand? Almost zero, Christopher. Two that we have found, by algorithm searching satellite map data. One, a private volleyball court. Two, a rich man's reconstruction of a Roman colosseum. But it is not these. There have been no movements near them for many months. We have live satellite data."

Wren grunted. "What about hacking the app?"

"We are working on it, but it is embedded deeply. FBI chatter says US President is considering total shutdown of all communications; Internet, phone, television, while Army and National Guard flood in and secure streets, institute lockdown and daylight curfew."

"They are panicking," said B4cksl4cker.

Wren thought it sounded like a good move. It was what he would say to Humphreys, if Humphreys would take his call now. Absolute quarantine. Take the poison out of people's hands. Without this app driving them on, the heat would abate. But with Rogers removed from the loop, he knew Humphreys would never listen to him. There'd be no 'catch' anymore. Only 'kill'.

It all came down to needing more data. It came down to the girl.

Gruber held the fly screen open. "She's upstairs," he said, "but she's refusing to say a word."

Wren pushed through the door. Just like the Pinocchios before her, she'd speak for him.

33

JESSICA

Climbing the stairs made Wren's whole side ache. At the top Gruber led him to a bedroom door with a crudely screwed-in bolt-bar.

"She's angry," he warned, slotting a key into the padlock. "Last time she tried to club me with a bed slat."

"She succeeded," Hellion corrected in Wren's ear.

"Open it," Wren said. Gruber did, looking unhappy. Now Wren saw the welt on his forehead.

She came at him like a jack-in-the-box. Must've been waiting there all along. As soon as the door swung inward, she lunged through with a sharp length of wood held out like a spear.

Wren slapped the wood away and scooped her up like a puppy. She screamed. Wren carried her back into a room that had been thoroughly wrecked; bed stripped, walls scored, furniture smashed. He deposited her on the edge of the bed and kneeled before her, holding her wrists firmly and shackling her legs with his elbows.

"Cut that nonsense out," he said softly. "We've been through this already." She tried to bite his face. "And that. You'll hurt the baby."

She went to headbutt him, then cursed long and loud as he leaned just out of reach.

"What are you, eight months along?" he asked calmly. Her eyes flashed. "You're ready to pop any minute. Tell me, have you picked out a name?"

The cursing slowed. She hadn't expected that.

"It's a girl, right?" Wren pressed on, keeping her off balance. Her eyes froze a second, and Wren corrected. "No, a boy. I've got one of each myself. I don't get to see them much. It's a tragedy, but I'm learning to take responsibility." He gazed calmly into her eyes, seeing a lifetime's worth of anger coming hard on the shame of her earlier admission. The best way to get through that was to slip around the side.

"That's the first thing you feel when you become a parent," he said, "the weight of responsibility. You can't imagine it until it comes, then, bam, it's all on you. This tiny life in your hands. All her prospects, all her hopes, they begin with you on day one and they never stop." He paused a moment, looking at her. There was fear in her eyes now, driving the rage. "If you start being responsible now, maybe you can steer this child to make better choices. She needn't end up in a suicide cult gargling a potassium-cyanide cocktail."

She strained against him again but was unable to budge in his firm grip.

"Now, we're going to talk. Last night you told me you were present at the arena. I need you calm and talking about that right now. I need it all. Short me and I'll know. You won't like what happens next."

She spat in his face. Not pleasant, but a waste of time. He wiped his face on her shoulder once more. "So think about this. I shot my own partner to get you out of there. You think I'll be nicer to you?"

"I'm not helping you," she snapped.

Better. At least now she was talking. "You already are. So let's come at it from this angle. Your compound, Anti-Ca, you all went to the Reparations arena. You already told me that; you were the audience. Was it by bus or plane?" She just stared. "OK. We'll work up to it. What interests me now is the cyanide. The orange juice. You knew about the order to commit group suicide. I'm even thinking you might've placed a call for help, soon as you heard about it. Was that you?" He saw the guilt flash across her eyes. Bingo. He'd picked the right person in the chaos of that safe room. "OK, you did. But you stayed anyway. Why?"

She went abruptly still. Wren felt the difference in his gut, like she was a suicide bomber about to pull the pin. The shame of her battlefield confession was shutting her down and her eyes were emptying out, like she'd just become a ghost.

He pulled back, not enough room to launch another headbutt attack, but room to breathe. Took ten seconds then carried on. "What's your name?"

She stared blankly back at him. Wren turned to Gruber.

"Jessica," he said.

"Jessica," Wren repeated, running those dizzy moments in the Anti-Ca compound through his mind again. A room full of dead bodies. The others just waiting for their turn. "That suicide order was about me, Jessica. You know that, right? They told you to die because they knew I was coming, and they wanted you dead, so all the evidence was cleaned up." She flinched slightly. "Your own leaders wanted you to die just to shut me down, and you wouldn't be the first. I think that's disgusting. They valued you and your baby less than their mission. Why don't you think about that for a minute?"

Her eyes widened slightly. Wren plunged on.

"Think about what that says about them, and about me. I would never tell you to kill yourself. I'd never tell you to kill your own baby." Her eyes began to shine with tears. Anger, confusion, shock. "They're playing a game here, Jessica, and to them you're a pawn, easy to sacrifice. Help me stop them before too many other pawns die." He gazed steadily into her eyes. "I know you believe in your message. The rich need to pay for their crimes, I'm one hundred percent behind that, but this is something else. For the people behind these videos, your movement is just a tool. They're not trying to save America; they're trying to destroy it."

A tear spilled down her cheek. He could feel the emotions burning inside her.

"But you made that telephone call, asking for help. You didn't drink the poison when I told you to. It's because you want to live, and you want your baby to live. So live, Jessica. Tell me how I can stop them. Tell me where the arena is."

In one smooth movement he let go and backed away, leaving her bowed protectively over her belly on the edge of the bed. Teary and red-eyed, staring at the sharp slat that lay on the floor.

"Wren," Gruber cautioned.

Wren ignored him.

"Jessica," he said. "It's a beautiful name. It comes from the Hebrew, 'Yiskah', which means foresight. Now it's time to live up to your name, Jessica. Show me what you really are."

He waited. For long moments she didn't budge. Deep processes turning inside. Maybe five minutes passed before she looked up, her eyes still red but intent.

"So ask your questions."

34

QUESTIONS

Wren dropped to one knee, closer to her eye level. "I need to know where that arena is, Jessica. I need to know anyone you saw there."

"I don't know where it is," she answered. "They put us on a bus from the compound, told us we were going to make history, but we had to wear blindfolds."

"Blindfolds? For how long?"

"For the whole trip. It was really uncomfortable. I think I fell asleep, at one point. So I don't know how long it took."

That didn't help any. A duration of travel would at least give Wren a search radius. Still, there were other ways of telling time. "So tell me what you know. Was it light when you left? Dark when you arrived?"

She thought for a second, eyes rolling up and to the left, accessing memory. "We left around noon, after lunch. I don't know if it was dark when we arrived. We wore the blindfolds even when we got off, until we were indoors."

"OK. We'll come back to that, but let's stick with the bus for now. Did they feed you while you were traveling? Were you hungry when you got off?"

She thought for a moment. "They didn't feed us on the bus. I was hungry, yes."

"How hungry?"

"Really bad. It woke me up."

"Painful? Like a knife in your stomach?"

She countered fast, like a tennis game. "Not that bad. Just hungry."

Wren estimated the hours. Less than sixteen, when hunger pangs really kicked in. More than eight, enough to wake you up. It gave a rough range of six hundred to one thousand five hundred miles, traveling at an average of sixty miles per hour. He had to narrow that range down.

"Did your legs hurt afterward? Pins and needles when you got off?"

She smiled, like she'd caught him out. "They hurt all the time. I'm eight months pregnant. Answer me this: how will you get me to a hospital, here?"

Wren countered just as fast. "We have a doctor here, better than whatever you had in that compound, I promise. Now." He started down a different track. "Tell me about faces. Who did you see?"

"I didn't see anyone. Not once. They all wore those white suits, like in the videos."

"Even when you arrived at the compound?"

"I didn't see them until we were in the arena. Only our leader actually talked to them."

"Where's your leader now?"

She barked a single laugh. "You broke his jaw. In the safe room."

Wren remembered. One elbow in the chin. He hadn't really seemed like leadership material, but you never knew.

"OK. So give me numbers; how many of them did you see up close?"

"I don't know. In the arena? Maybe two came close."

"Voices? Men or women?"

"They barely spoke. I don't remember."

"How many total then? In the video it looked like a dozen, plus perhaps a dozen more in various production roles."

"I don't know." She rubbed her belly. "Yes, maybe."

"OK. So walk me through the process from the bus to the arena. Were you outdoors when you got off the bus?"

She frowned. "I don't think so. It was cold, and echoey. Like an underground parking lot? There was the sound of a metal door coming down, like they were sealing us in."

"A loading bay," Wren murmured. "OK. What next?"

"They led us to a waiting room."

"Still in your blindfolds?"

"Yes."

"A long distance? All indoors?"

"What does that matter?"

"I'm trying to get a handle on the size of this place. So they take you to a waiting room. How big is it, how many people, and how long are you there?"

Her eyes narrowed. "Big. Like, a football field? It looked like a warehouse, bare walls, concrete. Um, there were a lot of people. You saw the video. They kept bringing more people in. We guessed it was other Anti-Ca cells, more coaches coming. Thousands, I think. I, uh…"

"This is all good. Good details, Jessica. Keep going. How long were you there?"

She gave a shy smile. First sign of trust. "Well, I don't know. There was no clock. They did feed us."

"Feed you what? How many times?"

"There was a buffet. I went up twice, I think. Also, I slept."

Wren tallied the facts. "So you're in one long hall. Did you see other halls?"

"I don't think so. But I don't know for sure."

Wren smiled. "I know you don't. Don't worry about that, I'm not trying to test you on things you don't know. Let's stick to your experience. Talk to me about transit to the arena from the hall. How did that happen?"

"They told us to put our blindfolds back on."

That was curious. "Oh? Why? Did they take you outside?"

"I don't know why. I don't think we went outside until the arena. Just, walking along corridors."

"How was it, cold, hot?" Wren tried to put himself in her shoes. "Did you feel the sun on your skin? Did the sound change as you walked along, like wood, or concrete? How did it feel underfoot?"

"I don't, uh… Hmm." Her tongue poked between her lips. "It was hard floors all the time, like concrete. Echoey, even when we were in the arena. I didn't feel the sun, at least, not until later."

"So the hall was connected to the arena," Wren confirmed. "This sounds like a large building. Especially if there were other holding halls. Describe the arena to me. Going in."

"I didn't see it going in. They didn't let us take off our blindfolds for a while."

"For how long?"

"I don't know. Maybe twenty minutes? They were directing us to empty seats. It was hot, but stuffy, you know."

"It was stuffy?"

"Right. Humid. They gave several warnings about the blindfolds. One guy took his off, they weren't happy about that. I think they escorted him out."

Wren considered. "Why do you think that was? You were already in the arena. What was the big deal?"

"I don't know." A pause. "Maybe they just wanted to keep the surprise."

Wren chewed his lip. "So then you took the blindfold off."

"Right," she began, then paused, and briefly a smile played on her face. "It was so strange. We were in this kind of Roman arena, but there was popcorn being handed out, beer, even hotdogs. The atmosphere was great, like we were at a ball game. There were people in the haz-mat suits coming up and down the tiers, handing us stuff. They even gave me a beer."

"They wanted you relaxed. A better response to the show. Did you drink?"

She laughed. "I'm not an idiot. I had a hotdog. Someone gave me a big foam hand."

"Dressing the set," Wren murmured. "So they've got you set up. Getting drunk, eating, like a ball game."

"Yes. But first there was another announcement; something about keeping all this a secret. How important for the cause it was. We were lucky, we were going to see the start of a new revolution. Get ready for amazing special effects, they said."

That caught Wren's attention. "Special effects?"

"Right," said Jessica. "About what came next."

Wren said nothing, just looked at her. What came next was the brutal murder of a man, followed by cheering. Perhaps she saw some of that suspicion in his eyes, because her expression soured.

"Wait. You think we thought it was real?"

Wren said nothing, didn't need to, just waited as her sour expression lapsed into anger. "No, of course we didn't! They told us it was a show, a special effects extravaganza, why would we not believe that?"

Wren just watched her. This was straining credibility. "Special effects."

"Yes!"

There was no point lingering on it. Either she'd known it was a man dying or she hadn't. "OK. So did you see anything else? Any buildings or mountains on the horizon?"

Jessica wasn't done. "Wait a second, you really thought we wanted that man to die? You thought we were cheering that he actually died?"

Wren eyed her. "We watched the video, Jessica, and we saw crowds cheering. Thousands of people. Of course we believed it."

"Right, but they lied to us! They just tried to make us kill ourselves. Don't you believe me now?"

He looked in her eyes, and the outrage seemed real. "I do. So let's figure this out. Could you see anything outside the arena?"

It took her a second, swallowing her anger. "No. I just saw the arena. It was so bright. It was breezy. The sky was blue, no clouds, and the sun was hot. People were everywhere. The walls were all stone, you know that from the video, and there was all that sand at the bottom. It pretty much started after that."

"The brought the billionaires out?"

"Yes. It all happened fast. Minutes only. We didn't even know who they were at first, just naked men, until the big screens started showing close-ups. I figured they were lookalikes, but it still felt good to see them laid low, humiliated. It made for a carnival atmosphere, like we were already celebrating a victory."

"So it happened fast. Soon they're on the sand, they're circling up."

"Right, then they hammered the big guy. It was horrible; but people near me were laughing. I just figured, yeah, it's not real. Special effects. This is the show, so go along with it. I even started to cheer."

Wren nodded. Helping her shed the guilt, as it would only get in the way. "You couldn't know it was real. You didn't know what was coming."

She stared back at him. "I didn't. None of us did. I may hate the one percent, but I'm not an animal."

"So they kill him. Then...?"

She swallowed. 'So they kill him' glossed over a lot, but Wren saw nothing to gain in digging in deeper. "Then that was it. Blindfolds back on, we were out of there in minutes. The event was over. They escorted us to the holding area, then the bus back."

Wren rocked back on his knee, one hand on his chin and picking through the story. There were clues, but not enough. Lots of buses arriving at different times from different Anti-Ca compounds. A large complex anywhere between eight to sixteen hours' drive away, directly connected to an open-air arena.

Except the arena couldn't be open-air. B4cksl4cker had said as much. Even a movie set arena would take time to assemble. That much sand, that scale of tiered seating, all that fake stone; even if it was just polystyrene sprayed gray, it would take at least a day to build, maybe more. You couldn't fake sand. Satellite overwatch updated constantly and would have seen it.

Wren spun back through Jessica's answers. The Reparations video was long, but much of that was the buildup and editing tricks. Actual raw footage of the arena in daylight, with the crowd roaring? Less than fifteen minutes. Easily short enough to evade crisscrossing satellites above. Timed, perhaps, to perfectly avoid being seen...

"Jessica," he said, leaning in, "this is important. You said 'breezier' earlier, after you took the blindfold off. Before that you said the arena was stuffy. What did you mean?"

She looked at him for a long moment. Thinking. "Stuffy, like a car parked in the sun."

"Hot. Like contained heat."

"Right. And then, yes. It was just breezier. I don't know. Maybe they turned the fans on."

Wren was on it now. Bigger than he'd considered. The scale of planning. "Did you hear fans?"

"Uh, I don't think so. No."

There it was. The key to unlock the data ghost. Only one way to explain it.

He stood. "You've been very helpful. Thank you, Jessica. The others will take care of you. Welcome to the Foundation, if you want it, coin one."

Striding down the stairs and out over the dusty clay, Wren's heart thumped hard. Rage rushed through him at what they'd done to Jessica, twisting a pregnant woman's mind so she'd come this close to killing herself. There were no words for how disgusting it was. He looked up and after-images of the Anti-Ca's dead children flashed across the baking sky, bubbles at their lips, forced to drink poison, and for what?

For some half-baked, anarchist vision of reparations. For what could only be the Apex's mad design, luxuriating in bringing America down. Just another psychotic game for his father to play with innocent lives.

By the time he stamped into the barn his limbs were trembling with fury. His new 'Board' were spread around the shadows, working on laptops or phones, but all eyes flashed up as he stormed into their midst.

"The arena was not open to the air," he announced, his head spinning through the possibilities. "I'm thinking they built it under a huge tarpaulin, in a large, roofless structure, then pulled the cover back just long enough to evade satellite overwatch." A pause, and his eyes beaded on them one by one. "How many completely flat roofs of that size went up in the last few months, within a six-hundred to fifteen-hundred-mile radius of the Anti-Ca compound? We're looking for at least two large adjoining halls, one with loading bay doors. Maybe a derelict factory or warehouse. They built their arena inside it like a cuckoo's egg in the nest. Do whatever it takes, use whatever assets you need, but find me that arena!"

The Foundation stared back at him. He touched one hand to his earpiece.

"Hellion, B4cksl4cker?"

"Yes, Christopher," Hellion answered.

"We're going to fight fire with fire. I want a line into the Reparations' app, and the means to make a video go viral. Can you do that?"

A second passed. "Yes, this is possible. We cannot shut it down, but we can manipulate it. What video?"

Wren was already ten moves ahead. "Our own. We're going to livestream my attack on the arena. The people want reparations for past crimes? I'm going to show them what real justice looks like. We'll need cameras, drones, hundreds of thousands of eyeballs prepped and watching. Can you get our feed into the Reparations app, boost it viral so their whole audience sees it?"

The sound of keys clattering came from Hellion's end. "This is possible. We will do it."

"And get me through to Humphreys at the CIA. He won't want to take the call, not after Rogers, but force it. I'm going to need his help to pull this off. If we fail to stop these videos, he needs to be ready to kill-switch the Internet. Turn it off at the source, shut down the Internet Service Providers and clamp the trans-oceanic pipelines, or just snatch peoples' phones out of their hands. Whatever it takes."

"Understood. Working, Christopher."

He took a breath. Hopped up on the surging pain and rage. He focused in on Teddy, standing thin as a grim reaper at the center of the barn. One more order he could give, since this was an accelerating crisis.

"I want Foundation members across the country ready to mobilize, if all else fails. Set up stings on the biggest Internet Providers, take out cell towers, masts, server arrays, as many as we can. If we can't stop this infection cold, then we slow it down." He took a breath, looking around at his team. His Foundation core. "This is everything. You asked for responsibility and a larger role, so here it is. I trust you with my life. Now fire me at these bastards as hard as you can. We're going to hammer them into the damn sand."

35

FOURTH

The fourth Reparations video came while Wren was in the air, an Eclipse 550 microjet after hopping a Bell 429-7 helicopter pick-up from the farm. Forty-thousand feet high and heading south-east at four hundred miles-per-hour, tracking the best intel Hellion and B4cksl4cker had yet produced on the arena.

Wren hunched over his phone in the expansive jet's seat, light flooding in through the window, he held up his phone. With only a blister pack of over-the-counter painkillers for company, he hit play and watched the video began.

It began with a raised stage festooned with American flags. The seven remaining billionaires stood in designer suits at seven lecterns, like this was some kind of political debate. Damalin Joes III stood at the center, a vast man in a tailored suit that made him look powerful, sharp and rugged at the same time.

The other billionaires flanked him like spokes in a wheel, Geert Fothers the oilman, Cem Babak the arms trader, Inigo De Luca and the rest. A voice was speaking, describing the format for the 'debate'. Each of the men would be given five minutes to make their case why they should be allowed to survive, and why the others should die.

At the end of the brief announcements, a wooden cart was brought out by haz-mats, cloaked with black velvet fabric. Its wheels squeaked noisily as they pulled it up a ramp to the stage. They left it in the center, every billionaire straining to see, then pulled off the velvet.

Beneath lay the price of failure. A large wooden block with a curved dip in one edge. A long-handled axe. A black hood. All the equipment you needed for an execution by decapitation.

Wren's mouth went dry. It was outrageous but compelling, and fully visible to everybody watching. Like a high-stakes political debate for the Presidency, twisted to some kind of Russian roulette. In response, the vote tallies began to spin like the dials on a casino slot machine.

Wren checked the viewership count. Hundreds of millions and rising. The billionaires' names danced in the ranking box like a stream of shells ejected from an autocannon, Joes then Babak then De Luca then Joes again.

The debate began. Opening arguments, it seemed, five minutes each. The billionaires took it in violent, raucous turn to rip each other to shreds, calling out hypocrisy after hypocrisy as reasons the others should die and they should live: murders they'd spent millions to cover up; countless rapes and abuses they'd buried with lawyers and NDAs; thousands of innocents crushed underfoot; thousands of careers destroyed out of spite, of rival companies decimated, of wars begun and ended in the name of personal profit.

The wages of corporate capitalism flowing unchecked.

It was sick, unmissable viewing. At various points tears erupted in self-pity, in anger, in attempts to elicit sympathy. Soon they moved from opening arguments to questions tossed by some unseen female moderator, focused variously on their contributions to humanity, their value to friends and family, their plans on how to use their billions for the betterment of America.

The billionaires wrung themselves out, turning red-faced to make promises and vie for trust, while still getting punches in on their competitors wherever they could. It was a verbal bloodbath. A fistfight broke out at one point, only broken by haz-mats with cattle prods, leaving two men with bloodied faces and rumpled ties. The onslaught of questions and answers went on regardless, guilty men roaring out vile accusations and proclaiming lie-filled promises, only to have vile accusations leveled their way in turn, with greater lies promised at each turn.

Only Damalin Joes III somehow managed to stay above the fray, as he had every time before. It was incredible to behold, as he held the center by diving into the filth and embracing it. He was indeed vile, he boasted proudly in his five-minute speech. A grotesque man. Yes, he'd done all the things they were accusing him of. He was proud of it. But that was the American way. The strong survive. The weak die. Forget decency, forget kindness, forget being 'polite'. He was not his brother's keeper. Human nature was red in tooth and claw, and if you wanted to succeed, you had to prove you were worth it. If you wanted to succeed, you had to be strong like him.

It wasn't the Damalin Joes Wren had come to know on his superyacht, during their week of interrogations en route back to the US. That Damalin Joes had been a ruthless man, but not blind to the negative impact of his choices, not trying to convince others they were the true American way. It certainly wasn't the man Joes had been in the process of becoming, with the coin system propelling him toward charitable actions to benefit his fellow man.

This was a new Damalin Joes III. A Joes who radiated

power, a man who'd blossomed within a very different system to the coins, one that catered only to strength. In this system violence was survival, and Joes had been an adaptive chameleon all his life. This was just his latest iteration, like a brand-new smartphone with a killer new app.

The people loved it.

The vote counters swung his way hard by the end of the debate. His unapologetic stance and powerful demeanor spoke volumes, where the others crawled and apologized desperately, abasing themselves in their own shame.

Damalin Joes stood cool and calm. When the time elapsed, and the vote counting ended, it hardly seemed important who had actually lost the 'debate'. Rather all eyes were on Joes' massive bulk, his swarthy face, waiting for their new winner to proclaim the loser. Longing for more billionaire blood.

Like the judge on a reality show sending one contestant home, Joes extended one long arm slowly, riding the wave of anticipation, until it could no longer be in doubt who he'd selected.

Cem Babak.

It wasn't the popular choice. The voting tallies had selected Inigo De Luca, but in the moment it didn't matter.

Babak realized it and ran.

De Luca was first to give chase. The rest fell over themselves to follow, and the cameras raced after them; shoulder-mounts held by jogging haz-mat operators, crane-cam gliding smoothly in, boom-operators racing to keep pace through the wires and detritus of the set's backstage. Crosscuts captured every detail in crystal-clear 4K with stereo sound, as five billionaires ran down one of their own.

Babak fell to a flying tackle from De Luca. He rolled and briefly tried to fight back, then the others descended and the destruction began, beating one of their own with all their strength, too terrified for their lives to do any less. The cameras and microphones caught every thud and cry.

Joes alone waited on the stage, holding court like a king.

"Enough," he boomed at last, a thundering bass that carried impressively through Wren's phone, and the beating ended. Babak lay still, just about dead already. "Bring him."

They dragged him like a dead dog. Joes stood still as a statue as they came, executioner's axe in hand. The cameras pushed in as Babak's eyes flickered faintly, capturing his recognition of what was about to happen. He made fleeting efforts to resist, but he was weak. They laid him before the wooden block, where he flattened to the stage like a deflated balloon.

"Hold him up," Joes commanded.

Again De Luca was first, lifting Babak and forcing his head onto the block. Geert Fothers the oilman helped. Joes took up position. He solemnly pulled on the executioner's hood then raised the axe. The studio went absolutely silent. Every eye craned forward. The cameras flowed right up to the stage, as desperate as the millions around the world to truly see.

"For your crimes," Joes said, and brought the axe down.

It was a clean stroke. Babak's head rocketed clear and tumbled noisily off the stage. His body went limp. The screen flashed to black.

YOU ARE OWED REPARATIONS
CLAIM THEM TONIGHT

The Internet went crazy after that.

Wren was left in shock. The impact was so stunning he watched the tail end of the video a second time, and still felt like he'd been sucker punched in the gut. As a work of populism it was incredible. He'd never seen anything like it. The power of it was entrancing. The effect it would have...

The familiar chill grip of fear rushed up his spine. Turn

the billionaires against their own. Debase their humanity until they were nothing but animals scrabbling for survival. Turn the rewards of capitalism on their head, make raw might seem more moral rather than reason, and give permission to any and every worst instinct the people had.

It was genius, and Damalin Joes III was their perfect avatar. In all, it was incredibly destructive.

Wren intended to respond in kind. He switched off the video and made the necessary call.

36

HUMPHREYS

"I'm going to kill you, Wren."

Gerald Humphreys, newly minted Director of the CIA, sounded nothing like the man Wren had known. In the echoing cabin of the Eclipse jet it sounded as if he too had been transformed by Damalin Joes' performance. The Reparations were working their alchemy on the minds of everyone in the country, turning neighbor against neighbor, ally against ally.

"Tell me you're going to take their phones," Wren said, ignoring the threat and diving right in. Hellion and B4cksl4cker had been working for hours to get the CIA Director on the line, and Wren didn't intend to waste a second. "Every phone, every house, every apartment in every city, you need to cut the flow of this poison before nightfall. It's going to be a bloodbath."

Nothing had come for a moment other than heavy breathing.

"I read your file again," Humphreys said, his rage transmuting to ice. "It's all there, every sign of this megalomania, narcissism, trumped-up self-righteousness.

James Tandrews spoke up for you, but he was a fool, like I've been a fool too. Thinking maybe we could wield you like some blunt weapon; our own pet cult leader, fight fire with fire." A pause. "We were arrogant fools. I don't care anymore if you're on our side or not. You're as much a poison as these videos. You're broken, Wren, and you cannot be fixed. I hate you for it."

"I-"

"You shot Agent Rogers. You dumped her at some country hospital. It was-"

"I'll pay for that. Arrest me when it's over. Right now it brought us a lead."

Humphreys barked a laugh; disbelief. "Arrest you when it's over? How much damage will you cause before you decide it's over? And it bought you a lead? In what world, you mad fool, is it acceptable to shoot your partner to get a 'lead'? She was the only person arguing for you! The only thing keeping us from unleashing every contract killer and mercenary in the world to hunt you down. And you shot her!"

Wren took a breath. This wasn't helping him or Humphreys. The Director was going to hyperventilate if he climbed any higher.

"The bill comes due at the end, Humphreys. We are all going to pay, myself included. Now stop grandstanding like you're a man of moral fiber and listen. This last video, it puts a clock on the Reparations. America explodes tonight if you don't take immediate steps to shut this app down. You need to activate every agent, officer, soldier, militia member you can. We need an overwhelming flood of bodies out there, switching off Internet lines and taking phones and computers right now. Do this or face total anarchy."

Humphreys' laughed sounded crazed. "Take every phone? Shut down the ISPs? Have you any idea how massive a logistical task that is? You're mad, Christopher. Really, I admire it."

"You didn't listen to me about the Blue Fairy. Listen to me now."

"It's impossible!" Humphreys crowed. "You're talking about hundreds of millions of phones alone, billions of SIM cards, and all the computers too? There are Internet-capable devices everywhere! You may as well ask me to go strip every American naked at once. It can't be done!"

"Then you better get started right now," Wren said, uncompromising. "You saw the debate video. It's a kind of propaganda attack we are not equipped for. There is no antidote but to crush it completely."

The laughter turned darker now. "Oh, Christopher Wren. You've done this to me. First Agent Rogers, now me. I just became Director. You're going to cost me everything."

"It's not me doing this. Start activating teams right now. I'm tracking the Reparations; I have a lead and I'm heading now to stop the flow of footage, but you need to be ready in case I fail. The copycats are the real threat."

Humphreys' tone changed abruptly at that, like a sailor glimpsing land through the storm. "You've found them?"

"I've found something. Maybe the arena."

"Where is it?"

"I'll let you know." A pause then as he ran calculations, deciding how much to share. "New Mexico. My team did some analyses on satellite data. I need boots on the ground, but they'll have to follow my command without question. A helicopter strike squad, six Marines minimum, on standby in El Paso. Can you do that?"

Humphreys was bewildered. "Wait, now you're actually asking me for a team?"

"Get me a team or I go in alone, and we'll see how that

shakes out. Probably you should have missiles on standby, a couple of Patriots out of White Sands base should do it. I'll release the coordinates when I'm on-site; blow me up if you like." A pause. "Don't overthink this, Humphreys. Order me the team, set the missiles and focus on building an army to quarantine this app." He checked the time until nightfall. "Can you be ready in seven hours?"

It took Humphreys five gaping seconds to get his feet back under him. "You really think it's coming apart tonight?"

"I think it's coming apart right now. Nightfall is the deadline when there's no going back. Take all that we've seen so far and ten-x it. Multiply it by a hundred. We're facing an all-out purge, the poor against the rich, and I don't think anyone's going to pull their punches after seeing that video. They want what they think's their due, and they won't stop until they have satisfaction. We have to make them stop." He took a breath. "Now focus. We're at the sharp end of an exponential curve here; things are only going to speed up from this moment, and you have to be ready."

A silence.

"I'll put it to the President."

"Not enough," Wren snapped. "You head the CIA. Send the order right now. Lead by example and get your people moving, that's a hundred thousand agents and support staff, plenty to begin with. The other agencies will follow."

"But I-"

"Forget about holding onto your Directorship if you don't get this right. The country will be in revolutionary pieces, nothing left to Direct. Now get me that team."

He killed the line, sat for a moment staring out the jet's oval window as intermittent chimes rang from his phone; notifications about fresh #Reparations atrocities. Far below, three hundred thirty million petty rages were transmuting to action. The Reparations videos blazed a trail around logic, reason and any sense of proportion, allowing blind animal rage to roar through the gaps. Building the chaos his father had always thrived on.

It would feel good. Reparations for so many crimes. Wren willed the jet on faster.

37

FACTORY

I n two hours Wren was there, a silicon chip factory.

Abandoned in the late nineties, busted down and dilapidated, circled by a half-hearted barb wire fence. Wren stood on the sand a mile out, southwest corner of New Mexico near the town of Antelope Wells, barely across the border.

The air was bitterly dry and hot like an oven, enough to gum your eyelids to your eyes. His rental Jeep ticked at his side as the radiator tried to cool the engine and failed; the air had no room to vent the heat. Baked yellow sand skirled by his feet; no rainfall here for a generation, it felt. Barely any cacti, pampas grass, scrub. A no-man's-land, nothing alive, perfect for the hermetically sealed environment required to manufacture precision-grade silicon chips.

This was the place, no doubt.

The factory lay ahead like a wrecked ship's hulk. Decrepit, twenty years out of business and showing its age in tarnish, rust and sun bleach. The parking lot was coated with sand; a few burned-out vehicles dotted here and there beneath defunct security lamps. 5 p.m. in the afternoon and not a hint of movement but for white blinds shifting in a low wind through the broken office windows.

The structures Jessica had described were all there: a huge warehouse with three elevated loading bays, each sealed shut; a huge roofless factory structure, called a 'fab' according to B4cksl4cker, five hundred yards of windowless metal siding stretching into the desert, big enough to fit the arena within it; a low office building that linked the two, corporate logo reduced to plastic shards on the ground, double door entryway devoid of glass.

Hellion spoke in his ear, and Wren half-listened. Apparently records showed the factory had shut its doors years ago, thanks to competition from China. Globalization. Outsourcing. Automation. The age-old enemies of the average working Joe, together with billionaires making up the four horsemen of the apocalypse for small-town middle America.

It made sense.

"This plan is reckless," Hellion said in his ear.

Wren said nothing. No way to be subtle with only five hours left on the countdown clock he'd given Humphreys, before the United States turned on its own people and started snatching up computers and phones.

Going reckless was the plan.

He brought up a pair of 10x42 USCAMEL binoculars, and a twinge of pain ran down his left side, threatening to drop him flat. He grunted, consciously slowed down his movements. This was nerve damage from the grenade shrapnel, he figured. Some surgery and a few hours in bed wouldn't fix something like that.

Instead he blinked and shook his head, trying to clear it. The pain was bad, walking was just getting harder and generic painkillers wouldn't cut it anymore. With every step stitches pulled tight down his left side, bleeding in pinprick stars through a new black shirt. When he opened his mouth, his left cheek sweated blood. He'd hoped to do this cold turkey and clear-headed, but that didn't seem possible anymore. Pretty soon he'd struggle just to walk.

He reached into the Jeep for medication and came back with two prescription bottles. From the first he popped a white oxycodone pill, swigged water, swallowed, then chased it with a tabs of methylphenidate; basically crystal meth, but the same thing they used as a stimulant for ADHD kids.

And they said the country had a drug problem. He slammed another swallow of water, and the hit came quickly: pain relief, a sharpening of the senses and a parting of the fog, plus some mild euphoria. Basically the same stuff they'd given to soldiers in Vietnam: wired for the kill. Add some antipsychotic chlorpromazine for the stress and guilt and he'd have the full GI cocktail.

The effects kicked in swiftly. The pain washed back; an intense sense of focus rolled in. He steadied himself and raised the binoculars again to his eyes.

"This is only clear match," B4cksl4cker had said hours earlier, back when he'd been on the helicopter off the farm. "Nothing else on radar similar."

"Talk me through it."

"It is simple satellite image search," B4cksl4cker answered. "Same as we searched for golden eye of sand, the arena. I program algorithm to search for roofs of certain size, all one color, on flat angle."

"You can program for the angle?"

"It is shadows, Christopher. Flat roofs have certain shadow. Inclined roofs have different one. Our tarpaulin will be flat, as walls of arena are same height."

Wren grunted.

"After that it is comparisons. There are many large flat roofs in your country: warehouses, offices, malls, fulfillment centers. It is not as distinctive as sand arena, but how many buildings like this were built in last few months?"

"Within fifteen hundred miles? Dozens, I expect."

"Correct. How many in isolated areas, on top of old factories?"

"Not many."

"Just one," B4cksl4cker said. "It fits our proportions."

He walked Wren through the factory's closure, the 'clean' fabrication rooms left behind that were easily large enough to accommodate the arena, and the white suits workers had to wear. "They are called 'bunny suits', Christopher, for ultra-clean environment."

Wren had grunted. Full-body white 'bunny suits' that looked just like hazardous materials disposal uniforms. The clues had been right there from the start. The haz-mat suits weren't a coincidence.

Somebody was trying to make a point

"What have you got on this factory?"

"Schematics. Looks like kids got into large fabrication room, or 'fab', after factory was abandoned, and burned it in the early 2000s. There was no roof after this."

"Surrounding buildings?"

"Two. One, large warehouse with underground levels to keep chips cool. Much concrete flooring, connected to the fab through office block. No need to go outside, plus several loading bay doors; everything the Anti-Ca girl described."

"Jessica."

"Yes."

"And the woman? The one Damalin Joes was having sex with in video three? You said she seemed to be the leader."

"Yes. We are still scrubbing our databases. It is like digging fossil out of rock; you start with jackhammers and dynamite then graduate to toothbrush. There is not much to see on in sex video, pixilated. The Foundation has collected long lists of rejects from film-school, dropouts with canceled streaming accounts, some Anti-Ca propagandists. Coming from the other angle, there were many techs on staff at chip factory with daughters; some would have been teens when the place shuttered."

"That's a prime age for radicalization," Wren said.

"Yes. We are cross-referencing records."

"Good. And mass movements of buses to this place?"

"We are winding back satellite record. We already know the Reparations are good at evading overwatch. As far as we can see, not one vehicle has gone near this place in last six months. One day two months back black tarpaulin roof went up, but nothing since. No people, no movement."

Nothing since.

Wren dialed the binoculars on the factory. Three buildings, pretty much what he'd expected. He tracked the path Jessica and the others must have taken from the left to the right. Pull into the warehouse on the bus while the sky was clear of satellites. Stay in its concrete depths for a time while other buses arrived, completely sealed-in with a buffet table for food, then blindfolds back on for the trek through the offices in the middle. Last they went into the arena, built inside the walls of the fab.

The billionaire prisoners were probably kept in the fab too, their long cells tucked underneath the arena's tiered seats. The second video had been filmed there. As for the third and fourth videos, the sex scene and the debate, they could've been shot anywhere: a re-purposed part of the fab, or the warehouse, or somewhere completely different.

The debate had closed out just hours ago. Maybe they were all here still.

"Where's my strike team?" Wren asked the empty air.

"In the air twenty minutes out of El Paso," came Hellion's crisp response. "Cheyenne gunship with eight-man Marine squad, all cammed up for livestreaming, as you asked. You have five minutes and they'll hit."

"And our feed?"

"Fifty thousand viewers so far. Reparations have secured their app against take-down attack, but they cannot prevent our piggyback. We are a go."

Wren grinned. Since the farmhouse Hellion and B4cksl4cker had led a massive botnet in hacking cell phones with the Reparation app; not enough to shut it down, but enough to force a new video to go viral. All the pieces were in place now to exploit the Reparations' soft infrastructure from within, using their own tactics against them.

"Set to livestream?"

"All feeds are ready. I have camera drones above, your bodycam, dashcam, chopper, troops also."

Wren spun the assault forward in his head. Using the power of viral videos to drop a justice bomb into the mass psyche. If you couldn't beat them, join them.

"Four minutes, Christopher."

He felt himself settling into a sense of calm. Eye of the storm. It happened sometimes on the battlefield, charging into the unknown, about to put his fate in the hands of the almighty.

He climbed into the Jeep. Started the engine. Put his hands on the wheel. With the windows down, he listened to the sand rustling by outside, his heart thumping blood up and down his left side, straining until he caught it: the faint sound of helicopter blades chopping closer.

"Three minutes," Hellion said, "your uplink is live to the Reparation app. Now is the time."

Wren swiveled the dash cam to point at his face.

"My name is Christopher Wren," he said gruffly. "I took down the Saints and the Blue Fairy, I took down NameCheck and WeScreen, now I'm coming for the Reparations, and maybe for you." He paused a second, staring long enough to let that settle in. "Anyone who picked up a hatchet, who put on a white suit, who strung cables from their car and ripped a person apart, believe that I am coming for you. Nothing comes for free. You will all pay reparations for the crimes you chose to commit. There will be an accounting for us all. Now watch; it's what you do best."

He spun the camera back around so it pointed out through the glass.

"Short and sweet," Hellion chimed in.

Wren laughed, hit the gas and revved the engine loud. Eyeing the dilapidated structure ahead. "What do you think about that office wall? Can I go through it?"

She laughed in turn. "I think we will find out."

He slammed the stick into first, punched the gas and the Jeep roared away.

38

FAB

The Jeep's tires chewed hard through crusted sand as Wren cranked up through second to third then fourth gear like a bullet down the barrel of a gun.

"Pushing your feed viral," Hellion said. "Chopper inbound. Make sure the camera sees it."

Wren just laughed and hit fifth gear, inclining the dash cam upward. Fifty miles an hour and eating up the distance, less than a minute out when the Cheyenne gunship roared in low overhead. Tactical black and massive, Wren saw its gun turrets, the Marines leaning out the open bay doors, and laughed harder.

The Jeep shot off a rise and caught air into the parking lot, spewing sand out back as it approached sixty, fishtailing toward the double-doors of the broken office structure with only seconds left then burst through the opening like a Tomahawk missile.

The truck pulverized the flimsy doorframe and cheap plasterboard walls, spraying inward like confetti, barely dropping any momentum. Beyond lay a completely empty cement expanse, an office space stripped of carpets, desks, light fittings, and Wren skidded into it, cranking the handbrake and spinning the wheel hard to the right.

A voice came in his ears, screaming out wild yahoos. His own. The windows were down, hot stuffy air pumped in.

"A hundred thousand watching now, Cheyenne dropping rappel lines to the tarpaulin roof!"

The tires squealed, cornering at forty and burning rubber, seeking traction until the treads caught a few yards before he pinballed off the rear wall.

Wren wrenched the wheel straight and started a head-on run toward the fab's entrance, hung with anti-static plastic strips.

"Pray it is clear," Hellion shouted over the roar of his engine, "or you will crumple on airlock; this is tons of reinforced air filtering equipment."

Wren just laughed and slammed the pedal down.

"Lights on!" Hellion shouted, then the Jeep hit the strips and whooshed through into darkness.

Almost at once the Jeep made contact, metal poles that whipped up and away with high pranging sounds as he smashed blindly into some kind of scaffold support network; likely holding up the arena seating above. The Jeep's engine screamed, Wren kicked on the flood lamps and saw the forest of poles lying ahead.

The Jeep hammered through and Wren spun the wheel left into a corner, chopping out support poles with his B column side-on, so sharp he had to swing the wheel back right just to keep his back end from spinning out, racing around the outside of the arena like it was an F1 track.

The sound of poles ripping from their supports and ricocheting away became an uproarious cacophony, demolition derby style. To his left Wren tracked the sheer wall of the roughly built arena in gray cinder blocks, to his right raced the plain concrete fab wall, and then-

The long cage cells lay dead ahead. Empty.

Wren yanked the Jeep straight and ran it like a ten-pin ball directly toward the wire mesh. There were no cameras here now but his own, no haz-mat operators, with the stage walls pulled away; a film set deconstructed. As the Jeep hit the cell dividers, they ripped out of their stapled foundations like pulled teeth, chicken wire spooling up and wrenching off his wing mirrors.

The Jeep slowed and he downshifted to increase torque, third gear and surging through the seventh, eighth, ninth cells and then he was clear and accelerating back into the wild turn, taking out more support poles down the far side of the arena.

"Virality is rocketing," came Hellion's voice in his ear.

Let them all see what would happen to the Reparations.

The sound of scaffolds tumbling like skittles became a tremendous, thunderous roar. Wren completed his first circuit and charged on faster, swerving to take out poles he'd missed the first time. The front of the Jeep was smoking now, and he pressed it faster, until through the crashing of poles and the engine's scream he heard the first huge crack as the structure above began to come apart.

By the red glow of his taillights in the rear view he saw a portion of seating come crashing down, beginning a domino effect. Dust filled the once-clean fab as the tiered seats collapsed behind him, destroying this monument to the lowest depths of humanity.

Wren stormed on until he was running up on rubble and light spilled in from above; the tarpaulin roof had cut loose and peeled away in the chaos, was now flapping in the wind like a giant kite. The strike team's Cheyenne hovered black and sudden as a tank in the sky beyond it, eight Marines already rappelling through the gap.

"Now, Christopher," came another voice in his ear.

"B4cksl4cker!" he called as he smashed a path through rows of plastic seating littered with cement dust.

"There are people in the arena. Try not to kill them."

"I'll do my best."

He pulled the wheel hard left, powering a four-wheel-drive run-up that smashed the truck into the cinder block arena wall and crunched it right through.

The windshield burst inward, and the lower ranks of the arena seating exploded outward, spraying across sunlit sand. The Jeep skidded through the gap, tires tearing on wreckage, to screech to a halt at the arena's edge. Overhead the tarpaulin lashed like a giant whip, like the sky itself was coming unstuck as its last mooring points pinged free, finally unveiling the Reparations' sickness to the light.

His Marines were on the sand already, circled up like the billionaires. Wren kicked the Jeep's door open, snatched up a tactical shotgun from the passenger foot well and lunged out. In the center of the arena, circled by five haz-mat suit-wearing camera operators, stood an Asian woman in a dark jumpsuit, staring back at him.

39

ARENA

"This is her," said Hellion in his ear as he strode forward, "the leader, one hundred percent."

"Don't shoot," Wren called to the Marine squad as they closed in like a noose. His voice barely carried above the beating rotors of the Cheyenne.

The woman was beautiful; slender, tan, dark hair hanging in wet-look tresses, chiseled features, mid-thirties. A model if she wanted, a CEO, a Hollywood actress. She watched him unafraid, as if she'd planned all of this. Her camera operators circled warily, filming her, him, the Marines, the helicopter, the whipping tarpaulin until finally the last pinions ripped away with a machine-gun flurry of pops, like a giant bandage torn clear.

The Cheyenne banked away. The Marines held position in a circle, rifles level. The cameras on the operators' shoulders pointed right back, blinking red.

"Dueling livestreams," Hellion said. "Her video feed just came out of nowhere. You're both hitting a million plus viewers right now."

She had a plan. She'd been waiting for him. She wanted this too.

Twenty yards and closing. "Can you ID her?" he asked Hellion low.

"Yes, from image search, local records. She is Yumiko Harkness. Japanese mother, Texan father; laid off when factory closed. Home schooled, never uploaded single frame of footage as far as we can tell. She is social media void."

Wren grunted. From above the receding chop of the Cheyenne was replaced by the buzzing of Hellion's camera-mounted drone. All shot in vivid 4K, and Yumiko was ready for it. There could only be one reason she was here now; like him, she recognized they were coming to the end of the road. Four hours until nightfall; time for the season finale.

"That's far enough," she said when Wren reached ten yards out, and held up a device with a red button on the front, depressed by her thumb. A cartoonish dead man's switch, triggered the moment she released her grip. "The arena floor's set to blow. One more step and we're all vapor."

Wren stopped, smiling now. He didn't believe her; not for a second. She wasn't going to die like that.

"Take the camera operators," he said. "Non-lethal."

Five shots rang out from his Marines. Five cameras fell, military-grade Taser shots in their chests or backs. Five bodies hit the sand and jerked.

Yumiko didn't break eye contact. Neither did Wren. Dark eyes, dizzy depths. With so many assets, such a complex game, there was more at play here than just rage about outsourcing.

"You're the director of the Reparations," he said.

She smiled. It looked practiced: white teeth, a perfect reality-show grin splitting sleek contoured make-up. Her fifteen minutes of fame. "Director, producer, cinematographer-"

"I don't need your whole CV," Wren interrupted. "I don't give a damn about you, Yumiko: who hurt you, who sowed this 'darkness' in your heart." He did air-quotes. "What I want is my father, Apex of the Pyramid, Damalin Joes the third, alive and well, and the Reparation app's source code, in that order. Hand them over."

Her smile stretched. A delicate pink tongue, dancing as she spoke. "You more than most should know, the urge for reparation is widely distributed. It lives on in the hearts and minds of those who've known injustice."

Wren laughed. His left side throbbed in spite of the drugs. "Now that's some BS. Come on, girl, you and I both know you're in this for the thrills. It's fun to stick the boot in some other guy's face, right? Tear down the system that tore down your pops. I can't even begrudge you your anger or your desire for reparation. I've spent my life seeking justice for secret crimes, but there's one difference between us. I never threw my lot in with the psychopathic leader of the country's most famous death cult. Justice is a scalpel, not a bludgeon."

Harkness smiled. "Spoken as a man who works within the system, for the system, upon the system's orders. You could never-"

"Let's get real," Wren interrupted, no interest in her excuses. "The ride's coming to an end, even you must see that. I guarantee we'll find Joes and the others three hours out, on the run, wearing wigs and sunglasses while they hide out in some gas station restroom. The dragnet is closing in, Yumiko. As for the app, well, after we get done here, you think your billionaires are going to keep playing along? And about my father? You used him to suck me in. Handing him over's non-negotiable. All must pay for their crimes, am I right?"

Her eyes flared a little. Some fire there. Wren set himself to fan it hotter, but she spoke first.

"The crimes of your father are not mine. They belong to you as much as anyone."

Wren frowned. "That sounds like some grade-A victim blaming there, Yumiko. What do you even know about the Pyramid?"

Her smile widened. Not so easily drawn. "I know you are a killer like the Pyramid's Apex, Mr. Wren. How many men have you executed over the years? How many Pinocchios have you executed in the last three months, chasing your father's ghost?"

"I can always kill more."

She laughed sharply. "Of course. You claim we're different, but we are not. Both acting out against the crimes of our childhood. You are barely even in the CIA anymore. Nothing you do is sanctioned or legal, they are in fact on the verge of turning their weapons on you, but still you act on their behalf. These men," she gestured to the Marines, "they are just mercenary extras in the Christopher Wren show."

He snorted. "If it's all just a show, then your cast is looking a little thin." He nodded at her camera operators, still writhing on the sand, then gestured around the ruined arena. "Your set's getting worse for wear, too."

"My set?" She laughed in a long high trill. "This is your inheritance, Mr. Wren. You know what we call you?" She waited only a half-second. "The ungrateful son. Your father gave you so much and you squandered it. So many gifts." She trailed off, sounding sad.

That spiked something into Wren. A hint of a buried memory, maybe.

"Enough, Yumiko. You stayed behind for a reason. If you wanted to kill me, you would've done it. I don't believe there's explosives underfoot. So let's find out."

He took a step forward.

"He spoke so well of you," Yumiko said, like she was reading from a script now, except her eyes genuinely glistened with tears. A better actress than he'd taken her for. "His Pequeño 3."

There it was, another hammer on the spike in his chest. Pequeño 3. The same old fear. The same old shortened breath, tunnel vision, crawling fear. Like she really knew his father.

"Steady, Christopher," came Hellion's voice, "your pulse is racing."

"I got your message in Deadhorse," he countered, playing for the cameras too. "What a pleasant gift, another Pinocchio wrapped up for me. I should have expressed my gratitude earlier."

Yumiko looked sad. "It won't save you, you know, this fake bravado. You can't bluff anarchy. In the end all your clever talk won't mean a thing. When you kneel before him once more, Apex of the Pyramid, and beg forgiveness for your many crimes, what do you think he'll say?"

There it was. His greatest fear of them all. Being at his father's mercies and whims like he'd been as a child. He'd tasted it in Somchai's mansion, when the name 'Pequeño 3' alone had sent chills of fear down his spine, coloring the world red and making the walls close tighter in. Fight or flight lapsing into fear...

"Christopher, you are going to have embolism like this," Hellion said in his ear, so very far away. "Control yourself!"

He took a shaky step closer, seven yards distant. "So you read my Wikipedia page. The Apex is an old bogeyman, long dead. Do better research, Yumiko. I've moved on."

It wasn't his best comeback. As if to show that she knew it, Yumiko took a step toward him, the dead man's switch held out.

"You really are a wonder to behold, Ungrateful Son. I have been looking forward to this moment. The last survivor of the Pyramid's rapture, in the flesh. I wondered what kind of man you would be. Could you defy my expectations?"

Another step, five yards, and now Wren caught a dizzy scent on the air; something familiar, acerbic and bitter, biting at his nasal passages. Her hair was clumped together and damp like she'd just taken a shower.

"How do I measure up?"

"You are a disappointment. So simple, like a clockwork toy following the same tired pattern every time. They bring a knife; you bring a gun. They bring a gun; you bring a squad of Marines." She gestured at the men around them. "Simple escalation every time. It makes you as blind as the child you were. Don't you get tired of running on the spot?" She took another step and the scent grew even stronger, billowing off her in a fog, making his eyes water.

"Christopher," Hellion said. "Something is strange here. I am sending in Marines."

He knew it. Couldn't put his finger on it. Yumiko's eyes were everything now, swallowing up his world. He felt lost in them. There was something there he had to understand. Something on the tip of his tongue, but he couldn't get out the words.

"Your every reaction, we knew it before you did," Yumiko went on. "From the Saints to the Blue Fairy to now, you have been utterly predictable." Four yards. "Ungrateful Son, ask yourself this: why did we want you involved at all? Why start this trail with Somchai Theeravit in Deadhorse?" She gave a smaller, secret smile. Like a lover. Three paces now, moving languidly, sensuously. Her jumpsuit dripped clear liquid to the sand. "And that message? They told me not to write anything, but I couldn't resist."

He flashed back to the flash drive. I THINK YOU'LL ENJOY THIS ONE, PEQUEÑO 3. That was her doing. He was struggling to follow along, and now she was only two yards away. The chemical stench was unbearable, burning into his nose and throat, some liquid clinging to her skin in a thin, shiny film. Her eyes were red, not from tears but from the fumes. Her jumpsuit was soaked. Wren felt seconds away from understanding, the revelation just inches away, but he couldn't quite reach it.

She leaned into the gap between them and whispered. "I am *your* director, Ungrateful Son. *Your* writer. *Your* choreographer. I delivered the script and you have been my lead actor ever since, reading your lines to the letter. Call this your last reparation; an original sin that will be made right today, as it should have been so long ago."

One yard. She was so close now, almost touching. All Wren felt was her breath on his face. All he saw were her red eyes, like the pull of some heavenly body sucking him in. She leaned closer still, so close his shotgun barrel pressed against her stomach, barely breathing the words.

"He told you what to do all those years ago, and you didn't do it. You defied him, Pequeño 3. Again and again, you defied him. You appreciated nothing, and now this is your punishment."

Wren opened his mouth to say something, but Yumiko Harkness closed his lips with a sudden kiss, sealing them with the burning chemical tang.

"From me to you, brother," she whispered, "a final gift."

Then she took a step back and raised the dead man's switch. Looking into Wren's eyes, ignoring the Marines circling close, she released the button.

There was no explosion.

Only a single flame. A lighter igniting. For a moment Wren felt relief. A misfire? But of course not. It all came crashing back. That stench overpowering him for hours as he'd painted person after person through the desert streets of the Pyramid's fake town.

Napalm.

Yumiko gave a last, secret smile then pressed the naked flame to her throat.

The napalm caught and she became an instant fireball. A blast wave of heat struck Wren as the flames engulfed her, thick and searing, angry orange and red. The inferno chewed into her skin, consumed her hair in a single greedy swallow, lapped down to her feet and sucked away the surrounding oxygen.

Wren fell to his knees, staring as she blazed; still standing, still burning, so glorious that-

It plunged him back into the fake town, holding the paintbrush dripping napalm, by his father's side and doing the good work all the way until the end. A thousand people had died just like this, on the Apex's command, at Christopher Wren's hand.

Call it a thousand and one.

40

BROKEN

Wren came back to himself walking in the desert. He felt the heat on his face still, and still smelled the napalm: equal parts petroleum and a thickening agent, to make the brew gelatinous and cling. Aluminum salts of naphthenic and palmitic acids. Na-palm. Burn you down to the bone, burn you underwater, kill you in seconds.

She'd just disappeared before his eyes.

He should have recognized the smell sooner. He'd been there at the mixing the first time in Arizona: the worst memory of his life, right there for the taking.

Punishment from the Apex. Reward. They were the same thing.

He limped. The pain was coming on hard. His mind felt slow and thick. Who the hell was he to just stand by and watch it happen all over again, like all those nights left with the children in their cages, with the believers in their pits. Only survive, that had always been the key.

Yumiko Harkness was right: everything that had followed was a reaction to that incredible atrocity. Becoming 'Saint

Justice' for the CIA had made him feel like he was paying off an old debt.

It was hard to breathe.

That was another effect of napalm. In Vietnam they'd dropped it on whole villages; terrorist camps for the Viet Cong, was the euphemism. Those who didn't burn up suffocated as the potent mixture blazed through all the oxygen.

Yumiko Harkness's death was a grisly message from his father, which meant his father was still alive.

It felt like twenty-five years of his life had been erased. His Foundation. His family. He didn't even have to close his eyes to see them all lining up for the napalm brush.

"I am so proud of you, Pequeño 3," the Apex had said.

He'd said it again and again as each one burned, making him worse than complicit; making him proud too. That all-consuming glory in Yumiko Harkness' eyes, to be making the Apex proud. He'd felt that exact same emotion himself, as a child.

On his knees he came back to himself, phone in his hand and already ringing; in line with what Dr. Ferat had ordered, right before he'd died.

Talk to your family. Not just your wife and kids; your whole family. Maybe it was time.

The line answered.

"Hello?" came the voice on the other end. Deep, authoritative, the once-adoptive father he'd avoided for twenty years.

Agent James Tandrews. His voice carried Wren back.

In 1995 Tandrews had been Commander of the FBI's Gold tactical Hostage Rescue Team. Two years after the Waco debacle, he'd been first on the scene at the smoking ruin of the Pyramid in their fake town in Arizona, to find one thousand dead and only one survivor.

A twelve-year-old boy with no name. Barely able to speak. Covered in burns and wearing blackened clothing, stinking of gasoline, dehydrated and wandering amongst the dead bodies.

Maybe it was guilt that drove him to take the boy in; for failing to stop the Pyramid, for the deaths at Waco. Maybe he was lonely. He was forty-two then; marriage dissolved by the job, children grown and flown with their mother, no longer the center of anybody's world, on the way out at the FBI after his twin failures.

He took on the child known only as Pequeño 3, and for five years molded him, channeling the boy's rage, pain and PTSD into action. He'd kept him away from other children for those early years, from school and the mall and the county fair until he was ready, and plunged him into a constant flood of fresh challenges. There were no friends for him back then, no family, only the two of them stalking the midnight forests of Maine, far from the deserts of his earliest years, learning to live off the land for weeks at a time. For long days and nights they barely spoke, just experienced the raw reality of nature.

It had rooted Wren in something different and real. He'd come to trust Tandrews; the man never buried him in a pit, never drowned him in a vat, never made him beg for more time in the cage. He only taught him how to use the natural skills of his body and mind; to ground himself in observable reality. Fighting. Shooting. Shelter. Family.

In time, high school had come. Wren got to experience a 'normal' life for a few years; make friends, have a girlfriend, until on his seventeenth birthday, there was the adoption.

Tandrews had waited until Wren was seventeen, when legal adoption would not carry the weight of control. It didn't mean much in the eyes of the law, especially after they'd already filed Wren's papers of emancipation. But it meant something still, a symbol of their connection. A certain respect. The young man once named Pequeño 3 had agreed. He'd been happy. Then the night before they signed the papers, a panic attack had hit like he'd never experienced before.

A sense of being trapped, like he was right back in the Pyramid. It wasn't logical but it consumed him completely. It burned up all his ideas of college, his high school life, his friends and his girl. It rooted him back in the Pyramid, in that fear, which he knew he would have to spend the rest of his life fighting.

He'd fled Tandrews in the middle of the night and never gone back. Signed up for the Marines the next day.

Now Tandrews sounded the same. Older, maybe. There was a lot of pain in that voice, and Wren didn't know what to0 say.

"Is that you, Christopher?" Tandrews asked.

Wren's heart skipped a beat. How did he know?

"Don't speak if you're not ready," Tandrews went on. "But you should know, Director Humphreys reached out to me. I saw what happened in the arena. The woman, the napalm. I know what it means for you."

Wren felt separated from his own body. It wasn't even him listening. It was someone else; this boy who'd chosen to call himself Christopher Wren, named after the great architect of London. Even that felt like a foreign ambition, to design great structures built out of people.

"I know what you're feeling. I woke up with you screaming enough times. Life was never going to be easy for you after that, but there is one thing I am certain of: you're a good man. The Apex twisted you the way he twisted everyone, the way he twisted that woman, but you never broke. Now we need that strength again."

Wren breathed hard. The darkness receded slightly, as

Tandrews' presence blocked it out. Who could have predicted that?

"I know you've been hunting him. I never stopped hunting either. He's doing this to us, and now he wants you at the center. That makes you our greatest weapon against him. Do not let him use you again."

Wren felt like the barriers he'd spent so many years building coming down. At seventeen formal adoption was a symbol only, a gesture of love, but he hadn't been able to accept it.

"I-" he managed, but his voice was just a croak.

"You're my son, Christopher. Not his. You will always be my brave, wild son, and that is what's real."

Wren felt the walls breaking down inside. So this is what Dr. Ferat wanted. It had been coming for so long, and turned him inside out.

"I wish I could have stayed," Wren managed.

"You don't owe me an explanation, an apology, not a damn thing," Tandrews said, his voice turning gruff. "I'm just proud of the man you've become."

Wren's breathing came easier now, and he pressed the phone tighter against his ear.

"I hope one day we'll see each other again," Tandrews said. "Man to man. Until then, I know you'll do what's right. You'll close this chapter and move on to the next, and you'll hunt that rat-bastard Apex down. He's a loser, Christopher, and that's all. Only losers do this, and one day we'll piss on his grave. You always had the strength to bring him down. I know he saw it, and I see it now more than ever."

The words entered Wren like a balm, far better than oxycodone and methylphenidate, shaking loose things he'd wanted to say for years.

"You saved my life," he said. "Thank you, Tandrews. I'll fix this, I promise."

He ended the call, then let the phone drop by his side.

The sun beat down, lowering over the horizon. Time marched relentlessly on toward nightfall.

He felt different, a flush of new strength rising within. He was the Apex's son, but he was also Tandrews' son, and now he could embrace them both.

In an instant, new possibilities spun out ahead of him. Now he finally saw the whole plan, clicking into place like the last pieces of a jigsaw. What Yumiko Harkness had said about him; always escalating. His reliable MO, and how they'd used him to further their own aims. He understood what she'd meant by calling him her lead actor, how every move of his was so predictable.

She might be dead now, but the show wasn't over. The final curtain call was coming, and she'd left him a part to play there too.

He knew what he had to do.

41

LIVESTREAM

Wren strode back toward the factory, phone squeezed tight in his hand.

FIND DAMALIN JOES he typed on his Megaphone app to the whole Foundation. THIS ENDS WITH HIM. DO WHATEVER IT TAKES. AND GET ME HUMPHREYS.

He shoved the phone in his pocket. The limp was coming through on his left side now, but he felt unstoppable; a product of his twin pasts, like naphthenic and palmitic acids brewed into napalm, becoming something fearsome.

The Apex didn't know what kind of monster he'd made.

He stamped into the stripped office, past his Jeep's twin burnt rubber trails on the flat gray concrete, past a red stain on the concrete and through the plastic curtains and out over the rubble of seating into the arena.

The air hung with greasy smoke and the drifting smell of exhausted napalm. Yumiko Harkness was a blackened charcoal patch in the center, circled by the hog-tied bodies of her operators. Three Marines guarded them with their rifles at the ready. The Cheyenne helicopter hung high overhead, rotor blades whipping up sand.

He tapped his earpiece. "Are you seeing this, Hellion?"

Her voice came through clear, the first time he'd really tuned into her since before the burning. Maybe she'd been there in his ear throughout, but he hadn't heard a word. "I am here, Christopher. I see you."

Time to ramp things up a notch. "Bodycams live? The drone feed?"

"There are many cameras, yes, but we are blocking all feeds. You do not look so well, Christopher."

He grunted. That had to be an understatement. "Put the livestream back up."

"What?" blurted B4cksl4cker.

"Do it now. Show them I'm alive and I'm coming. Put the fear into them."

"Are you sure this is good idea? I do not-"

"Hellion," he said, calm and intense. "Trust me. This is the right thing to do."

Keys clattered down the line. "Done. All cameras are up."

"On me," Wren said.

"I have drone incoming."

Wren watched it come in a surging buzz of rotors, falling like a rock to catch itself in a hover at head-height two yards away from Wren, camera pointed dead at his face.

"You are live," Hellion said. "There are still some hundred thousand left watching, even after we cut the feed."

Wren stared into the lens, feeling more ready than ever. Everything he said and did now would be heard by the wider world, but that was all right. He was done covering up the past. Time to let all his demons out. He gazed into the lens, feeling like a laser boring straight through to his father.

"You thought you could destroy me," he said, and his voice came out resonant and intense. "You thought I'd be ashamed, afraid, a broken man when I saw the depths of that poor woman's madness." He pointed to the cinders of Yumiko

Harkness and the drone spun to take her in. "But you were wrong. It's true that I was part of the Pyramid suicide cult as a child, but I was only a child. Sick people twist children every day." He took a breath. "People are cruel. Fate is not kind. The pain mounts up and the cruelty circles on until at some point, we all want justice, but what the Reparations are offering is not justice. It is blind, aimless vengeance." He paused a moment, letting the momentum build. "The Reparations do not care who your revenge is against. They simply want the circle to spin faster. More pain. More violence. More chaos. More death. But it has to stop. There cannot always be the justice your heart craves."

He paused. Staring. Thinking. The pain down his side was coming on fast, brought on by the adrenaline burst, and he had to stay ahead of it.

"As of this moment, I'm declaring an amnesty." His voice boomed around the ruin of the arena. "All minor crimes committed during the reign of the Reparations are hereby forgiven. I don't care what you did. I will not come for you. But if you committed serious crimes? If you hurt people, killed people, tortured or tormented people? If you plan to commit those crimes tonight, then I swear, I will find you, and there will be justice. Do not run from this. Accept it and seek to pay your own reparations, before I come for blood."

"View count is a stampede," Hellion said in his ear, her voice flushed with a rare excitement. "This is going very viral, Christopher. Tens of thousands joining every second." She paused a moment, breathless. "The people want this!"

"Back from the dead," chimed in B4cksl4cker, deep voice rumbling. "You are topping all rankings."

Wren went on. "Your first step is to halt the cycle of violence immediately. The app you are viewing this video feed on is a crime. All your shares, your likes, your copycat videos condemn you." He felt like he was staring into the soul of America. "So delete them all: your videos, your shares, the app. It's time for the bloodletting to stop, and this is the only time I will warn you." He took a raspy breath. "We are all the victims of the greatest act of brainwashing in history. Our pain has been co-opted. Our hurt has been weaponized. But the Reparations will not help us heal. Delete the app and let the real healing begin."

He was panting now, almost toppling over as his left leg trembled. Maybe a minute left.

"If you don't do that, then I will come for you." He pointed again at the corpse of Yumiko Harkness. "I was twelve years old when one thousand souls in the Pyramid cult burned alive. You may know I was the sole known survivor. What you don't know is that I burned those people myself. My father drove me on, but I was the one who painted napalm onto the skin of those thousand people. I was the one who lit the spark on each and every one."

Wren felt a stunned silence stretching out, through the cameras and on into the world. Not the Apex. Him. He'd never told a soul. He hadn't even known it himself until recently.

"What is this, Christopher?" whispered Hellion.

"We just hit one billion viewers," B4cksl4cker said. "That is large part of global population."

"I burned a thousand people alive, and I will do it again, if I have to," Wren said. "I will find you, I will soak you, and I will burn you to the ground. So turn off your feed now, there is nothing left to see."

For a long moment his fierce gaze blazed down the drone's lens, then he said, "Kill it," to Hellion, and the red light on the drone cut out.

At once Wren dropped to one knee, no longer able to hold himself up. What he'd just done felt like a seismic shift. The truth was out there for once and all, who he was and whom he'd killed. There was no turning back now.

"It is happening," B4ckscl4cker said, sounding stunned. "They are cutting out. View count dropping.

Hellion laughed in his ear. Magic. He felt like laughing himself. He had both in him. The cult leader. The cult survivor. The Apex's gift. Tandrews' gift. He was transmuting now like lead to gold into something new.

Wren 2.0

42

WREN 2.0

Wren fought for breath, looking around the wrecked arena from one knee. Sand was mounded over the heaps of fallen seating, blown by the Cheyenne's downdraft. Wren turned to the nearest Marine.

"Tell them to bring the chopper back down."

It came in moments, blasting the sand away and revealing the wreckage again. Wren watched it descend, shouting over the roar. "Hellion, report."

"Copycat videos are bottoming out," she said. "Users are deleting the app in the millions. Pings confirm it."

Wren breathed a cautious sigh of relief.

"About half of all video content has been pulled down. Shares and likes coming down too, but not all. We have analytics running, behavioral projections say ninety percent will delete the app and erase their presence."

Ninety percent was an excellent number. Not enough, though. Ten percent could still precipitate outright chaos in the streets. "What about the rest?"

"Our target demographic. I am tagging them all. B4cksl4cker and I have long memories."

Wren smiled. At best he'd won a moment to breathe in. The country still stood on a knife edge, and Yumiko Harkness had known it. She'd even called him out, a windup clockwork toy, she'd said. His MO was always to escalate, and it made him predictable enough for her to script out his role.

He'd already played it in large part, telling Humphreys to send out an army of federal officers to raid every single American home and snatch the phones directly from peoples' hands. When spun the right way, it was the most damaging visual possible.

Federal officers storming a million homes around the country, forcefully snatching private property from people's hands, cutting their free access to information. It would be the biggest government incursion into the private lives of the citizenry in history, busting through about half the Constitution and most of the Amendments.

Yumiko Harkness had baited him, and he'd responded. All she had to do next was set cameras to watch it. With just enough people left over to watch those videos, she'd flip her popular uprising against the rich into a revolution against the state itself.

It was brilliant. Genius really.

He couldn't let things go that far.

"We have to find Damalin Joes," he said to Hellion. "He's going to be at the center of what's coming. He must be nearby. You're running satellite sweeps?"

"We are."

"They'll be evading overwatch. Search for bands of geography outside our satellite coverage, patches where they could pass through unseen, and sync those blank spots to their schedule."

"This is vast range." Hellion's keys were already clacking frantically. "Number of blind corridors through satellite overwatch is large and shifting. Can you narrow this,

Christopher? Departure time would help, plus means of transport, some idea of their final destination."

Wren's mind buzzed. He ran it all backward and forward, working through the Reparations' track record, their actions, their MO. Always prepared, that was one. Within an hour of Wren signaling an interest in the Anti-Ca compound, they'd passed down a suicide order to wipe out the evidence, activating a store of potassium-cyanide and orange juice.

They'd been ready for him. Within a day, Yumiko Harkness had accelerated her billionaires' 'knockout' games to the final stage: political speeches. He'd moved fast and she'd adapted; getting the penultimate video out before Wren could nail them in the silicon chip factory.

"They must have had vehicles here," he said, "prepped for an emergency evac."

"Yes?"

Wren looked up at the nearest Marine. "What's your name?"

"Acton, Sir."

"OK, Acton. I need you to go check the warehouse." He thought a second. "Run searchlights over the ground near the loading bay doors. You're looking for drops of gasoline, anything that glistens." He thought more, piecing it out. "The vehicles wouldn't have been fully fueled in advance, which means they fueled them in the last few hours. I'm thinking you'll find spots; soak some up with gauze. If it's clear, that's regular motor gas, meaning they left by road. If it's blue or green, those are dyes added to aviation grade gasoline, which means light helicopters. Go."

Acton started away at a run.

"Light helicopters in the warehouse?" Hellion asked.

Wren worked the math. "The loading bay doors are wide enough for a semi-trailer. You could park two Vertical Hummingbirds on one of those, nose-to-tail. Two trailers,

246

that's four Hummingbirds, a sixteen-seat passenger capacity total, enough to get all the billionaires and crew out. Way faster than anything by land. It's what I'd do for an imminent bug-out."

"Lining that up for search algorithm. We will pull in local radar data; four helicopters will stand out, help narrow radius." Wren heard keys flying madly. "Next is when, and where?"

Wren rewound again, stripping his memory for clues. There'd been something in the entrance to the empty office, like a puddle of mud right before the Jeep's burned rubber slug-trails began. Except it hadn't been mud.

He reached out and grabbed another Marine. "In the middle of the office there's a red stain, maybe blood. Go find it."

The man ran. The Cheyenne's blades wound down, and Wren staggered over to lay a hand on it, holding himself steady as his left side throbbed, thinking hard and breathing harder. In less than a minute the second Marine came in through the radio. "I see it. It's blood."

Wren nodded, playing the scene through in his head; a pack of homicidal billionaires being shepherded out of captivity. Accidents happened. Arrogant men who'd been wound up to fight would be capable of extreme violence.

Somebody had been beaten there, maybe died. One of the haz-mats, most likely, he figured. They must have taken the body with them, too much evidence to leave behind, but there'd been no time to sop up the blood.

"Describe the color," Wren said.

"You went through the patch with the Jeep," the Marine said. "Brown around the edge, still red at the center."

Wren ran the numbers. When blood left the body, it began evaporating water immediately, ultimately leaving behind only a reddish-brown crust. This was basically rust, made primarily of iron. It took time, of course; you could date a sample with some precision by how much it had evaporated its water content.

Still red at the center, the Marine said. Still wet, which made the death more recent. In a hot environment like this, with a dry wind blowing through, he figured the death had happened within hours. Call it two max. Any longer and the evaporation would be complete.

"Departure between one and two hours ago," he said to Hellion. "No sooner than one, they wouldn't cut it that close."

"Better," Hellion said, and the keys flew. "Finally, where are they going?"

Wren spooled Yumiko Harkness' script forward. She wanted to turn his nationwide phone raid into a mass revolution, synced to nightfall. Wren checked the sky, saw the sun was below the wall of the fab. Not long now.

So where? The action was clear, the script of tyrannical government overreach coming into the lives of private citizens, but what would the setting be? She could choose any stage set she wanted, to maximize the impact. What environment would be most likely to offend Middle America the most? His mind raced. It couldn't just be a set, either, couldn't look contained or fake in any way. It had to look real. It had to be real.

"A small-town suburb," he said, as the words came to him. "Picture perfect. Nice green yards, neat roads, white picket fences, porch swings, pure Americana." He played it further, like he was reading Harkness' own stage directions. "I think the billionaires will be waiting inside a regular house. Like the fab, it'll be a purchase within the last six months, maybe a year. Waiting for our strike forces to hit." He stopped, thought again. "Scratch that. No."

He played the idea forward and back. Harkness wouldn't take the chance of waiting for the actual federal strikes to come. No way to know for sure where the feds would hit first, or when, and no way to control for that outcome. If they came too late, raids across the country would already have snatched millions of phones by the time their feed went live, and nobody would see it. That meant...

"They're waiting, but not for us," he sped on. "Look for a cluster of federal-marked vehicles, ATF, FBI, whatever, probably under cover near a small town or suburb." He put the last pieces together. "The whole thing's going to be fake. Actors dressed as police rushing in for the phone-snatch." He kept on calculating. "It'll happen soon, so they can get their video of resistance out and prime the people before the real raids come. The billionaires will fight them off, at least Damalin Joes will, and it'll show the people the government can be beaten. She's turning Joes into a people's hero!"

The weight of the ambition floored him. It was like clockwork. He checked it in his head but saw no flaws. Every genuine federal raid after that would be met with hardened resistance. It would be Waco all over again, spread across the entire United States.

"Winding back through overwatch, looking for emergency vehicles converging on a small town or suburb," Hellion said, typing rapidly.

Nearby a speaker crackled and Acton's voice came through clear.

"I found the drops, Sir. The gasoline's blue."

Wren perked up. "Hellion?"

"Heard it, light helicopters. Search algorithm programmed and going live."

Wren looked to the Marines around him. Still feeling weak. He looked at the step up into the Cheyenne and figured there was no shame in asking for help.

"Get me on this helicopter right now."

43

PHENOMENAL INTUITION

The Cheyenne lifted off; the sound of rotors elevated to an eardrum-splitting storm. Wren sat slumped flat on a seat taking every second of rest he could get.

Odd thoughts danced in his mind. His son, Jake, loved helicopters. Every time one had passed by overhead, whether a traffic copter, a police unit or an Air Force transport heading to or from Fort Hamilton, he'd wanted to rush out and watch it.

Quinn, his daughter, hated the racket they made. She preferred trains. Every time they took the subway, she'd glue her face to the window and watch carriages rattling by in neighboring tunnels, seemingly awestruck. Wren could understand that. Different people on different tracks, briefly brought into alignment side-by-side before pulling apart again, in different directions.

Yumiko Harkness was like that. She'd called him brother.

He missed his family. All of this was supposed to be for them. To find his father and make the world safe, but he wasn't sure if he was achieving it. Wasn't sure what he was achieving but more vengeance. The exact same thing he'd accused Yumiko Harkness of.

"Christopher," came Hellion's voice in his ear, dragging him back to the present.

"Have you got Humphreys?" he asked on throat-mic.

"Working on it," Hellion answered. "Seems he's busy."

Wren snorted and let his head rock to the side. Through the half-glass of the Cheyenne's door he watched the silicon chip factory recede. With no tarpaulin roof and no sand in the arena it didn't look like anything special at all; just another abandoned structure in America's crumbling industrial core, left to rot. Soon it was gone, swallowed by the desert.

"Where are we going?"

"North," Hellion answered, "unless you think they'll film in Mexico."

"Four helicopters over the border," Wren said, considering, "I doubt it, too conspicuous on military radar."

"We agree. And you said perfect Americana, picket fences, green yards? This is not Mexico. There are few in New Mexico also; image search exhausted these in seconds. There are many picket fences in nearby towns: Antelope Wells, Hachita, Playas, Anima, but none of these have green yards. It is all desert."

Wren second-guessed himself. It seemed a lot to bank on a hunch. Maybe the Reparations didn't care about green yards. But then, yes, they would. Image was everything, when it was all you had. The power of propaganda lay in the imagery. It had to be right.

"Anything more?"

"Not yet. Look out though, here is Humphreys. He sounds angry."

When did he not? "Put him on."

His earpiece clicked.

"Humphreys, we need to-"

251

"I always knew you were a killer, Christopher," Humphreys fumed. "I didn't know you'd killed a thousand people when you were twelve."

That took Wren by surprise. For a moment he'd forgotten about his confession. But what did it matter; was Humphreys going to hunt him down harder? Line up outstanding warrants for the thousand dead, brought forward twenty-four years? Stacked atop the Pinocchio executions, it would put Wren away for a thousand life sentences.

"It's true," Wren said. "But now-"

"I'm sorry," Humphreys interrupted. He sounded different, like his anger wasn't at Wren anymore, but at some joint enemy. Finally. "I didn't know. It's easy to forget what you went through when you're out murdering Pinocchios every day. So listen to me now. Earlier I said we wanted you as a blunt weapon, our own pet 'cultist', and that was true, but it's not the whole truth." He took a fortifying breath. "We always knew you were a genius. Temperamental, dangerous, but on the Emotional Quotient scale you were like nothing we'd seen before. The intuitive leaps you made at seventeen? They were phenomenal. And the things you do now, Christopher, the way your mind works…"

Wren didn't know what to say. It sounded like an apology. He wasn't sure.

"I needed to say that," Humphreys added. "It doesn't let you off the hook for what you've done. There is the possibility you may have been licensed for the Pinocchio executions. It'll be the President's call."

Wren almost laughed. Licensed by the President, to kill? He cleared his throat. "Humphreys, we need to-"

"Let me enjoy the quiet for one second more," Humphreys said. "The great Christopher Wren struck dumb, basking in the glow of my praise, not immediately just telling me what to do."

Wren gave him a second. Several, in fact.

"OK," said Humphreys. "You called me. Go ahead."

"You need to cancel the strikes to grab phones. All of them, right now."

There was a long, painful silence.

"You're joking. Ha ha, Christopher. Very funny."

Wren took a deep breath, pressed on. "I'm not. It's not funny. I'm for real."

"Unh."

Wren imagined Humphreys face-palming.

"Think of all the money you'll save."

Humphreys groaned. "Christopher! Why do you do this to me? Money we'll save, are you serious? We've spent billions already. Have you got any idea how much it costs to mobilize millions of people across different sectors, train them, equip them, arrange logistics to transport them, not to mention the analytics required to split America into sectors for a simultaneous strike?"

"I don't know. A lot." A pause. "I'm sorry."

A long sigh. "A lot. Well, at least you're sorry. I can dine out on that when Congress hauls me up for gross incompetence."

Wren saw a gap opening up. Humphreys had shifted. This wasn't the man he'd spoken to earlier: burning cold with anger, blaming Wren for everything. This was a man who'd re-balanced his perspective.

"I'll use my Emotional Quotient," Wren tried. "Phenomenal intuition, wasn't it? Maybe I can pull some strings with the President."

Steel crept back into Humphreys' voice. "Don't push it. We've got you on dozens of murder charges."

Wren almost laughed. Not back the way it always was, but better than before.

"Fine. Either way, the Reparations are counting on those

strikes. They've been using me as a foil. They knew I'd escalate at every provocation, because that's what I do. They push me with their app, and I push for the strikes. They're going to use it as a call for revolution. An over-reaching government; it's the great American fear. We can't give them that."

Humphreys took a moment, then cursed loud and inventively.

"Right. I'm not such a genius now."

Humphreys laughed; it sounded almost like a sob. "So call off all the strikes?"

"Not quite all. Hellion's sent you the analytics? People are deleting the app themselves. We've got ten percent projected to stay on and try to keep the revolution rolling. You need to focus your best on them. Don't raid them, give no provocation, just watch them and let them see you're watching. Let them see it's futile. We'll arrest the worst of them later, when the heat's gone out of this thing."

"What about your amnesty?"

Wren chuckled. "I was wondering when you'd mention that."

"I must say, I am glad you carved out some room for us, when you made that announcement. Gave us permission to make arrests for murderers and such. Thank you."

Wren knew he was mocking him, but took it seriously still. "I don't want them to fear you. You're not the enemy of the people. I want them to fear me."

Humphreys just laughed. "They will definitely kick me out of the CIA for this."

"Maybe make you VP."

"Ugh. All right. I have to go face the music." He paused and Wren almost killed the call, but Humphreys had one more thing to say. "Oh, and thank you for the chance to meet your hackers. Hellion, I think it was? She called me a 'pussy wearing a dick-suit'."

Wren tried and failed to stifle a laugh.

"I'm glad it amuses you. That's ten years, for maligning an officer in pursuit of his duty."

"Well, you always had the best suits," Wren said. "Now I have to go kill some bad guys. Good luck."

"See you in jail, Christopher."

The line went dead.

"He is pussy in dick-suit," Hellion said flatly.

Wren laughed. It didn't hurt that much. Somehow, he felt good. So what if he went to jail? He'd just been preaching the importance of making atonement, of paying down your debts. He had so many to pay: Ffamilies of the Pyramid deceased he owed apologies to, a thousand now and counting, debts he'd never even realized were his; members of his Foundation that he hadn't been able to properly help. He just had to kill the Apex, try and make things right with his kids, then jail would come as a relief. It'd give him time to set up a payment plan on those debts. Ten steps for ten coins. Get into writing letters.

He blinked. The exhaustion was playing havoc with his head.

"Do we have a destination yet?"

"Tentative," Hellion said. "There are few towns in light helicopter range, with matching gaps in oversight and green yards and flood of blue light vehicles coming in. What I am seeing, either these are Reparations or this is criminal convention. Many ghost movements, changes between satellite overwatch cycles."

"Where?"

"Twenty minutes north of you, a little place called Pie Town on other side of Gila National Forest. And get there fast Christopher, Reparations app is warming up new livestream now. It is still shot of your Constitution, but viewcount is climbing."

The Constitution. Wren had been ready to run it underfoot, and he cursed silently. This was a lesson.

"Yeah," he said, and looked out of the glass again. The sun was sinking low to the west, nightfall was coming fast. His giddiness burned away. The Cheyenne tore on. It all came down to this.

44

PIE TOWN

The Cheyenne swooped in over trailer park homes interspersed by yellowing yards and dark green Douglas Firs. Wren should have known it; Americana but leaning poor, like the majority of the country, the people with the most to be angry about. There were picket fences, but the effect of downward social mobility was everywhere. A few had fresh coats of paint, but not nearly enough.

The place felt like defeat.

Blue lights flashed ahead. Wren pushed himself upright and nearly tipped off his seat as the Cheyenne banked tightly over dirt roads and scrub.

"Sir," said Acton at his side, catching Wren by the shoulders and steadying him. "Are you sure you're fit to engage?"

"Just be there if I fall, son," Wren said. He was maybe only ten years this Marine's senior, but whatever; it gave him the privilege to call him son.

"Yes, sir. Now, we've got AR-15s, more shells for your shotgun, magazines for the SIG .45, or you can-"

"Don't need them," Wren said, holding up his hands. "All I want are these." He made fists, but they didn't feel tight, the knuckles barely whitening. He was as weak as a six-year-old. "Just keep me alive."

"Sir," the guy barked.

"And whatever you do, try not to kill the billionaires."

Acton's brows pushed slightly closer together. "Sir? Aren't they considered hostiles by now?"

Wren looked around at his team; eight Marines in tactical black, armed to the teeth. "They are, but I repeat, do everything you can not to kill them. This is a special operation with far more at stake than immediate life and death." He took a breath, saw the doubt on his squad's faces. "You know Stockholm Syndrome? Consider these men hostages who've been co-opted. Forget about what they've done, that was all under duress. They've been brainwashed. If we kill them, and those deaths are caught on the livestream, we may win the battle, but we will lose the war." He sucked air. Speaking so much winded him. "Am I understood?"

They'd surely had few directions like that before. Most propaganda wars weren't actually fought in the streets.

"Oo-rah," they replied.

"Coming in," shouted the pilot.

The Cheyenne swung hard right barely ten yards above the roof line. A cluster of emergency vehicles was parked at the head of a blacktop road, clearly recently tarred and painted with fresh yellow lines. More set dressing, thanks to some unnamed benefactor to the county council. It beat out the dirt roads that linked the rest of the tiny burg and completed the picture-perfect image.

Just your average American suburb.

The Cheyenne stopped sharp in back of a neighboring house, then the doors kicked open and the first two Marines jumped out on rappel lines.

Gunfire began; outgoing and incoming. To Wren it was all a lot of noise.

"I'm tethering you to me," Acton said, and clipped onto Wren's jump harness with a karabiner. "You can't make this jump alone."

Wren just grunted and rose to his feet. His head spun with the sudden surge of blood, making him dizzy. "Go," he said and stepped out into air. Acton was already ahead of him and paying out line for their rapid descent. Wren fell, was caught in the harness then closed the last few yards under Acton's smooth control; Wren just watching the yellowing grass spin up toward him.

They hit the ground together. Wren's left leg gave out and he dropped to his knees, beyond dizzy already. Automatic gunfire ripped on all sides. Acton hoisted him back to his feet.

"Go," he barked.

"Go," Acton amplified, and the team moved; eight-strong with Wren at the center. It took five fast steps, punctuated by gunfire with the trees and faded white siding a blur. Acton held one hand to Wren's harness as they ran, holding him steadier.

They ran around toward the front of the house, where a haz-mat camera operator swung to film them with a look of shock on his face. Ahead lay the carnage of a fake gunfight in the street, haz-mats and billionaires in the house fending off the over-reaching arm of the State.

One of the Marines cold-cocked the haz-mat as they hunkered briefly beside the front porch. Wren stared at the manic battle in the street. Up close it didn't look fake. It looked real. Bodies lay scattered and bleeding. Bullets sparked convincingly off the bodywork of patrol cars. A woman in a police uniform lay on the blacktop, bleeding from a vicious head wound. You couldn't fake that kind of injury with makeup.

The Marines split and fired: one squad flanked left around the fake emergency forces, dropping them in a spray of lower leg shots; the other mounted the porch, Acton helping Wren with the ascent. A flashbang grenade went off nearby and stunned him; smoke billowed out through an open window. His team were rolling in, black-clad bodies streaming into smoke with goggles on and firing. There were screams. Wren tried to run after them, but Acton held him back.

"Wait, sir," he said.

They waited. Smoke enveloped them. Covering fire kept the forces on the street at bay, the few of them who were still standing. Haz-mat camera operators moved through the firefight like it wasn't even there.

"Now," said Acton, hoisted half of Wren's weight and ran in.

Smoke was everywhere, biting at Wren's eyes. He could barely see a thing; dark shadows moving in the gray, Marines firing disabling shots, throwing blows, leaving…

Wren saw his target.

"Let me go," he said to Acton.

The man melted away. Wren almost fell at once, but managed to lock out his left leg and just keep his feet. Through the bitter smoke, there he was. Bare-chested and enormous, his prodigious weight powered by muscles as big as watermelons, arms wide, pale skin sprayed with blood, wounded bodies quivering at his feet.

Damalin Joes III. The people's billionaire. Lips pulled back tight and eyes wide with the fire of some newfound righteousness. In both hands he held hatchets. Wren smiled. Of course. Haz-mats spun around them, capturing it all. A hell of a finale. Wren steadied his legs, took a stance, and raised his fists.

Damalin Joes saw him and laughed. "Christopher Wren," he boomed, "you barely look like half a man anymore," then flew in with the hatchets arcing back.

45

DAMALIN JOES III

The right hatchet came in first, a haymaking chop from above, powerful enough to split Wren right down the middle. He barely sidestepped it, but Joes redirected his vast momentum with a nimbleness incredible for a man of his size, spinning out a hooking left strike.

Wren staggered three steps backward to evade it. On the fourth step his heels hit something, a body maybe, and he fell, rolled, then came up on his knees by instinct.

Damalin Joes III stood massive before him in the clearing smoke, a too-wide grin on his face, like clown makeup, clearly enjoying this.

"Not so fast as before," Joes said appraisingly. "Try that choking trick now."

Wren pushed himself to his feet, and Joes danced two lightning steps forward to swing both hatchets at once, a pincering blow that would lop Wren's head off like a dandelion. He barely flung himself away in time, feeling the rush of the blades passing near, then thumped into a wall.

The wind slammed from his lungs. This time Joes didn't press forward immediately. Instead he just watched, like he was studying a bug with its wings removed, struggling to fly.

"I saw your speech," he boomed through the smoke. "In the arena, after Harkness died. I thought it was so sad. An alpha surrendering."

Wren's mind spun, slowly straightening up. Damalin was a different man, there would be no reasoning with him. Kill a couple men in an arena, and your personality could change like a summer flood. Wren just needed to find the angle.

"Better than a beta rolling over on their whole life," he countered, hoping an adrenaline dump would come soon and speed up his sluggish reactions. His whole body felt out of sync and disoriented. "Are you a billionaire titan, Joes, or are you Yumiko Harkness' wind-up toy?"

Joes laughed, a deep rumble. "You can ask Cem Babak about that." He darted in again, right hatchet sweeping down hard. There was no time, nowhere to go, so Wren threw up a hand like Merriot Raine had, fingers splayed, but as the blade flew in he shoved off the wall, managing to slip the metal head and snag the handle.

It felt like catching the pumping piston of a steam train. The tendons in his wrist wrenched back, only just halting the hatchet's metal head within an inch of his scalp. Joes didn't hesitate and sent his left hatchet in a tight scythe toward Wren's extended arm, but Wren was already kicking off the wall. The momentum sent him barreling straight into Joes' chest.

He hit, Joes staggered a step then together they went down, hatchets clanking on the hard wood floor. Wren rolled away fast, eyes streaming with the smoke, maybe feeling a trickle of adrenaline pushing through, enough for one or two more concerted efforts.

On his feet, fists up again, for the first time he got a real sense of the room as the smoke cleared. It was a den, but devastated, littered with the dead and dying. Police, FBI, SWAT; bodies like props in their terminal performance. There was blood sprayed on the ceiling, there were wounds. All real. Joes had been in here for minutes only before Wren's Marines arrived, and he'd worked a whirlwind of devastation. The man was as powerful as a bull.

Nearby black-clad Marines surged through the smoke, battling the billionaires hand-to-hand. Wren caught flashes of weaponry, but no gunshots rang out, in line with his orders. Everything was tracked by the Reparations' camera operators, four of them weaving smoothly around the action in their red-stained white haz-mats suits, streaming video to the ten percent.

The message was all that mattered now. No help was coming from the Marines. Wren was on his own.

He turned back to Damalin Joes. The huge man was on his feet. A thin trickle of blood rolled down his jaw, but he was grinning still. Wren knew he couldn't take the man hand-to-hand, not even with the adrenaline, not in his current state.

"She's using you, Damalin," he said, and felt his father's firebrand voice ring out from his throat, stronger than expected. "You're the poster boy for a vengeance you don't even understand."

Damalin Joes just laughed, advancing as Wren circled around a toppled coffee table. "Like you used me? And do you think I care?"

He came in fast, this time leading with a big front kick. Wren rolled it with his left forearm, spun and bounced a backhand off Joes' head. Joes barely noticed, spinning tight to slam his right-hand hatchet into Wren's injured side.

The Twaron vest blocked the edge but still the force carried through, thumping the wind out of Wren's lungs for a second time and sending shooting pains deep into his spine. Wren acted through the pain: with his left hand he trapped the hatchet-head against his ribs, with his right he hooked Joes' upper arm and for a second they looked into each other's eyes, locked in an embrace so close they could kiss. Then Wren put a stinging head-butt into the bridge of Joe's nose.

The big man broke away, hatchets flailing for balance. Wren himself staggered and almost fell. Hard to breathe after that, head spinning. Ignoring pain was one thing, but you couldn't ignore damage. He had minutes left before that blow in the side took him down; the shrapnel wounds re-opened, maybe some internal bleeding if he was unlucky. He had to make it happen now.

Damalin Joes caught his balance and stamped back, lips awash with blood pouring from his broken nose. He spat blood at Wren, red on the Twaron, and whirled his hatchets.

"Try that again," he said, and lunged.

Wren barely slipped the left swipe, dropped and rolled under the right. It took it out of him; he came up slow and wheezing.

"You're tired," Joes said, advancing. "You've had a hard day, half man. Lie down and rest."

Another swing, another duck. Wren managed to bat a follow-up strike clear, but it was close, just barely deflecting off his thigh armor plate and almost burying in the meat of his leg.

Joes kept advancing as Wren limped backward across the den. "This is all you've got? It's so sad. I can do this all day, but you?"

Another powerful swing: Wren backed into the sofa and rolled over it awkwardly, calves smacking down hard on a fallen chair, arms slipping off a wet body. Joes stalked him like a predator.

"To see the mighty so fallen. I know all about your 'Foundation' now. It's pathetic. To think I ever let you guilt trip me? You should have burned in that town thirty years ago."

Wren had only seconds left, maybe one good play left

before one of Joes' hatchets landed. His body was exhausted but his mind wasn't, and he'd done this countless times before. Deprogramming cult members. It took days, weeks, a lifetime sometimes, but these were extreme conditions, coming on the back of an extreme conversion, and extremity helped move the needle.

"How does it feel," Wren asked, barely lurching out of range of another haymaker behind the sofa, "knowing that all this was for me?"

Joes sprang over the sofa and came at Wren direct, hatchets high. "What are you babbling about? You're a footnote."

Now Wren laughed, hobbling behind the dining table and clutching his side, managing to bark out a few more words. "You're a reality show contestant, Damalin!" He skipped back from a chop that smashed splinters out of the table. "A billionaire reduced to nothing more than an actor on a stage, recruited solely to capture *my* attention." Another wild slash. "This doesn't lead to anything for you, and you must know that. I survived Harkness' attack. The Reparations app is gone. There's nothing left for you to do. Even if you win here, what do you think you'll get?"

Joes grinned, bright blood outlining each of his perfect white teeth. "Have you heard of mindfulness, Christopher? It's all the rage. I didn't really know what it was until a few days ago. Now I understand."

Wren laughed. "You think killing is mindful?"

"It's the only thing that is." Joes lunged forward and Wren staggered back. "The way it feels when you look a dying man in the eyes. I think you more than anyone know what I mean. You killed a thousand, didn't you?"

Wren tried to catch his breath, limping and reeling. So Joes had watched the video. He had only a couple chances left. "I did. I saw that look in their eyes and it broke me,

266

Damalin. There's always a cost. The rush of power comes right along with the shame. But you get to choose how far you twist yourself inside to deny the existence of either."

"Pretty words," Joes hissed and flung out a downward swipe.

Wren barely sidestepped and pressed on. "Words are everything! Yumiko Harkness used them to brainwash you. Just like I was brainwashed. We're both victims. Right now I know it seems as if the whole world has shifted and permission has been granted, but the world hasn't changed, Damalin." He spread his arms wide. "There is no permission for this."

"You're making excuses," Joes said, twirling his blades so blood flicked like sparks from a Catherine wheel. "It's what weak men do right before they die. It's what Merriot Raine did. He begged me. He kept on begging as I brought the hatchet down."

"What about when you ripped Handel Quanse apart, Damalin? Was it the same then?"

That froze Joes for a second, standing between the coffee table and sofa. A strange mixture of emotions played across his face. Maybe uncertainty. Taking him back to the first moment of indoctrination and exposing the illogic; a standard deprogramming tool.

"He was weak."

Wren laughed. "Handel Quanse was weak? He was as strong as any of you. Your cellmate. So he had to go." Wren circled into the kitchen, cameras following tightly. "Were you were happy to lead that charge? Rip him up before he even had a chance?"

"That wasn't me!" Joes spat immediately, words out of his mouth before he could stop them. "I didn't want that."

Now Wren smiled. An opening. "Didn't you? Then who

did? Was it Yumiko Harkness, should I be talking to her, your boss? Except she's dead, leaving you holding the bag."

Joes' glare darkened. The exultation was fading, replaced by defensive rage. Wren knew that feeling well. It was the ugly face men showed to avoid feeling shame. "You don't know what you're talking about."

"Don't I?" Wren edged around the granite-topped island, half a retreat, half an advance. "I've seen the videos. I've been to that arena. Hell, son, I just got done tearing it down. The cages, the stage, all of it. That was a silicon chip factory, Joes. It was rich assholes like you who killed it; outsourced the work, automated it away, and your boss, Yumiko Harkness? Her father worked there! He lost his job, so she went bananas. It's as simple as that. You're just the instrument of her revenge." He paused as he circled, watching Joes' expression. "A smart woman. She thought she knew who I was too. She directed me step-by-step, just like she directed you with that electroshock collar, like a dog running to the command of a bell. She thought I'd over-react when she burned herself alive, double down on shutting down free speech, but she had me wrong. I think she has you wrong too."

Joes' face remained dark and angry, but Wren felt the uncertainty building in him like an explosion. Recognizing your own failures could feel like an act of self-destruction.

"Because you were weak," Joes said.

Again Wren laughed. Not mocking now, but mournful. "Listen to what you just said, Damalin! I didn't destroy freedom of speech, one of the pillars of this nation, because I was weak? It was strength that got me through. Like you on that horse, yanking Handel Quanse behind you. You didn't want to do that, no matter what she told you afterward. You did what you had to to survive. But there's nobody here pulling your strings anymore." Wren gestured to the smoky,

268

bloody room. "You can let it go; show your real strength and get back to the old version of Damalin Joes."

Joes stood perfectly still now, like a suicide bomber with his finger on the trigger. "The old version's a fool."

"The old version's a billionaire!" Wren snapped back. "*You* achieved that. Sure, maybe you started with a loaded deck, a nice inheritance, but what you built was still extraordinary, far more impressive than killing a few men with your bare hands, especially when every single death was fake!" He sucked in a breath. "Think about it! The arena, the slaughter in the cages, even the stage; she wrote your role for you! She put you in a set with a script and a well-rehearsed cast and watched you recite your lines like a good little boy."

Wren was close to shouting now, about all the energy he had left. "And as a reward, she screwed you. Explain all this some other way." He gestured at the bodies lying on the floor. "You must know that these people are all just extras in costumes ready to die for her cause. People she brainwashed too. What does it even mean to kill them, when their deaths were scripted before this thing began?" He paused, reading Joes' breathing, the flicker of his pulse in his temple. "You're wearing the costume she picked out, playing your part in her grand production. Maybe the lead role, but you think you're in charge? Don't make me laugh. She wrote the whole damn movie!"

Joes' breathing grew faster. Wren could feel the fight-flight state building to climax. Like Simon back in Deadhorse. One step either way and everything would change. Part of him would only want to chop Wren to bits, to revel in the thrill and kill his doubts. Another part would want to hear more, was crying out to be saved.

Finishing touches.

"You're a victim here, Joes. Like Merriot Raine, like Handel Quanse, like me. We're all just clockwork toys waiting to be wound up and set loose. That's not strong! What's strong is you think for yourself, you make your own choice about who you want to be." He panted, exhausted. "You were a Rhodes scholar! You clerked for the Supreme Court! You came up hard, bloodied a few noses along the way, but you were not afraid to face the truth. You made billions, and now you're ashamed of that? Think again. Just think."

Joes stared. Worlds turned inside his eyes. Permissions being granted, being revoked. It was a lot to swallow; what he'd done, what had been done to him. It would take years, but it always began with one step.

His arms twitched. Imagining using the hatchets. Maybe the onset of an attack. Wren steeled himself. He couldn't dodge any more. Take a few more hits on his Twaron, maybe, but then...

Then he'd be dead.

"Order them to shoot."

It was Hellion's voice in his ear. She had his bodycam. She saw everything he saw, first-person perspective, and thought she knew better.

He ignored her.

"I'll order them," she said.

From the corner of his eye Wren saw one of the Marines lift his rifle, listening to Hellion's orders, but Wren couldn't turn away now. He couldn't say another word, just had to trust the Marines would trust his instruction, while Damalin Joes III remained frozen in indecision, eyes shining, hatchet blades trembling in the air.

All he needed was one more push to close this out.

"Nothing you've done so far condemns you, Damalin. You can come out of this stronger. Plead insanity; it's the truth, and it doesn't make you weak, only human. You were kidnapped from the safety of your home, man! Drugged, stripped naked, dehumanized, treated worse than an animal. The tactics they used on you will be studied for years to come; advanced psychological warfare, enough to crack the strongest minds we have. No person could have held up against the onslaught, and that was the point. That's why it worked; if the best amongst us can be turned against their own interests, then nothing matters, nothing means anything anymore." Wren gasped for breath, silver lights flashing before his eyes. "But our actions do matter, Damalin! What we say and do has meaning, and the balance lies in your hands. Turn away now, I guarantee you will be a hero. You resisted, your better angels won out, you're a case study for a new model of humanity. Push through though, you get to be king of the ashes. You get to kill me, but is that really the limit of your ambition? All addicts know the drug is bad for them. Few addicts become billionaires. I don't think you're the one bad penny to break that mold. Tell me I'm wrong."

Hellion shouted orders in the background.

His own pulse raced. Marines held their weapons high. At any second the whole thing could implode.

Then Joes let go.

Wren saw it first in his eyes, the opposite of that first decision on the arena's sand. Next the hatchets fell from his hands. He transformed in a heartbeat, back to the man he'd been before. Imperfect, yes, cruel, even vengeful, but not a murderer.

"I don't-" he began, but nothing more came.

Marines rushed in. They handled Joes gently, onto his knees, arms behind his back, putting on the cuffs like this was a routine police matter. No black bag over his head, and that was good. Wren turned to the haz-mat operators, half of them watching Joes, half watching him. He stared down their lenses.

"He's the last," he said. "No more forgiveness after this."

Then he walked out.

He didn't make it far. Out the door and onto the porch, looking over the scene of blood and wreckage. The Cheyenne had touched down in a neighboring yard, rotor blades still spinning. There were bodies everywhere, cars shredded by automatic weapons' fire, broken glass.

On the yellow grass he fell to his knees. Too exhausted. He had nothing left. Hellion was talking. More forces were inbound. Humphreys had the location now. A team was winging its way closer.

Then there were hands hoisting him up. It was hard to see, with his vision blurring. He saw the contours of a familiar face.

"Man says mobilize, I mobilize."

"Wha-?" Wren managed.

"Teddy sent us," Gruber answered, getting under Wren's arm, holding him up along with someone else. Was it Doona? "You'll be OK."

"Man says OK," Wren managed.

46

MAN ON THE INSIDE

nother bed, another building. Drip cables fed into Wren's wrist. There was a window and a dresser with a mirror, flowery wallpaper looking a little worse for wear, a medical chart within reach on a side table. He took it.

'Medically-induced coma', it said. Three days. Ruptured left kidney. Displaced vertebra. Early-onset sepsis. Internal bleeding.

Wren felt hungry. His face hurt, and his back, and his side. He reached one hand up, touched his cheek. Stippled with scar tissue from the Anti-Ca grenades. Even with the best plastic surgery money could buy, he'd carry some remnant of these scars. His children might not recognize him when he saw them next.

He pushed the blanket away. It was thin cotton, but even that much exertion left him sweating and faint. His bare chest was yellowy with bruising, emanating from a dark purple blot above his left hip, as big around as a dinner plate. The scarring wasn't so bad here, thanks to the Twaron vest; it seemed his arm and face had taken the worst of it.

He swung his legs out and stood, barely holding himself up.

"Lie down," came a voice through a croaky speaker. Wren looked around slowly; it hurt to turn fast. Not a speaker in sight, but a teddy bear nannycam sat on the chest of drawers, dark glass eyes watching.

"I can see you," the voice went on. "I've called security."

"Hellion?" he asked, then, "security?"

The door opened. In came Steven Gruber, NSA Analyst. He looked pale and drawn. His face showed a lot of emotions. Happiness, yes, but also a kind of expectant concern, like he was very worried about what Wren would say or do next.

"You're up," he said cautiously, "ahead of schedule."

"And you're security?" Wren asked.

Gruber shrugged awkwardly. "Hellion likes playing games." Like that explained everything.

Wren looked at him, around the room. Just the two of them. "You've been looking after me?"

"I volunteered." Gruber took a step further in. "It only seemed right, given how we started this thing together."

Wren nodded. That was true. Breaking NameCheck felt like a very long time ago.

"Are we in the Oregon farm?"

"No," said Gruber. "A different one. Teddy set it all up. We're all busy now. A lot of private jets, doing surveys, 'resource investigation', he calls it. I've got a role there, but I wanted to do this first. To make sure."

"He's been doing everything," Hellion's voice came through the nannycam, mocking. "Sponge baths, comb your hair, brush your teeth, little goodnight kiss…"

Gruber reddened. "I didn't-"

Wren sighed. You couldn't stop the kids from being kids. "That teddy bear is starting to freak me out. Can you turn it off?"

Gruber looked surprised. "I, uh. Teddy, I mean, I know that's a kind of in-joke, Hellion's joke I think, but Teddy wanted-"

"Is Teddy here?"

A pause. Maybe Gruber was fighting the urge to look around and be sure. "Uh, no, he's-"

"So turn it off."

Gruber took a few hesitant steps.

"Do not terminate this device," Hellion's voice came through firmly, "it is condition of Christopher's new parole status, one-coin negative that-"

Gruber reached the bear, looked to Wren who nodded, then pushed the power button.

There was a silence.

"I'm one-coin negative?"

Gruber reddened further. "I... uh, I mean. I think they're trying it out. A lot of new ideas, you know?"

Wren fixed him with a glare. "Trying it out on me?"

"Uh."

Wren cursed under his breath. If Teddy couldn't steal the Foundation, he'd end up changing it so much it was unrecognizable. But Wren had left him in charge, and this is what he got.

"I think there's a Board meeting scheduled for the day you wake up," Gruber said, trying to be helpful. "The room's all set for it, I can-"

"Hold on."

Gruber stopped talking.

There were a lot of things to ask. To say. Three days in a coma, things would change. There were things that really mattered. There was no question what mattered most, though.

"How's Rogers?"

Gruber looked at his feet. "I think we should set up the meeting, get the full debrief, because-"

"Steven."

Gruber looked up, clearly at war inside himself, but making the decision fast. "I don't know. FBI took her from the hospital, and we haven't heard anything since. We think she's OK, but we don't know..." He paused a moment, then went on more brightly. "FBI swept the Anti-Ca compound too, right after your last transmission. There were surrenders, I heard, looks like they didn't go the suicide route, so that's good, isn't it?"

He smiled encouragingly.

"And the Reparations?"

"The app's dead. Most of them have gone silent. We have many of their IP addresses, the ones who wouldn't delete it. Most of them did, after Pie Town. It was..." Gruber seemed lost for words. "Inspired. The way you turned it around."

"I was half high on oxycodone," Wren said. "The whole time. Let's not read too much into it."

"Of course," said Gruber, though he clearly didn't think so. "Well then."

"And copycats?"

"Stopped cold. On TV they've been debating your amnesty. Pundits, talk shows, late night." A pause. "You're a major topic, too. You're famous now, your story is out there. People are coming down on all sides." He stopped, maybe reading the disapproving look on Wren's face before hurrying on. "But the amnesty, Congress is considering some kind of legislation. I doubt they'll get anything real through, but there seems to be a sense that people want to do something about inequality. It makes sense, right? If we weren't so unequal, this thing never would've gotten so crazy." He paused, thought a moment. "Following on from that, it seems nobody wants to hunt down the thousands of citizens who committed lesser crimes. graffiti, public disorder, property damage and so on."

"And the major crimes?"

"Arrests are ongoing. The billionaires, Damalin Joes foremost, are asking for insanity pleas, just like you said. It looks like they'll get them, if public opinion is anything to go by. They're not popular men, but there's a certain kind of understanding, right now? They've been talking about the experience on chat shows, about how it overwhelmed them, and nobody can really argue with that."

Wren nodded. "We all had a weaponized dose of manipulation. Make sure Teddy pushes that narrative. If it's good enough to get the billionaires off, it should get others off too."

Gruber stared. "Uh, you mean, I should tell him?"

"You're on the Board, aren't you?"

"Um, yes? I suppose so."

"So raise it. You're my man on the inside." Wren winked.

Gruber just stared. Probably he was wondering what he'd let himself in for. "I, uh, thank you?"

"Don't mention it."

They looked at each other. Wren smiled. He felt good somehow. There was the pain, it would be there for weeks now as he healed, but still he felt better. His father had done this, and he'd lost. Wren had come out of it stronger than before. He could think back on his past in a new way now. He'd even spoken to Tandrews. It felt like a dream, but it was real. Dr. Ferat would be proud.

Gruber shifted uncomfortably. "So, was there something I could get for you, or…"

"What's a guy gotta do to get some food in this place?"

"Oh, yeah," said Gruber, so relieved he laughed. "Of course, I'll get some. Hash browns, bacon, beans. Pancakes if you like, eggs too. It's around breakfast time."

Wren grinned sunnily. "Sounds perfect."

47

REPARATION

Five days later, Wren arrived in the little town of Frederica, Delaware not knowing what to expect. Deep black skies and a watery white moon. The past seemed very far away. The future too. He no longer had his phone set to a 4 a.m. alarm, because there was no need. He was planning to see his family soon.

The new family duplex had a grass yard, picket fences, just like Pie Town. He pulled up fifty yards away under the streetlamps, then sat with his heart pounding like crazy, hoping just to catch a glimpse of them when they woke. To see Jake rushing out to try out his BMX. To see Quinn pacing thoughtfully around the yard, checking on her plants. To know they were OK.

At sun-up he'd get out, go over and knock, try to explain things to Loralei as best he could. Try to get back in their lives, even a little bit...

Then the voice came.

"You're getting slow."

It came from behind him, through the open window. He turned and recognized the figure standing in the darkness, splashed by the streetlights. Just behind the C-column of his

278

truck, holding a gun trained on him, with more figures in the shadows drawing near. Rifles, body armor, creeping up.

He watched her in the wing mirror, thinking that maybe this was always how it was going to go. Family was a weakness; he'd known that since he was a child. At least, seeing her came as something of a relief.

"Agent Rogers. You're alive."

"No thanks to you." A pause. "You promised me you'd come in."

There was a lot of hurt in her eyes. Anger. Leave it too long, and there'd just be nothing.

"I hoped I could see them first."

"The answer's no." Another pause, freighted with the past. "You shot me, Wren."

He gave a sad half-smile. She'd never called him Wren before. There was a lot he could say, but even in his head it all sounded like excuses: that she'd been wearing a bulletproof vest, that he'd been packing slow-velocity bullets, that she'd lost faith and pulled a gun on him first. All pointless, because in the moment he'd made the choice and put her at risk.

"I'm sorry, Sally."

Rogers said nothing. Wren looked ahead at the lights of the duplex. The truth was staring him in the face even now. It had been for hours, and maybe he just hadn't wanted to see. A light on in the living room window. He'd seen the curtains twitch a few hours back and ignored it.

"She called you, didn't she?"

He heard Rogers take a step closer. Unclasping handcuffs from her belt, sliding her fingers into the door handle. "You should've checked in with me, saved yourself a trip. Your family's been under my protection since you started slaughtering Pinocchios."

He couldn't smile through that. Didn't know what to feel.

That Loralei was afraid of him. That his kids might be afraid. He turned in the seat, looking back at her. "Can I at least see them? That's all I want. Before you put me under."

Rogers tilted her head, and a stray wash of yellow lamplight caught her, cast through tree branches. She looked well, as solid as ever, blond hair tied back, no longer red-eyed and exhausted.

"You know the answer's no. They don't want to see you, and I couldn't allow it anyway. You're still on a catch/kill order."

That hit like a punch in the gut. Catch/kill. He'd allowed himself to dream, that the forgiveness extended for minor Reparation crimes might extend to him. Might extend to the past.

"Humphreys said I could be licensed for the Pinocchio deaths."

Rogers snorted. Her team moved up closer. "You should've known that was BS. He's a professional liar."

Of course. You didn't become Director of the CIA without telling your share of lies along the way.

"My father's out there, Rogers. I know it. This isn't over."

"We'll finish it for you."

Not much to say to that. They couldn't. Not against the Apex. But he'd let himself be cornered. "Catch/kill," he said softly. "Which are you betting on?"

"Neither," she answered. "A third option."

"Cooperation?"

She leaned in closer to the window. He'd always admired that about Rogers; she acted even when she was most afraid. "That, or something very much like it."

Wren smiled sadly. It was moments like these where you made decisions that forever affected your life. Who you were going to be. He had promised to come in, after all. Maybe his family would come see him in prison.

"Cooperation," he repeated, and just sat there, in the shadowy driver's seat while her team moved in front, rifles pointing right at him through the windshield. He wondered how much they were even following Rogers' orders, and how much this was on Humphreys. "He wants the Foundation."

"Above my pay grade," Rogers answered.

Wren squeezed the wheel, feeling any hopes he'd nurtured for the future crumbling. Not everyone forgave.

"I'll never cooperate," he said. "Not like that. I won't hand them over."

"Tell that to your interrogators," Rogers answered, "I don't care anymore. Now put your hands out through the door, Christopher, palms up."

He looked ahead, to the duplex and the yard, to the lit living room window where a silhouette now stood, looking back. Loralei.

A dozen plans played through his mind: steal Rogers' gun and turn it against her, take out the guys dead ahead, get the truck started and ram through the rest, spin out of Frederica and back out into the darkness. It wasn't impossible. He'd done things like it before. His Foundation would support him. He had doctors to extract bullets. He had the darknet to cover his tracks. They'd never come near him again.

Then there was Rogers, and her eyes. Hard eyes. Angry too. Angry at him, at what he was thinking even now. It felt like she could see right into his soul, like she knew what he was planning. What had he come all this way for, after all?

He put his hands through the window and let her cuff him. She opened the door and pulled him out onto his knees. He could withstand their interrogations. Maybe Humphreys would come through with the license. Maybe not. What else did he have to offer, now?

"Reparation," he said.

Rogers just grunted, then opened a black bag and brought it down over his head.

THE NEXT CHRIS WREN THRILLER

His friends. His colleagues. Someone's coming for them all.

Ex-CIA legend Chris Wren is locked away in a black site, withstanding daily torture. His old colleagues want his 'Foundation', an off-book network of friends in intelligence with paramilitary skills.

Wren will never give them up - but it doesn't matter. Someone is burning CIA assets alive and blaming it on the Foundation - a false flag attack that brings the entire US government down on their heads.

Now Wren's friends are dying on both sides of the divide. He cannot let that stand.

AVAILABLE IN EBOOK, PAPERBACK & AUDIO

www.shotgunbooks.com

HAVE YOU READ EVERY CHRIS WREN THRILLER?

Saint Justice
They stole his truck. Big mistake.

No Mercy
Hackers came for his kids. There can be no mercy.

Make Them Pay
The latest reality TV show: execute the rich.

False Flag
The CIA's hunting his friends. He cannot let that stand.

Firestorm
The President has been co-opted. The storm is coming.

Enemy of the People
He's public enemy #1. Can he survive?

Backlash
He just wanted to go home. They downed his passenger jet...

Never Forgive
5 dead bodies in Tokyo, Japan. Wren's name's all over it.

War of Choice
Russia came for his team. This time it's war.

Learn more at www.shotgunbooks.com

HAVE YOU READ EVERY GIRL 0 THRILLER?

<u>Girl Zero</u>

They stole her little sister. Now they'll pay.

<u>Zero Day</u>

The criminal world is out for revenge. So is she.

Learn more at www.shotgunbooks.com

HAVE YOU READ THE LAST MAYOR THRILLERS?

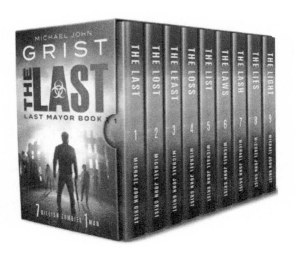

<u>The Last Mayor series - Books 1-9</u>

When the zombie apocalypse devastates the world overnight,
Amo is the last man left alive.

Or is he?

Learn more at www.shotgunbooks.com

JOIN THE FOUNDATION!

Join the Mike Grist newsletter, and be first to hear when the next Chris Wren thriller is coming.

Also get exclusive stories, updates, learn more about the Foundation's coin system and see Wren's top-secret psych CIA profile - featuring a few hidden secrets about his 'Saint Justice' persona.

www.subscribepage.com/christopher-wren

ACKNOWLEDGEMENTS

Deep thanks to Julian White, Bruce Simmons, Britta Morrow, Tony and Aileen Grist, Sue Martin and Ana Schaeffer for sharing their feedback and thoughts, which helped make the book what it is.

- Mike

Made in the USA
Las Vegas, NV
06 June 2023

73058241R00173